D0389192

# HOUSE
# STANDOFF

Also by Mike Lawson

*The Inside Ring*

*The Second Perimeter*

*House Rules*

*House Secrets*

*House Justice*

*House Divided*

*House Blood*

*House Odds*

*House Reckoning*

*House Rivals*

*House Revenge*

*House Witness*

*House Arrest*

*House Privilege*

*Rosarito Beach*

*Viking Bay*

*K Street*

# HOUSE STANDOFF

A JOE DeMARCO THRILLER

MIKE LAWSON

Atlantic Monthly Press
*New York*

FIRST EDITION

*Published simultaneously in Canada*
*Printed in Canada*

First Grove Atlantic hardcover edition: April 2021

This book was set in 12-pt. Garamond Premier Pro
by Alpha Design & Composition of Pittsfield, NH.

Library of Congress Cataloging-in-Publication data is available for this title.

ISBN 978-0-8021-5856-7
eISBN 978-0-8021-5857-4

Atlantic Monthly Press
an imprint of Grove Atlantic
154 West 14th Street
New York, NY 10011

Distributed by Publishers Group West

groveatlantic.com

21 22 23 24  10 9 8 7 6 5 4 3 2 1

I'm dedicating this novel to all the doctors and nurses who remained on the front lines throughout the COVID-19 outbreak. As Winston Churchill said about the RAF pilots during the Battle of Britain:

"Never was so much owed by so many to so few."

# 1

A small town was a bad place for a night owl like her to be.

It was past midnight and she couldn't concentrate and felt like taking a break, but Waverly, Wyoming had pretty much locked its doors, turned off the lights, and gone to bed. If she was still living in Boston, she might have gone to this one hole-in-the-wall bar near her old apartment and had a glass of wine, or maybe to a coffee shop that was open until two a.m. But here there were no cozy coffee shops or quiet bars playing soft jazz that stayed open until the crack of dawn. There was a twenty-four-hour convenience store at the truck stop that served bad coffee and stale pastries but that was about it. The diner was closed and the other restaurant in town stopped taking dinner orders at nine and closed at ten. The one bar in town was open until two but the last thing she felt like was getting hit on by some lonely roughneck who'd had too much to drink.

She looked out the window and across the highway at the diner. It appeared as if Harriet had gone to bed. Harriet wasn't a night owl like she was; the poor woman just had a hard time sleeping. There'd been many a night since she'd been in Waverly when she'd look out her motel room window and see a single light on over a booth in Harriet's place and the silhouette of the old woman sitting there. Some nights she'd cross the highway and rap on the window and wave, and Harriet would unlock the café door and they'd spend an hour or so talking. These gab sessions had not only been fun but also useful in that they'd contributed significantly to her research on the little town and its inhabitants. She doubted, however, that there would be another late-night session with Harriet, not after what she'd done to upset her. That had been a big mistake.

She turned back to her laptop and read the paragraph she'd just written. It was awful. It was total crap. If she'd been using an old-fashioned typewriter as Hemingway had, she would have yanked the page out of the carriage and let it flutter to the ground like a dead bird. But since she was using a laptop she couldn't resort to anything so dramatic. She just blocked out the text and hit "delete" emphatically. Some nights were like that. Some nights the words flowed from a literary wellspring in her mind and she actually impressed herself. Other nights were like this one, where she produced nothing but unprintable shit. Such was the life of a writer. Maybe she should go for a walk to clear her head; she wasn't worried about walking alone late at night, not in Waverly.

She knew the time had come for her to leave Wyoming. She'd immersed herself in the setting, had captured it completely in her mind, and the characters in the novel would be born from the people she'd met, yet would not be those people. There was really nothing to be gained by remaining any longer. Then there was the fact that she'd unintentionally alienated some residents, and she had definitely worn out her welcome with them. Yes, it was time to go back to California—she lusted for the sight of the ocean—and start writing the novel in earnest. She wondered idly what would happen to the people in this scandalous little town but their fates weren't integral in any way to her book. She'd probably give Harriet a call in a couple of months—assuming Harriet would speak to her—to see how things had played out with the adulterers, the potential killer, and the king who was losing his potency thanks to the ravages of time.

The knock on the door made her jump in her chair and she almost gave herself whiplash spinning her head around. What the hell? She wondered if it was his wife, coming to yell at her again. Or maybe it was Harriet. What more reassurance could she give her?

She opened the door, but before she could speak, she felt something slam into her chest, as if she'd been hit in the breastbone with a sledgehammer. It didn't occur to her that the sound of the gunshot had been mostly muzzled by the noise of two eighteen-wheelers barreling down the highway.

As she lay on the floor, she could feel her body shutting down. She couldn't move; she couldn't speak. Her vision began to blur.

Her last sight on earth was a leg clad in blue jeans stepping over her. The world, and the promise of a glorious future, faded to black.

# 2

DeMarco looked over at the bedside clock. Eight a.m. A respectable hour to begin the day. He swung out of bed, walked to the bathroom, took a leak, and brushed his teeth. He glanced in the mirror and decided he needed a haircut. Or maybe he'd let his hair grow and tie it up on top into a little man-bun, like some kind of Italian samurai.

Yeah, like that was ever gonna happen.

DeMarco was almost six feet tall and muscular. He had a prominent nose, blue eyes, dark hair he combed straight back, and a cleft in a blunt chin. Clad in red boxer shorts and a sleeveless white T-shirt, he padded barefoot to the kitchen, filled the coffee maker with ground coffee and water, and punched the ON button. From the kitchen, he walked, still moving slowly, only half awake, to the front door of his Georgetown townhouse to get the newspaper. He still had the *Washington Post* delivered to his door; he liked the feel of a newspaper in his hands and didn't want to read the news on his iPhone.

He opened his front door to a gorgeous morning. It was the first day of June, sixty degrees outside, a cloudless sky, no wind at all. In other words, a perfect day for golf. It was a shame he had to go to work, which he would do eventually, but he wasn't in any rush. He didn't punch a clock. For that matter, he rarely went to his office.

He looked down at the porch for his paper and saw it wasn't there. It was about halfway down his sidewalk, a good thirty feet away. Son of a bitch. He looked around and didn't see anyone on the street. He walked briskly down the sidewalk in his bare feet, bent over to pick up his newspaper, and just then a car drove by with a woman at the wheel who was treated to the sight of DeMarco in his underwear. Probably made her day. Or maybe not.

Back in his kitchen, he poured a cup of coffee, added cream and two packets of sweetener, and pulled the sports section from the newspaper. The almost always depressing news on the front page could wait. He scanned the box scores to see which baseball teams had won and lost and looked at the teams' standings. The Washington Nationals were only one game out of first place, but as it was only June, that hardly mattered.

He read an article about two Houston Rockets basketball players. One was a six-foot-nine power forward and the other was one of the best point guards in the NBA—and they'd decided to get married. Since the two guys combined for over forty points a game, DeMarco was betting that the super-conservative, evangelical who'd just bought the Rockets was going to have a Road to Damascus moment.

The important news out of the way, DeMarco scanned the front page. The banner headline was TORNADO IN KANSAS KILLS 62. Too depressing, so he skipped the article. On the right side, above the fold, was a story about two soldiers killed in Somalia. Also too depressing; he didn't read that either. On the other side, above the fold, was an article about a guy who worked in the White House being indicted. This wasn't depressing; it was just business as usual in our Nation's capital. DeMarco decided he didn't care enough to learn why the guy had been indicted and flipped the paper over to see what was on the bottom half of the front page.

The headline in the lower righthand corner read: *AUTHOR SHANNON DOYLE KILLED.*

Oh, Jesus. DeMarco closed his eyes. For a moment, he couldn't breathe and felt lightheaded. His next thought was: It can't be her. Maybe there was another writer named Shannon Doyle famous enough to make the front page of the *Washington Post*—but he knew there wasn't. He knew it was her.

DeMarco had known Shannon Doyle. He'd slept with her. He'd been in love with her.

He'd met her in Boston when he was doing a job there for Mahoney. At the time, she was working nights in the bar of the hotel where he'd been staying. During the day, she worked on the novel she was writing. While he was in Boston, her novel—the first one she'd written—was sold to Random House for over a million bucks and took off like a rocket. Oprah picked it for her book club; it was #1 on the *New York Times* Best Sellers list for fifty-four weeks. The film rights were bought by Reese Witherspoon, who would star in the soon-to-be-released movie. Shannon became rich and famous overnight and began to appear on talk shows.

DeMarco's involvement with Shannon had only lasted a few weeks. He'd known it was going to be hard to sustain the relationship with her living in Boston and him in D.C., but he'd been willing to make the effort. But when she hit the big time with her novel, she decided to move out to California to work with Witherspoon on writing the screenplay for the movie—and she left DeMarco behind.

But it wasn't as if she'd abandoned him. They hadn't been married or lifelong lovers. The fact was that she just hadn't felt as strongly about him as he'd felt about her and she'd simply moved to the other side of the country to live the life she'd always wanted. The choice to pursue her career instead of staying close to him probably hadn't been a hard one for her to make, although she claimed it had been.

He could still see her, the last morning they woke up together. She'd been a beautiful woman with long dark hair and gray eyes and a long-legged, narrow-waisted, athletic body. She wasn't a brooding, introverted writer type. She'd been approachable and gregarious. She'd had a booming laugh and a wicked sense of humor. She'd been an avid hockey fan and had played hockey in college. DeMarco took her to a hockey game on their first date and she was as raucous as the rest of the Bruins' maniacal fans. He couldn't imagine someone who'd been so vibrant, so alive, being dead.

He read the article, barely able to focus on the words with the image of Shannon still in his head. It said that she'd been killed in a town called Waverly, Wyoming, where she'd been doing research on her next novel. She was killed in her motel room. Shot once in the chest. The motive for the murder appeared to be theft as her purse, laptop, and phone were all missing. But that was it. There were no suspects identified or any other details provided to make sense out of what had happened. Her death appeared to have been as random and inexplicable as a person being struck by lightning.

Most of the article was about her famous novel, *Lighthouse*, and the praise it had garnered. Other prominent writers were quoted in the *Post*, all of them basically saying the same thing, that the world had lost an incredible literary talent. The book was about a woman who'd fled an abusive husband and had gone to live in a lighthouse in Nova Scotia with her pregnant teenage daughter. DeMarco had read it, and although it wasn't the sort of book he normally read, he had to admit that it had moved him. Even he, a guy who mostly read crime fiction, had been able to appreciate the way Shannon was able to place the reader in the wild coastal setting and make the characters come alive. Her writing was lyrical, poetic, insightful, and profound—something he'd never expected based on her outward personality—and it was easy to understand why the book had been so successful.

Now there would never be a second brilliant novel by Shannon Doyle.

Finally, DeMarco pushed himself away from the table and went to take a shower and shave and dress for work. But before the day was over he was going to find out more about her death and see what the cops were doing to catch the son of a bitch responsible.

# 3

DeMarco was a civil servant with an office in the subbasement of the U.S. Capitol, although how much he actually served was debatable. According to the paperwork on file with the Office of Personnel Management, he was a lawyer who served members of Congress on an ad hoc basis—meaning that when one of the legislators needed legal help, they might call upon him.

The truth was that although DeMarco had a law degree, he'd never practiced law and he served only one person, John Fitzpatrick Mahoney, the current Speaker of the House.

John Mahoney was arguably the most corrupt politician to ever serve in the U.S. House of Representatives, but through a combination of luck and skill he'd never been indicted, much less incarcerated. Despite his flawed character—or maybe because of it—he was amazingly popular with his working-class constituents in Boston and had been a member of Congress for forty years. His critics quipped that you couldn't buy Mahoney's vote, but you could certainly rent it. And the list of Mahoney's defects continued. He was an alcoholic. He lied frequently and shamelessly. He cheated on his wife, although incidents of adultery had become less frequent as he'd aged. He was vain, self-centered, and unpredictable—and could literally charm the pants off women and figuratively charm them off members of the press.

DeMarco had gone to work for Mahoney after college. DeMarco's godmother—one of the many women Mahoney had slept with—blackmailed Mahoney into giving DeMarco a job. Armed with his new law degree, DeMarco arrived in D.C. thinking he would become a member of Mahoney's staff and be used to untangle knotty legal issues facing the legislature. This was not to be. Mahoney stuck him in a windowless box down in the bowels of the Capitol. In the beginning, DeMarco worked for another man to learn the tricks of his trade—the word "tricks" not a euphemism—and when his mentor retired by way of a heart attack, DeMarco sallied forth on his own. He became Mahoney's bagman—the guy who collected the rent for Mahoney's vote. He was also Mahoney's off-the-books troubleshooter. In this capacity, Mahoney gave him jobs he didn't want his legitimate staff to handle, jobs where DeMarco might have to commit acts that were not entirely legal. But he was not identified as a member of Mahoney's staff nor was there any paperwork or organizational chart tying him to Mahoney in any way. And the reason for this was so that Mahoney could deny that he was responsible if DeMarco ever ran afoul of the law—which on several occasions he had, but like Mahoney, he'd never been caught. Well, he was once, but that was a complicated story.

DeMarco's current assignment was to identify the person who had leaked something to CNN—something that had embarrassed Mahoney mightily. Mahoney wanted the leaker's bleeding head on a platter and DeMarco had been ordered to collect it.

DeMarco was supposed to meet today with the person who'd most likely leaked the story. The objective was to see if she'd admit that she was the source. If she didn't admit it, he would call a guy who could obtain the likely leaker's phone records to see who she'd been calling—like maybe that skinny snake Anderson Cooper at CNN, the guy who broke the story. But today DeMarco didn't care who had leaked the story or what Mahoney wanted. He had to find out what had happened to Shannon.

---

DeMarco walked into the Rayburn House Office Building and took the stairs to the second floor where Republican Congressman Wilbur Burns of Wyoming had his office. He was hoping to convince Burns to use his congressional clout to get more information from law enforcement in Wyoming regarding Shannon's death. He was worried, though, that Burns might not be willing to meet with him, and mainly because of the way Mahoney had treated Burns in the past.

Only seven states have a single congressman, Wyoming being one of those states as it has a population of less than six hundred thousand people. Mahoney delighted in saying that Burns represented more cows than humans. Burns was also an easy target because he was a flamboyant character who often wore cowboy boots and a cowboy hat, and when he was campaigning he'd appear in ads riding a horse. In one of his past ads, Burns rides up on his horse, whips a Colt revolver out of a holster, and puts six bullets into an Osama bin Laden target—then turns to the camera and says: "Wyoming needs a congressman who knows how to deal with them dang terrorists." So when Mahoney was asked to comment on something Burns had said one day, Mahoney's response had been: "Oh, you mean Yosemite Sam. Hell, his horse is smarter than he is."

---

DeMarco entered Burns' small office. He was not a ranking member on any committee; hardly anyone in D.C. knew his name, and the size of his office reflected this. Sitting in a reception area that was barely big enough for her desk, was a plump, pleasant-looking woman with a curly gray perm. Cat-eye reading glasses hung from a lanyard around her neck. The plaque on her desk identified her as Executive Assistant, Ida Burns. She was the congressman's wife.

DeMarco said, "I'd like to speak to Congressman Burns about a woman who was killed in his district,"—Burns' district being the entire state of Wyoming. "I was close to this person and I was hoping that he might be able to learn more than was reported in the papers about what happened to her."

"Who are you talking about?" Ida asked.

"Shannon Doyle, the writer."

"Oh, my God. You knew Shannon personally?"

"Yes."

"I met her once when she did a book signing here in D.C.," Ida said. "I just loved her book and I loved her too. I thought, because of the book, she'd be all brooding and serious, maybe even a bit, oh, you know, other-worldly. But she wasn't like that at all. She came across as this ordinary, fun-loving young woman. And she had a great sense of humor, which you'd never guess from her book. Like I said, I just loved her. When I heard on the news that she'd been killed I actually cried, and I told Wilbur that he needed to poke around and see what happened to her."

"So, do you think he'll talk to me? As I said, she was a friend."

Ida studied his face for a moment and said, "I can see she was more than a friend. Wilbur's not doing anything important right now, although he probably thinks he is. I'm sure he'll see you."

---

DeMarco entered Burns' office. It was a typical politician's office with one wall devoted to photos of Burns posing with celebrities who probably didn't know his name; there was a signed portrait of the Republican god, Ronald Reagan; in one corner was an American flag hanging limply on a pole stuck into a flag stand. His desk and the credenza behind his desk were piled with bills that were hundreds of pages long that Burns would vote on without ever reading.

Burns was at his desk, on the phone, looking out a window and his back was to DeMarco. He finished the call, saying, "That's great, Bob. I'll meet you at the restaurant at one." He spun his chair around and started to smile—then stopped.

DeMarco couldn't see Burns' cowboy boots as they were hidden by his desk, but a white Stetson of the ten-gallon variety was prominently displayed, hanging on a coat rack. And DeMarco had to admit that Burns actually did look a bit like the cartoon character, Yosemite Sam: He was short, as plump as his wife, and had a shaggy brown mustache. The first words out of his mouth were: "Hell, I know you. You work for that jackass, Mahoney."

For two decades, hardly anyone knew who DeMarco was, much less that he worked for John Mahoney. He was just one of about twenty thousand mostly anonymous people employed by the legislative branch of the U.S. government—but then he had the misfortune to be arrested for murdering an unpopular Republican congressman. He was actually framed for the crime and eventually proven innocent, but when it came to his relationship with Mahoney, the cat was out of the proverbial bag. DeMarco's picture was plastered on the front page of the *Washington Post*, perp walking toward the courthouse in an orange jail jumpsuit. And clever reporters, assisted by leakers working for the FBI, learned that he had some vague connection to John Mahoney. He'd been seen frequently in Mahoney's office and phone records tied him to Mahoney.

Mahoney, of course, vehemently denied that DeMarco, a man accused of murder, worked for him. He claimed that DeMarco was exactly what his civil service position description said he was: A freelance lawyer who worked for any member of the House who wished to use him. No one, however, believed Mahoney, a man who lied as often as he told the truth. The journalists all concluded, although without any actual evidence, that DeMarco was Mahoney's "fixer"—the word fixer laden with implications of corruption and underhandedness. Nonetheless, Mahoney continued to deny that DeMarco was his guy, no matter what the papers said. And that's where things currently stood: Nearly everyone in the Capitol knew who DeMarco was because the murder case had made him a celebrity, but both DeMarco and Mahoney maintained the fiction that Mahoney was not his boss. Wilbur Burns clearly wasn't buying it.

But rather than deny who employed him, DeMarco said, "Congressman, Mahoney didn't send me. He doesn't even know I'm here."

"Horse shit," Burns said.

"It's like I told your wife: I was a friend of Shannon Doyle's and all I want is to know more about how she died. I figured, being who you are, you might be able to get more information out of the cops in Wyoming. The article in the *Post* only said that she was killed in a motel room in what appeared to be a robbery, but that's all it said. I'd just like to know what happened and if the police have any idea who might have done it."

"And what if the cops don't know any more than what the papers said?" Burns responded. Before DeMarco could answer the question, Burns said, "Well, I know what Mahoney will do. He'll piss all over the cops in Wyoming, just like he's always pissing all over me, saying how they're a bunch of yokels who can't catch a killer."

"Congressman, I'm telling you that Mahoney isn't involved in this."

"Horse shit," Burns said for a second time. "This is just another one of that bastard's dirty tricks. You get the hell on out of here."

DeMarco could see it was hopeless. The guy hated Mahoney so much that it didn't matter what DeMarco said.

"Well, thank you for your time, sir." DeMarco put one of his business cards on Burns' desk and said, "If you change your mind or learn anything more about what happened, I'd appreciate you giving me a call if you're so inclined." DeMarco knew his business card would end up in the trash can.

He left Burns' office and as he walked by Mrs. Burns' desk, she said, "You through already?"

"Your husband wouldn't talk to me. But thanks for getting me in to see him."

DeMarco left the Rayburn Building, thinking about what to do next when it came to Shannon. He was about halfway back to the Capitol when his phone rang. He answered, saying, "Hello. This is Joe."

"This is Ida Burns. My husband changed his mind about talking to you. Come on back."

---

Burns said, "I never met Shannon Doyle and I never read her book, but Ida did and she told me if I didn't help you I'd be sleeping in the kennel with my beagles tonight. But I swear to God, if Mahoney—"

"Mahoney is not ever going to know we talked. I give you my word."

Burns glared at him for a moment, then put the phone on his desk in speaker mode and started punching buttons.

DeMarco said, "Who are you calling?"

"The sheriff of Sweetwater County."

The phone in Wyoming was answered by a woman who said, "Sheriff's office."

Burns said, "Darling, this is Congressman Wilbur Burns. Can you put that rascal, Clay, on the line?"

"Oh, of course, Congressman. Just a minute."

A moment later, a man said, "How you doing, Wilbur?"

"Just fine, Sheriff. And how's your lovely wife?"

"She wants me to retire next year and buy us a fifty-foot RV and travel all around the country. You know, go see national parks and relatives

I've never met. I tell you, Wilbur, if I have to be around her all day, I'll probably end up shooting her."

Burns laughed. "Tell me about it. Look, Clay, the reason I called is I wanted to hear what's happening with the murder of that woman writer in Waverly. In case you haven't figured it out by now, she was a big deal and a lot of folks are interested."

"Yeah, I know. I've been getting calls from the goddamn communists at the *New York Times*. I'd never heard of her—I'm not a big reader—but my wife knew who she was."

Burns rolled his eyes. "Yeah, mine did too."

"Anyway, I've got one of my best guys in charge of the investigation, a deputy named Jim Turner. Jim actually lives in Waverly where the murder occurred. My forensic guys are still there but so far haven't turned up anything useful."

"What do you think happened?" Burns asked. "About all the papers said was that she was shot in her motel room and her purse and her computer were stolen."

"That's true. It appears that she was shot sometime between midnight and four a.m. It also appears as if whoever killed her knocked on the door and she let him in. She was shot right inside the doorway and there was no sign of a forced entry. Also, she was fully dressed, not wearing a nightgown or pajamas or anything like that. So whoever did it, didn't wake her up. It looks as if she opened the door and was then shot once with a small-caliber weapon. Don't have the slug yet as the autopsy hasn't been completed."

DeMarco whispered, "Cameras?"

"Does this motel where she was staying have security cameras?" Burns asked.

"No. She was staying in a place that's a motel combined with a trailer park. The motel was slapped up during the gas boom, has about twenty cheap rooms, and nobody wasted money on cameras."

"So you don't have any idea who might have done it?"

"No, but we have a theory. The motel is on I-80, and across the road from it is a café and a truck stop where long-haul drivers will sometimes spend the night. The Doyle woman was in one of the motel's ground floor rooms, and you can see her room from the truck stop. We know she was alive at ten because she had dinner at a restaurant in town and stayed until the place closed at ten. So one possibility is that she drives back to the motel and some trucker sees her go into her room and he walks over, knocks on her door, and for some reason she opens it, which is when he shoots her and steals her things."

DeMarco shook his head.

"What was she doing in Waverly?" Burns asked.

"Researching some book she was writing. She'd been living in the motel for two months and everybody in town knew who she was. I was told she was real popular, especially with the women there, and didn't have any enemies that my deputy could find. So right now it looks as if she was killed in a straight-up robbery and most likely by an outsider. As you surely know, Waverly isn't one of those places with a big drug or crime problem because Hiram Bunt won't tolerate junkies or lowlifes in his town."

"Who's Hiram Bunt?" DeMarco whispered.

Burns waved the question away.

"Mainly what we're doing now is getting the names of truckers who drove through that day to see if any of them have criminal records."

"How are you doing that?" Burns asked.

"There are two weigh stations on the highway, one near Laramie for traffic going west and one near Rock Springs for the eastbound rigs. The trucks have to stop at the weigh stations and they record the license plate numbers. But we just started looking into that and so far don't have anything that points to a trucker who might have killed her."

"Well, okay," Burns said. "I appreciate you taking the time to talk to me, Clay. And say hi to Arlene for me."

"Will do. And you keep kicking those damn Democrats in the ass."

Burns hung up the phone.

"You happy now?" he said to DeMarco.

"Yeah, and thanks for making the call."

"So what are you going to do?"

DeMarco shook his head. "Nothing, I guess. There's really nothing I can do." DeMarco hesitated, then said, "I could tell the sheriff is a friend of yours, but would you say he's competent?"

"He's been the sheriff of Sweetwater County for twenty-five years. They wouldn't keep electing him if he didn't do his job."

DeMarco thought for a moment about asking again who Hiram Bunt was, the man who wouldn't tolerate junkies in his town, but didn't see the point. He thanked Burns again for his assistance, although he was no closer than he'd been before to knowing what had actually happened to Shannon.

As he was walking out the door, Burns said, "Hey, I saw Anderson Cooper talking about how Mahoney stepped on his crank. Ask Mahoney who's dumber than a mule now."

# 4

The story broken by CNN's Anderson Cooper was that Mahoney had met secretly with the billionaire CEOs of two telecommunications companies that wanted to merge. To make matters optically even worse for Mahoney, the meeting was held five miles off shore in Chesapeake Bay on a two-hundred-foot yacht owned by one of the CEOs, and Mahoney was transported by helicopter to the yacht. The yacht's owner, a man named James Morton, was a celebrated playboy and his yacht had an all-female crew whose uniforms of choice were typically very small bikinis, although no one knew how the crew had been attired the day of the meeting. Cooper did, however, display a photo of the yacht pulling into Fort Lauderdale the previous summer in which the anatomy of the "sailors" had to be partially obscured, as they were all topless.

According to what Mahoney had told DeMarco, only five people were on the yacht that day: Mahoney, the two CEOs, the lady who piloted the yacht, and another stunning young creature who served appetizers and drinks. The rest of the crew had been given shore leave to better ensure that whatever was discussed remained private.

The reason for the scandal was that the Democrats, including their fearless leader Speaker John Mahoney, claimed that they were adamantly opposed to the merger of the two companies, making the usual noises that these companies, if combined, would control too large a percentage of the media market and competition would be stifled. The fact that both CEOs tended to lean conservative exacerbated the matter as far as the Democrats were concerned. Well, what Anderson Cooper learned from his unnamed source was that Mahoney had been persuaded by the CEOs to support the merger, and if he did so, he would be able to ensure that the merger wouldn't be blocked by the FCC.

After the story broke, Mahoney loudly and vehemently denied that he was in favor of the merger—and he demanded that Cooper name his source, the despicable coward who had propagated this horrible lie. Mahoney said that he simply met with the CEOs to hear what they had to say—he had an obligation to be open-minded, for Christ's sake—but no way did he agree to their demands. And the fact that the meeting had taken place on a yacht staffed by women who looked like Victoria's Secret models was irrelevant. When the two CEOs were asked about the meeting, they both refused to comment. A few days later, the merger was effectively squashed with Mahoney leading the charge to assure that outcome. He made it clear, however, that he was still determined to prove that Anderson Cooper's anonymous source was a lying scoundrel.

The one thing that had surprised DeMarco was that when Mahoney gave him the assignment, he did so in a room filled with people, two of those people being senior Democrats who chaired committees in the House. Normally when Mahoney gave DeMarco a task he did so privately and often in some dimly lighted watering hole far from the Capitol. DeMarco figured that Mahoney had wanted his political brethren to be witnesses to his sincerity about finding the leaker and proving the allegations false.

The most likely culprit, according to Mahoney, was the young lady who had served drinks to him and the CEOs. She was standing nearby the whole time and would have easily been able to hear the discussion.

The two CEOs certainly wouldn't have leaked the story and the lady who had piloted the yacht had been on the bridge the whole time the meeting occurred.

The drink server was one Candy Ross, *Candy* actually being the name on her birth certificate. She was a stunning blonde, six feet tall, only twenty-one years old. She had cornflower blue eyes and a slight overbite, which DeMarco found appealing. He had seen pictures of her in a *Maxim* magazine photo spread where she and her crewmates were nude but artfully posed to cover strategic body parts. DeMarco had rationalized looking at the online photos as something that any thorough investigator would do to learn more about a viable suspect. Before he'd learned that Shannon had been killed, he'd been looking forward to meeting Candy.

---

CEO Morton's yacht was moored at a marina in Annapolis, but as the yacht wasn't constantly at sea—it wasn't an oil tanker—the female sailors all had other jobs at businesses owned by Morton. Candy was currently employed as a hostess in a restaurant in Baltimore's Inner Harbor.

DeMarco walked into the restaurant and the first person he saw was Candy. She was wearing a short black skirt, a low-cut top, and high heels. With the high heels she was two inches taller than he was. The word *statuesque* came to mind. She was standing at a lectern, talking on the phone, taking down a reservation. As it was only eleven a.m., the restaurant had only a couple of customers in it and waiters were still putting silverware on the tables for the expected lunch crowd.

DeMarco waited until she finished recording the reservation then said, "Candy, my name's Joe DeMarco. I'm—"

"Hello," Candy said, treating DeMarco to a brilliant smile. "Would you like a table?"

"No. Ms. Ross, I'm a congressional investigator."

"A what?"

"I'm a lawyer who investigates things for congress. Legal things. Serious things."

DeMarco took out his wallet, flipped it open to his congressional ID, showed it to her as if he were flashing a badge, then flipped the wallet shut and put it back into his pocket.

"I don't understand," Candy said.

Maintaining a stern expression, DeMarco said, "Can we go someplace where we can talk privately? It's important."

"Yeah, I guess," Candy said, a frown line now wrinkling her forehead. She led him into a bar that was empty of customers and over to a corner table. "So, what's this all about?" she asked.

"The reason I'm here is I need to know if you've done something inappropriate."

"Inappropriate?" Candy said. "Like what?"

"Candy, a week ago you were on Mr. Morton's yacht and you served drinks to Mr. Morton, Mr. Hamilton, and—"

Hamilton was the other CEO at the meeting.

"—and Congressman John Mahoney, the Speaker of the House."

"What's your name again?" Candy asked.

"DeMarco."

"Well, I'm confused, Mr. DeMarco. How could me serving drinks to three people be the subject of a congressional investigation?"

"Candy, CNN recently broke a story about the meeting held that day on Mr. Morton's yacht. Did you see it?"

"Nope. I'm too busy to spend my time watching CNN."

"According to CNN, Mr. Morton and Mr. Hamilton discussed plans for merging their companies during the meeting, something that's a very big deal, something that requires approval by the FCC, and which many members of congress and the public object to for a variety of reasons. The problem is that someone who had knowledge of that meeting told CNN that John Mahoney had agreed to support the merger, which Congressman Mahoney strongly denies. Congressman Mahoney wants the person who leaked the story to CNN to step forward and admit that he—or she—lied."

"Aw, now I get it. You think I'm the one who leaked the story."

"That's what I'm trying to find out. Did you?"

"What if I did? Did I commit a crime?"

"You may have. You might be prosecuted for libel or slander. And if you benefitted in any way from the lie, for example if CNN paid you, that could be considered fraud. Case law when it comes to making false statements versus protections provided by the First Amendment is complicated, but there's a possibility you could be prosecuted."

What DeMarco knew about case law when it came to the First Amendment would fit into a vessel smaller than a thimble—and Candy was apparently bright enough to know this.

"Oh, bullshit," she said. "I'm not a lawyer, but I know there's not a chance in hell I could be prosecuted."

"Or Mahoney might sue you," DeMarco added. "Can you afford a lawsuit? Look, if you'll just admit that you were the source and say you made a mistake, you can avoid a whole lot of potentially expensive and unpleasant problems."

Candy cocked her pretty head to the side and said, "You know, I'm not sure a lawsuit would be a bad thing. The publicity might be good for me. Plus, I'd win the lawsuit."

"So you are saying that you leaked the story to CNN."

"No, I'm not saying that. I was just curious about what could happen to me if I did. The truth is, I didn't pay any attention to what those guys were talking about that day. I just brought them drinks, and when I wasn't doing that, I was reading a book for a class I'm taking and texting my sister. About the only thing I remember about that meeting was that Mahoney drank like half a bottle of Maker's Mark. He drinks like a fish. Now if I was to say that to CNN, would that be slander? Or is it libel?"

Before DeMarco could respond, Candy stood up and said, "I need to get back to work. This place is a madhouse at lunchtime."

DeMarco sat in the bar for a moment after she departed. He'd completely misjudged Candy, and most likely because of her name. He'd thought she'd be an empty-headed blonde bimbo—which Candy clearly wasn't—and he'd figured that if she had leaked the story, he'd be able to get her to admit it. That obviously hadn't worked. Furthermore, he couldn't tell if she'd told him the truth or not. His gut told him that she was being honest, that she hadn't leaked anything, but now, goddamnit, he was going to have to call Neil and see if he could get her cell phone records to see if she'd talked to anyone at CNN.

Candy smiled slyly and waggled her fingers at him as he left the restaurant.

---

As he was driving back to D.C., he spent a few minutes thinking about other sources of the leak. It could be a person who worked for one of the CEOs and had prepped him for the meeting, but that didn't make a whole lot of sense either.

He phoned Neil.

Neil called himself an *information broker*, which sounded better than saying he was a guy who hacked into databases. He had an office in D.C., on the banks of the Potomac, within sight of the Pentagon—which the Department of Defense should have found alarming. Neil owned the building where his office was located because he made a very good living by obtaining privileged information and providing it to people willing to pay.

Corporations found him useful in getting a leg up on the competition. Rich people getting a divorce hired him when they wanted to find out how much the person they were divorcing was really worth.

Politicians used his services to help win elections. (In spite of recent history showing how inappropriate emails could end careers, politicians couldn't seem to stop themselves from sending them.) And DeMarco had used Neil's services several times while carrying out his duties for John Mahoney.

For something as simple as getting Candy's cell phone records, DeMarco suspected that Neil wouldn't have to touch a computer keyboard or slither through a corporate firewall. All he'd do was make a couple of phone calls. Neil had been in business long enough that he had contacts in organizations that stored data, such as Google, Facebook, telephone companies, and the IRS. He paid people in these organizations to give him what he wanted then passed on the cost to his customers.

DeMarco told Neil that what he needed was proof that Candy had called anyone associated with CNN. "Yeah, okay," Neil said. "But I'm in the middle of something big right now. I'll get back to you as soon as I can."

"All right," DeMarco said. "And thanks."

"You can thank me by paying me promptly, unlike the last time. I thought I was going to have to send a guy named Guido over to break your legs."

The truth was that DeMarco didn't really care if Candy was the source of the CNN story. And whether she was the source or not, he suspected that Mahoney had indeed plotted with the CEOs on the merger—and who knows what Mahoney might have done if the story hadn't leaked. But DeMarco didn't care.

The only thing he cared about was learning what had happened to Shannon.

# 5

DeMarco just couldn't believe that Shannon had been the unlucky victim of a random killer passing through a small town in Wyoming. He could understand her being mugged if she'd been walking around a big city late at night and the mugger losing control and killing her, but some guy at a truck stop just happening to see her entering her motel room, then knocking on the door and shooting her when she opens it—No, that sounded wrong. Shannon wouldn't have opened the door to a stranger after midnight, or at least he didn't think so.

As he'd never heard of Waverly, Wyoming, DeMarco googled the place on his phone. He learned that Waverly was on Interstate 80 in south central Wyoming about halfway between Salt Lake City, Utah and Cheyenne, Wyoming. Based on the 2010 census, 410 souls dwelled there. Why would Shannon be doing research in such a place? What was there to research?

DeMarco knew that Shannon had a younger sister named Leah and that Shannon had been close to her. He decided to call Leah and express his condolences, but mostly he wanted to know what Shannon had been doing in Wyoming. He knew Leah's married name was Donovan, that she had a couple of kids, and lived in Newport, Rhode Island—but as he didn't have her phone number he had to go online and pay one of those people-search companies to get a number.

He called Leah, but his call was sent to her voicemail. Not recognizing his number, Leah might have thought it was a robocall or maybe, and more likely, she was too grief stricken to feel like talking to anyone. He left a message saying, "Leah, you don't know me but my name is Joe DeMarco. I was a friend of Shannon's. I called to tell you how sorry I am for what happened to her and I also wanted to ask you a question. Would you mind calling me back when you can? Thanks."

Less than five minutes later, Leah called back. She said, "I'm glad you called, Joe. Shannon really liked you and she told me all about you and how you flew to Montenegro to get the woman who tried to kill that girl in Boston."

"You know," DeMarco said, "Shannon was the one who gave me the idea to go to Montenegro."

"Yeah, she told me. She said—" Leah's voice broke. "Oh, God I'm going to miss her. She was so funny and so smart."

"I'm going to miss her too," DeMarco said.

"Shannon said that the one big regret she had when she moved to California was that she most likely wouldn't be seeing you anymore. It sounded as if you were the one who got away."

DeMarco could see no point in telling Leah that he wasn't the one who got away; he was the one left behind.

"Leah, do you have any idea what she was doing in Wyoming?"

"Not really. I know she was doing research on her next book. She did the same thing when she wrote *Lighthouse*. She spent three months in Nova Scotia, in the winter, freezing her ass off, so she could experience firsthand what it was like living there. But she never told me what the new book was about. Something to do with wild horses or grazing rights or something like that."

"Wild horses?" DeMarco said.

"That's what she said. But when Shannon would call, we'd talk mostly about my kids. About the only thing she said about Wyoming was that she'd encountered some real characters out there and she told me a couple of stories about people she'd met that made me laugh. Shannon could always make me laugh." Leah started crying again and DeMarco was starting to feel bad for having called her.

Leah said, "Joe, Shannon's memorial is being held this Saturday here in Rhode Island. I'll text you the invitation. Her agent will be there and he might know what she was doing out West. I'd like to know myself. I'm just having a hard time believing that someone killed her to steal her purse."

Shannon had been raised in Newport, Rhode Island. Her parents and her sister still lived there. Her memorial was held at St. Mary's Church, a Gothic structure built in the 1800s. It was filled with Shannon's childhood friends, women she played with on the Boston College hockey team, and famous writers who'd mostly come from New York and Boston. DeMarco was surprised to see Stephen King there; King had been one of the many renowned authors who had endorsed Shannon's book. The biggest shock was that the keynote speaker was the actress Reese Witherspoon, who had bought the film rights to Shannon's book and would play the lead character in the movie that was being made. Shannon had spent a lot of time with Witherspoon as she'd adapted her book for the screenplay, and they'd apparently become close. DeMarco didn't know if Witherspoon had written Shannon's eulogy herself or if it had been written by a Hollywood screenwriter, but it was moving and eloquent and completely captured Shannon's personality, the impact she'd had on others, and how the world had lost one of its greatest writers. Like every other person present, DeMarco had tears in his eyes by the time Witherspoon finished.

After the service, the mourners moved to a nearby hall for wine and hors d'oeuvres. DeMarco gawked at Witherspoon and the other big-name celebrities; Witherspoon struck him as being down to earth. He eventually walked up to Leah and introduced himself. She had Shannon's dark hair and gray eyes but was shorter than Shannon and heavier. Two kids, a boy and girl, who were probably five and six years old respectively, were clinging to her.

She said, "You look just the way I imagined you would from what Shannon told me about you." When she smiled, he saw she also had Shannon's smile; the same dimple appeared in her right cheek.

DeMarco wondered what that meant about the way he looked: Like a hood? Like a slick political operator? He had no idea, but the way Leah said it, her comment had sounded like a compliment.

DeMarco again expressed his sorrow for her loss, commented on how wonderful the memorial had been, then asked, "Can you point out Shannon's agent? I want to ask him what she was doing in Wyoming."

Leah's head swiveled as she searched the crowd, then pointed. "There he is. The guy with the goatee in the blue suit near the bar."

"What's his name?" DeMarco asked.

"David, uh, David something. I don't remember his last name."

---

DeMarco went over to the bar, ordered another glass of wine, and stood near David. He was a tall man with thinning dark hair and a neatly trimmed goatee. He was talking to a heavyset woman wearing enormous earrings and based on the bits of conversation that DeMarco overheard, they were complaining about something that Amazon had just done. Finally, the woman turned to the bar to get another glass of wine for herself and DeMarco stepped up to David.

"Hi, my name's Joe DeMarco. I was—"

"Oh, so you're the famous DeMarco," David said. "Shannon told me about you and that thing you did in Montenegro when the two of you were dating. She said it would make for a good book but it wasn't the sort of thing she was interested in writing. I was thinking about having another writer I represent contact you to get some of the details."

No way in hell was DeMarco going to talk to a writer about what had happened in Montenegro.

"The reason I wanted to talk to you," DeMarco said, "is that I'm curious about what Shannon was doing in Wyoming. I'm having a hard time accepting what the newspapers have said about her being killed by some guy who wanted to steal her laptop and her purse."

"Are you thinking about investigating what happened?" David asked.

"I don't know what I'm going to do. But I've been wondering if her death could have been connected to whatever she was doing there."

David said, "If you don't mind, let's step outside. I want a cigarette. I don't usually smoke but today, well—"

"Sure," DeMarco said.

Outside the reception hall, DeMarco was struck by what a lovely day it was. It shouldn't have been. The skies should have been gray and the rain should have been drizzling down to match the sadness of the occasion.

David lit a cigarette and said, "I'm not exactly sure what she was doing in Wyoming. Shannon was one of those writers who felt the need to completely immerse herself in the setting of the book she was working on, the way she did when she wrote *Lighthouse*. She spent three months in Nova Scotia to absorb the setting, the people, the atmosphere, whatever. I guess she just couldn't google things like other writers do."

"Yeah, I know, her sister told me that too. But what was the new book she was writing about?"

"All I really know is that Shannon was fascinated by a standoff between some guy in Wyoming and the federal government. This guy apparently faced down a bunch of FBI agents armed with assault rifles and refused to let them come on his property."

"Why?"

"I have no idea. Something to do with wild horses."

"Who was the guy?"

"That I remember. His name was Hiram Bunt. I mean, isn't that a great name for a fucking nut who'd take on the federal government?"

DeMarco shrugged. "And this standoff, it was the focus of her book?"

"I don't think so. She told me she was writing a love story and that the standoff was peripheral to the whole thing."

"A love story?"

Now David shrugged.

"Did she submit anything to you?" DeMarco asked. "A synopsis, an outline, a couple of chapters, anything like that?"

"No. Shannon refused to write a synopsis or an outline for her books. She said she wanted people to read the book not a *summary* of the book."

David dropped his cigarette on the ground and crushed it with his shoe. Then, apparently feeling guilty for littering, picked up the butt and put it in a pocket.

He said, "You know, there is a person who might be able to tell you more about what she was doing in Wyoming. I represent a writer named Gloria Brunson. She writes a series about this female sheriff in Wyoming. She's a good writer but she's never hit it big the way Shannon did. Anyway, I introduced Shannon to Gloria over the phone one day because Gloria lives in Rock Springs, Wyoming, which is close to the place where the standoff occurred and I know Shannon had been planning to see her when she arrived in Wyoming. I'll give you Gloria's number."

The memorial was held on a Saturday and DeMarco drove back to D.C. that same day. The following morning he went to Clyde's, where he'd have brunch accompanied by a mimosa or two. Clyde's is a popular bar and restaurant on M Street in Georgetown—and a great place to go for Sunday brunch, when it would be filled with young men and women who worked on the Hill or in the White House or for lobbying firms on K Street. Most of them appeared to be extremely pleased with themselves, and based on the snippets of conversations DeMarco would overhear, they seemed to think they were running not just the United States but the entire world. The scary part was that maybe they actually were. Today, however, he ignored the crowd around him, and while waiting for his omelet, he pulled out his phone and googled "Hiram Bunt, Wyoming."

After reading half a dozen articles, he concluded Hiram Bunt was a dangerous megalomaniac who belonged behind bars. The gist of the story was that Bunt had been engaged in a decades-long battle with the federal government over the use of public land in Wyoming. DeMarco learned that almost half the land in Wyoming, about thirty million acres, is public land, and about eighteen million acres were managed by the Bureau of Land Management. Ranchers were allowed to graze their livestock on some of this public land, but they were required to pay a fee for doing so. The grazing fee was currently about $1.50 per head of cattle per month, which to DeMarco didn't seem excessive.

Well, Hiram Bunt didn't care what the grazing fees were and he'd decided that he wasn't going to pay them. He argued that public lands belonged to the *public,* and the goddamn federal government had no right to charge him anything. Bunt went so far as to claim that what the government was doing was unconstitutional and he sued to make his case—and one judge after another jammed his lawsuit up his ass. But

Bunt didn't care what the judges said and he refused to pay the grazing fees—he refused to pay them for more than ten years. And when the amount he owed added up to almost a million bucks, the BLM decided to round up some of his cattle that were eating the public's grass for free, intending to sell the cattle to offset some of what he owed.

Which was when Bunt decided to take on the BLM at gunpoint.

Bunt, people who worked for him, and other ranchers who felt the same way that he did, armed themselves with AR-15s, shotguns, hunting rifles, and pistols, and confronted the BLM agents while they were doing the roundup. The BLM immediately called in the cavalry, and the FBI and other law enforcement agencies sent in about fifty guys in body armor, packing automatic weapons. The FBI agents, with the cameras rolling, started screaming at Bunt to stand down and Bunt screaming back that he wouldn't, saying that he'd shoot any government son of a bitch that tried to rustle his cattle.

The feds blinked first. They walked away without arresting anyone or taking any cattle. When the agent in charge was asked *why* he backed down, he said that he wasn't about to get into a gun battle where a bunch of civilians were likely to get massacred. Not over a bunch of cows, he wasn't.

Wild horses fit into the story in a peripheral way. Wild horses were all over the western United States and most ranchers didn't like them; there were too many of them and they were munching on the grass the ranchers wanted for their cows. Protecting and managing the wild horses was the responsibility of the BLM, and Bunt wanted the BLM to get all the damn horses off his land, which, by the way, was not fenced in any way to separate public from private land. And if there had been fences, Bunt wouldn't have liked that either, as fences would have made it more difficult for his cows to wander over from his property to chew the government's grass. Not long after the standoff occurred, a dozen wild horses were found dead on public land near Bunt's ranch but no one could prove that Bunt had killed them and he loudly denied having done so.

And that's where things stood today. Bunt owed the federal government a million bucks, was never held accountable for killing a bunch of horses, and he was still grazing his cattle on public land without paying the grazing fees. One odd thing—or at least DeMarco found it odd—was that several politicians in Wyoming, including Congressman Wilbur Burns, had sided with Bunt, saying that the federal government shouldn't have as much control as it did when it came to public lands. DeMarco was also surprised to learn that Bunt's feud with the government wasn't unique or all that uncommon. Ranchers and the BLM had been engaged in squabbles for decades in a number of other Western states like Nevada, Arizona, and even liberal Oregon.

DeMarco wondered, however, if Shannon's research could have uncovered something new that would have posed a threat to Bunt. Maybe she'd found proof that he had slaughtered the horses. Most people considered horses to be beautiful, magnificent animals. Killing a dozen of them would affect people emotionally, and much more so than Bunt refusing to give the government the money he owed. Even Bunt's political allies, who most likely had a lot of animal lovers for constituents, might turn against him if they knew he'd shot the horses. Taking on the government over grazing fees might have made Bunt a local hero, but killing the horses would have made him a pariah. And if Shannon had found proof that he'd done it, it didn't seem totally unlikely that a nut like Bunt, a guy willing to engage in a gun battle with the FBI, might murder a woman who threatened him. But DeMarco was just speculating. He needed to know more. And what he really wanted to know was what else the fucking cops were doing to catch Shannon's killer. He just couldn't accept the looney trucker story.

DeMarco owned a narrow, two-story townhouse on P Street in Georgetown. It was made of white-painted bricks, had a front yard the size of a postage stamp, and an equally small backyard. It was about the only possession, other than his clothes, that he'd managed to keep after his first—and only—wife divorced him.

He went back to his place after brunch, thought briefly about mowing his lawn, then thought: *Aw, fuck that.* If the grass grew another couple of inches, who cared? He certainly didn't. His next thought was to go to a driving range and hit a bucket of balls—for him, whacking golf balls was often therapeutic—but that didn't appeal to him either. He just couldn't get Shannon off his mind. His head was filled with images and memories of her.

He took a seat on the patio in his untended backyard and started to call the number Shannon's agent had given him for Gloria Brunson, the writer in Wyoming that Shannon had most likely met with—and again thought: *Fuck that.* He decided, at that moment, that he was going to go see the woman in person. Then after he heard what she had to say, he'd mosey on over to Waverly and speak directly to the deputy in charge of the case—the one with the implausible theory that some truck driver passing through town had killed Shannon.

Shannon may have been famous enough to make the front page of the *Washington Post* but the media had the attention span of a hummingbird and would soon move on to other things. No hotshot investigative reporter was going to be assigned to make sure the Wyoming cops were doing their job. Nor did she come from a wealthy, connected family that could apply a political blowtorch to the cops if they were dragging their feet. And what all this meant was that her death could very likely become an unsolved homicide, which would then become a cold case, and Shannon's killer might never be caught—unless someone was pushing. Well, DeMarco knew how to push. All going to Wyoming would cost him was the price of an airline ticket and a day or two, and he'd be more likely to find out what the cops were doing to catch her killer and apply some pressure if they weren't doing enough. Also, if he talked to the cops in person, then the authorities would know that someone outside of Wyoming cared about what had happened to her and would be on their backs if they didn't get results.

He did, however, have the problem that his boss wanted to know who had leaked the merger story to Anderson Cooper. DeMarco knew if he called Mahoney and told him that he was flying to Wyoming to look into the death of an old lover, Mahoney would tell him to stay in D.C. and do his damn job. And although DeMarco had already decided that he was going to go whether Mahoney liked it or not, he'd just as soon not lose his job. So he needed to come up with a lie. Lying to a liar like Mahoney didn't bother him a bit.

He mulled the problem over. Okay. He'd say that his widowed mother, who lived in Queens, had fallen, broken her hip, and he needed to go home and help her out and set up some kind of nursing care for her. Not a great lie, but the best he was able to come up with after five seconds of deliberation. But as he knew that Mahoney, the callous bastard, wouldn't care about his poor, old mother's broken hip, he wouldn't speak to Mahoney directly. Instead he would call Mavis, Mahoney's secretary, and have her pass on the lie. He figured that by the time Mahoney was informed, DeMarco would be in Wyoming. Yeah, that sounded like a plan, maybe not a great plan, but he couldn't come up with a better one.

Mavis answered the phone saying, "Why are you calling me on a Sunday, DeMarco?"

Mavis had worked for John Mahoney since she was a teenager. She knew where all the bodies were buried and God help Mahoney if she ever decided to become a whistleblower. She was now about Mahoney's age and looked it, but when she'd been younger she'd been a stunner, and DeMarco was convinced that she was one of the many women Mahoney had slept with. Whatever the case, she was as loyal to Mahoney as a gangbanger's pit pull.

DeMarco said, "I need to talk to Mahoney. I called him but he didn't answer his phone or—"

"Of course he didn't answer his phone. He's on his way to China and from there he's going to Vietnam. Don't you ever watch the news?"

He didn't bother to tell Mavis that his television was almost permanently set to the golf channel, but this was perfect. Sometimes luck was better than a lie. "No, I didn't know about him traveling," DeMarco said. "And I'm sorry I bothered you. What I need to tell him will have to wait until he's back. There's nothing he can do while he's in China. How long is he going to be gone?"

"He's spending two days in China then he's scheduled for three more in Vietnam, although his Vietnam schedule hasn't been finalized. He'll be gone at least a week because when he returns he'll probably be attending a fundraiser on Cape Cod."

"Well, okay. I'll talk to him when he gets back. Again, sorry to bother—"

Mavis hung up.

Only because he was curious, DeMarco googled, "Mahoney, China, Vietnam." The all-knowing Internet informed him that Mahoney was attending some sort of trade meeting in China with a gaggle of other Democrats. Vietnam, however, appeared to be a personal mission for him, a stroll down memory lane. When Mahoney was seventeen, he'd been a Marine and had served in Vietnam and was rewarded for his service with shrapnel from a grenade, some of which was still embedded in his right knee. The article said Mahoney was planning to visit some of the places where he'd fought and would be meeting with some of the guys who'd been on the other side lobbing grenades at him. All those guys would be about Mahoney's age by now, and all the hatred they'd once felt for each other had most likely dissipated. DeMarco was sure, however, that Mahoney would make a point of rolling up his right pant leg and showing all the old Viet Cong soldiers the scar on his knee. Mahoney showed people the scar every chance he got.

For a moment he wondered why Mahoney hadn't called him before flying to China to ask what he'd learned about the leaker. Mahoney had been adamant that DeMarco had to identify the rascal but, for whatever reason, he hadn't bothered to harass him. Whatever the case, it looked as if he could spend a couple of days in Wyoming and Mahoney wouldn't even know that he'd been gone.

# 6

Not surprisingly, there were no direct flights from Washington D.C. to Rock Springs, Wyoming, the city where the writer, Gloria Brunson, lived. Vast parts of the United States are called "fly over country" for a reason. The quickest way for DeMarco to get to Rock Springs was to take a four p.m. nonstop from Reagan National to Salt Lake City—then rent a car and drive for three hours. He arrived in Rock Springs close to midnight on the same day he had talked to Mavis and checked into a Holiday Inn. It had been too dark for him to appreciate the Wyoming landscape during the drive.

The next morning he woke up around eight, had breakfast, and at nine o'clock called Gloria Brunson. He figured that by nine she should be up.

He said, "Hello, my name is Joe DeMarco and I was wondering if you'd talk to me about Shannon Doyle. Your literary agent in New York gave me your number."

"Are you a reporter?"

"No, I work for Congress but—"

"Oh, you're *that* DeMarco. Shannon told me about you."

This surprised him, just as it had surprised him that Shannon had told her sister and her agent about him. He'd obviously made a bigger impression on her than he'd thought. Which was good, but which also made his heart ache.

"What did you want to talk to me about?" Gloria said.

"I'm actually here in Rock Springs. I was hoping I could meet with you. Maybe I could buy you lunch or something."

"You don't have to do that. Just come to my house."

---

Rock Springs, Wyoming, a town with a view of White Mountain, is known for mining the coal that kept the Union Pacific Railroad's steam engines chugging back in the 1800s. Its population is only about twenty-five thousand; nonetheless, as of the last census, it was the fifth-largest city in Wyoming.

Gloria Brunson lived in a boxy, white, two-story clapboard house on C Street, close to the Rock Springs Library. There were two red rocking chairs on the front porch, the paint on the chairs peeling. Parked in the driveway was a dusty Jeep Cherokee. The grass in the front yard was about three inches high and dandelions were thriving. It appeared as if Gloria had about as much interest in yard work as DeMarco did.

He knocked on the front door and was greeted by a tall, thin woman in her sixties. She was wearing a plain white T-shirt, faded blue jeans with a hole in one knee, and sandals that looked as if they'd been made from old tires. Her hair was gray and straight and reached her shoulders and DeMarco's first impression was: Hippie. She shook his hand and said, "It's good to meet you. Shannon liked you a lot, so I figure you must be okay. It's a beautiful morning. Let's go sit in the backyard and talk. You want coffee?"

"Sure," DeMarco said.

DeMarco followed her into the house. The interior was cluttered with old but comfortable looking furniture. Books were everywhere:

in bookcases, on end tables, on the floors. A Native American blanket was tossed on a sofa; a cat sat on the blanket and a pair of scuffed tennis shoes lay in front of a recliner. The dining room table was littered with stacks of paper and more books; an open laptop sat on the table. DeMarco imagined the table was the spot where Brunson wrote her novels.

Gloria's backyard had a small flagstone patio and they took seats across from each other at a round table shaded by a beige umbrella. The grass in the backyard was as high as the grass in the front, but then he noticed three white, wooden boxes, each box about four feet tall, and he realized they were beehives. He could see the industrious little critters darting in and out of them.

Gloria saw where he was looking and said, "Those are my children as I don't have any of the human variety. You're not allergic to bee stings, are you?"

"Uh, no," DeMarco said.

"That's good. So what did you want to talk about?"

"I'm trying to find out what Shannon was doing in Wyoming. The cops here think she was killed by some trucker passing through Waverly, but I'm having a hard time accepting that. I want to see if her death could be connected in some way to whatever she was doing out here."

"Are you conducting an official investigation into her death?"

"No. I don't have the authority to investigate anything. I'm just a lawyer who does odd jobs for Congress."

"I think you're being modest. Shannon told me about that woman you tracked down in Montenegro because she tried to kill a young girl."

"Well, that was an extraordinary circumstance and not what I normally do."

DeMarco didn't see any point in mentioning that what he normally did was function as Mahoney's bagman and track down people who leaked unflattering things about his boss to the media.

DeMarco said, "Do you have any idea what she was doing in Waverly? Her agent thought she was researching some nut named Hiram Bunt who got into an armed standoff with the feds."

Gloria shook her head. "Shannon was intrigued by the standoff, but it wasn't the focus of her book. What interested her were the people."

"You mean Bunt?"

"Not so much Bunt as the men who work for him. They think of themselves as cowboys. They may use GPS devices to track cattle, and ATVs and pickups more often than horses, but they identify with the old-time cowboys who fought Indians and went on cattle drives back in the 1800s. A lot of them come across to outsiders as John Wayne wannabes, but they're not acting. It's who they are. They're tough as nails because you have to be to do the kind of work they do. Their idea of sport is riding a one-ton bull in a rodeo. They don't go around picking fights but they won't walk away from one. They make good soldiers, and a lot of them are veterans. They're often laconic and soft-spoken, and many of them tend to be painfully shy around women. Shannon was particularly impressed with how capable most of them are. When your car breaks down, you probably call triple A. These guys can fix cars and well pumps and windmills and just about every piece of machinery you see on a modern ranch or farm. They also all hunt and fish, and Shannon always said that come Armageddon, they'll survive while the rest of us will starve to death in the dark when the power grids come crashing down."

Gloria took a breath. "Anyway, that's what fascinated Shannon, what she called the cowboy persona. As for the book she was writing, I have no idea what it was going to be about. She told me she was writing a love story, but Shannon's approach to storytelling was so unique that I have no idea what kind of book it would have been and I doubt Shannon even knew when she first came out here."

"So what was she doing?" DeMarco asked. "Interviewing these people she found so interesting?"

"Interviewing them. Studying them. She spent a lot of time just riding around and looking at the country. *Lighthouse* was as much about the setting as it was about the women in the novel, and I think she was trying to do the same thing here: Capture the magnificence of the open range and the people who live on it."

"Do you know if she recorded these interviews?"

"Oh, no. Shannon just talked to people and soaked in everything about them. I doubt any of them would even consider a conversation with her an interview. And I actually helped her get started in Waverly. Waverly's a small town, but they have a book club there, and I've spoken to the club a couple of times about my novels. I introduced Shannon to the lady in charge and she was just thrilled that a big-name writer like Shannon Doyle would be willing to meet with her group. So Shannon immediately became friends with about twenty women in town and after that, she just sort of settled in. She'd go to the bars and the restaurants there and chat with folks. She told me she met a lot of the men who work for Bunt, even danced with a few of them, and she genuinely liked them."

*Liked them? How in the hell could she have liked a bunch of assholes who'd get into an armed confrontation with FBI agents?*

"What about Bunt? Did she ever talk to him?" DeMarco asked.

"I don't know. I imagine she would have wanted to, but I don't know if she ever did."

"What do you know about him?"

"I know his family has owned the Bunt Ranch going back to the days before Wyoming was even a state. His ancestors actually fought the Shoshone and the Ute when they first arrived out here. He's rich. In addition to what he's made from raising cattle, he's made a lot of money off natural gas. The area around Waverly is loaded with natural gas. He also owns property and businesses in Waverly and Rock Springs and Red Desert and the other little towns along I-80. When it comes to Waverly, he's basically a feudal lord. He handpicked the mayor and the city council, and the county sheriff probably wouldn't arrest him if he committed murder in broad daylight."

"I don't understand that. Why would the sheriff be close to a guy who got into an armed standoff with the government?"

"Well, first of all, Wyoming is no different than any place else. Politicians cozy up to rich people because rich people help them get elected. And Sheriff Clay Webber may be a cop, but he's also a politician who has to get elected every four years and Hiram Bunt helps make that happen. But you also have to understand that a lot of people in Wyoming take a dim view of the federal government in general. As far as most Wyomingites are concerned, the people in Washington, D.C. are representing the interests of city dwellers who live in California and New York, cities where millions of people live, and places that have nothing in common with the towns in Wyoming. People here don't want the federal government imposing a bunch of rules on them; they figure they can make up their own rules without any outside help. As for the standoff, the sheriff and other state politicians are basically on Bunt's side when it comes to the federal government having too much control over the use of public lands and the sheriff refused to get involved. He said Bunt hadn't broken any county laws and the feds were going to have to resolve the issue without his help. He never said he approved of Bunt's facing down the agents, but he never said he disapproved."

"Huh," DeMarco said, thinking that Congressman Wilbur Burns, for either personal or political reasons, had also sided with Hiram Bunt in his battle against the government. What the hell was wrong with these people? But he didn't see how the sheriff's position on the standoff would be connected to him investigating Shannon's death. Murder wasn't a federal crime; it was a local one.

"Let me ask you this," DeMarco said. "Did anything at all happen in Waverly while Shannon was there, something big, something involving Bunt, that might have interested her?"

"The only noteworthy thing that's happened in Waverly recently was that a BLM agent was killed near Bunt's ranch about a month ago."

"Really. Who killed him?"

"No one knows. But the case is being investigated by the FBI, out of their office in Casper, and not by the sheriff."

"Was Shannon looking into the BLM agent's death?"

"I don't know, but I doubt it. Shannon didn't write true crimc or crime fiction. But I know she knew the BLM agent. She told me he was a sweet young guy who she'd see having dinner by himself at the main restaurant in Waverly and she felt sorry for him. He ate by himself because folks in Waverly mostly consider the BLM the enemy."

Gloria paused and said, "You know, the person who might be able to tell you more about what Shannon was doing is an old gal named Harriet Robbins. She owns a café directly across the highway from where Shannon was staying, and Shannon told me that Harriet was the best source of gossip in Waverly. Anyway, I got the impression that she and Shannon became close. I don't know if she'll talk to you, but you might want to give her a try."

# 7

The town of Waverly, Wyoming is about a forty-minute drive east of Rock Springs. It straddles I-80 for about two miles and is a ramshackle collection of small businesses, gas stations, modest houses, a single church, an elementary school, and a couple of restaurants. There didn't appear to be any zoning laws. Next to homes were fenced-in areas containing equipment and bundles of pipe that DeMarco assumed were used for extracting or transporting natural gas or oil. The houses ranged from dilapidated shacks to well-tended middle-class homes. Surrounding the town were miles of flat land covered by sagebrush. He didn't find the place the least bit picturesque and he doubted it was a magnet for tourists.

DeMarco's first stop was the motel where Shannon had been staying. Behind the motel were approximately thirty travel trailers and RVs, ranging in size from twenty to forty feet. The motel itself was a two-story structure with twenty-four rooms, twelve rooms on each floor. As he'd learned when Congressman Burns talked to the Sweetwater County sheriff, Shannon had been staying in a room on the ground floor, but DeMarco didn't know which one. Across the highway from the motel was a café, a truck stop with an array of gasoline and diesel pumps, and a 7-Eleven-like convenience store. All the rooms in the motel faced the truck stop.

DeMarco hadn't bothered to call ahead to reserve a room, figuring that finding accommodations in a small town in the middle of nowhere wouldn't be a problem. What he didn't realize was that thanks to natural gas drilling and exploration near Waverly, every room in both of the town's motels, as well as bedrooms rented out in private homes, were almost always filled with workers. DeMarco saw one of the rooms on the ground floor of the motel had a sign on it saying OFFICE. He walked over to it. The door to the room was open and there was a stout man sitting on a couch, legs up on a small table in front of him, watching television. He appeared to be Native American, his skin reddish-bronze and grooved with creases, and he had two long, gray braids hanging down to his shoulders. He could have been anywhere in age from sixty to eighty; it was impossible for DeMarco to tell. He was wearing a turquoise Western shirt with snap buttons, worn jeans, and scuffed cowboy boots.

DeMarco said, "Hi. I'd like a room."

The man studied DeMarco for a moment, then said, "Well, you're in luck. A guy just checked out because he had some kind of family emergency and had to get back to Texas. How long you going to want the room for?"

"I don't know. Probably just a couple of days. Can I pay day to day?"

"Sure, if you got a credit card that works."

DeMarco smiled. "I do," he said.

The man got off the couch with a grunt; he was about five foot six and bowlegged. He limped over to a small dining area with a table that would seat two; there was something wrong with his left leg, maybe a bad hip. Near the table was a two-burner propane stove and a half-size refrigerator. He took a plastic box off the top of the refrigerator, a box that might have once been used for holding fishing tackle, and pulled out a registration form printed on a five-by-eight index card. He put a credit card reader on the kitchen table and plugged it into a phone jack. Not a high-tech operation. He handed the registration form to DeMarco and said, "Fill that out."

DeMarco completed the registration form and handed it back to the motel manager. The manager looked at it and said, "Washington D.C. We don't get too many folks from back east out here. What brings you to Waverly?"

DeMarco thought for a second about saying he was on vacation and just wanted to see Wyoming. Then he thought: *Why lie?* The whole point of him being in Waverly was to find out what had happened to Shannon and to do that he needed to talk to people and ask questions. He wasn't on some secret mission; the more people who knew what he was doing the higher the likelihood of someone telling him something useful.

DeMarco said, "What's your name?"

"Sam," the motel manager said. "Sam Clarke."

"Call me Joe," DeMarco said. "And the reason I'm here is a good friend of mine was killed right in this motel."

"You talking about that pretty, writer lady?"

"That's right. Shannon Doyle. She meant a lot to me and I'm just trying to understand what happened to her."

"Jim Turner thinks— "

"Who's Jim Turner?"

"The deputy in charge of the investigation. He thinks it was some trucker passing through, maybe some guy addicted to drugs who needed money, and he spotted Miss Doyle going into her room and decided to rob her."

"Yeah, that's what I heard too, but I have to tell you, Sam, I'm having a hard time buying that story. I mean, and no offense intended, but this motel doesn't strike me as catering to a rich clientele. Why would anyone think that someone staying here would have much money on them?"

"Hell, I don't know. And what doesn't seem like much money to you can be a lot of money to some guy who's broke."

"That's true. But do you have any other theories as to what might have happened to her? For example, could she have made an enemy out of someone living here?"

"That girl? No way. Everybody liked her. I liked her. Plus people here don't go around killing people. The last time somebody was murdered in Waverly was ten years ago. This poor vet who had PTSD and shot his wife, then killed himself."

"What about that BLM agent who was killed recently?"

"That didn't happen here in town. And except for Miss Doyle, that's the only other murder that's happened in, like I said, at least ten years."

"Anyone know why the BLM agent was killed?"

For the first time, Sam looked away and seemed uncomfortable. "No one knows what happened to that kid. The FBI is investigating that one. Look, I need to track down my daughter and get her over to clean your room. Why don't you go get some lunch and your room should be ready by the time you're done."

Seeing he wasn't going to get much more out of Sam, DeMarco said, "The food in that café across the highway any good?"

Sam smiled. "Depends on who's cooking. If it's Harriet, the lady who owns the place, it's pretty mediocre. Sometimes worse than mediocre. If it's Billy, then it's okay. When you walk in there, if you see a Mexican-looking guy in the kitchen you can order anything on the menu. If Harriet's cooking, I'd stick with a sandwich."

---

Sam stood in the doorway to his room/office, watching as DeMarco crossed the highway and proceeded to the café. He didn't know what to make of DeMarco. For some reason—and maybe only because of the way he combed his dark hair straight back and had an Italian sounding name—he reminded him of the hood played by Robert De Niro in that mafia movie *Goodfellas*. But it was hard to imagine why a mafia hood would come to Waverly. Plus the guy was from D.C.—a place known for crooked politicians, not gangsters.

He pulled his cell phone out of a pocket and called his daughter.

She answered the phone, sounding groggy. He said, "Are you still in bed?"

"No," she said. "I was just doing some things around the house." He was sure she was lying and he'd woken her up. He was also about ninety percent certain she was using again. And he suspected that might not be the biggest problem she had, although he found it hard to believe she could have done something like that.

"You need to get over here and start cleaning the rooms. And start with Room 9. A new guy just checked in and I imagine the guy who checked out left a mess."

"Yeah, yeah, all right," she said.

Goddamnit, he thought. She was destroying her life. It was a good thing her mother wasn't alive to see what she'd become and that none of the assholes she'd dated had knocked her up. And now, as if her luck couldn't get any worse, some guy from Washington was poking into the writer's death. He had to find a way to ask her about the gun, not that she was likely to tell him the truth. And about the earrings too, to see if he could get her to admit what she'd done, but at this point the earrings hardly mattered.

After he spoke to his daughter, he sat for a bit gnawing on a toothpick. It occurred to him that maybe the best thing to do when it came to DeMarco was to get the law involved. That was dangerous because Jim Turner might decide to help DeMarco, but he doubted that. Turner wouldn't want an outsider digging into his business. Then there was the fact that Turner had his own big secret he was trying to keep. No way would he want that getting out, not if he wanted to keep his job. Yeah, Turner might just move DeMarco along.

He called Turner, saying, "Jim, it's Sam Clarke. I thought you might want to know a guy from Washington just checked into the motel."

"Washington?" Turner said.

"Washington, D.C."

"Okay, but why are you calling me?"

"Because he said the reason he's here is he's looking into the death of that writer who got killed."

Sam heard Turner inhale sharply and he didn't say anything for a beat. "What's this guy's name?"

"DeMarco. Joe DeMarco. I got his address if you want it."

"Yeah, give it to me."

Sam read off the address written on the registration card.

Turner said, "You got any idea who he is? I mean is he a reporter or a private investigator or a cop, anything like that?"

"I don't know. All I know is what's on the registration form. And he didn't tell me anything about himself. Anyway, I just thought you'd like to know about him being here."

"I appreciate that, Sam. And do me a favor, will you?

"What's that?"

"Keep an eye on him and if you learn more about him or if he does anything that strikes you as strange, let me know."

---

Turner disconnected the call and closed his eyes, thinking: *Would this nightmare never end?*

He didn't think she'd killed the writer—but she might have. She had the stones to do something like that, particularly if she felt threatened, and Doyle had posed a threat. And as bad as he felt about what had happened to Doyle, he had no intention of doing anything more than he was already doing. He wasn't going to probe any deeper. He wasn't going to risk everything—her, himself, his family—for a person he'd barely known.

He sat for a moment, mulling things over, then called Clay Webber and told the sheriff that there was a guy from D.C. in Waverly who appeared to be looking into Shannon Doyle's murder. As much as he hated to tell his boss anything, he had to keep the sheriff in the loop when it came to such a high profile case. Naturally, the sheriff wasn't happy to hear about DeMarco, but only because he didn't want any outsider poking into a crime under his jurisdiction, and particularly not someone from D.C. As he'd expected, the sheriff told him to find out more about DeMarco, to keep tabs on him, and to keep him informed.

He sat a bit longer, then made a second call, figuring it couldn't hurt. And maybe it might even help. Hiram had his own way of dealing with folks he didn't like hanging around town.

A gruff voice answered, saying, "Yeah?"

"It's Jim Turner."

"I can see that on my phone. I'm in the middle of something. What do you want?"

*What a prick.* "I'm sorry to bother you, Mr. Bunt, but there's something I thought you should know."

# 8

The café had a counter fronted by six red-topped stools and there were eight tables with white Formica tops and red Naugahyde-covered chairs. On the walls were photos of what DeMarco suspected was the land around Waverly: large, grassy areas that seemed to go on forever, striking red rock formations, windmills standing like sentinels, everything photographed with dramatic morning or evening skies in the background.

Four men were in the café, all wearing jeans, T-shirts, and baseball caps. One man wore a *Peterbilt* cap, and DeMarco figured the men were most likely truckers who'd parked their rigs at the nearby truck stop. Two were sitting at the counter; another was at a table by himself fiddling with an iPad. The fourth man was standing near the cash register paying a stout, gray-haired woman. The woman's hair was thick and cut short, no more than an inch long. She wouldn't have to brush or comb it in the morning; all she'd have to do was rub her hand across her head. She was a tough-looking old bird.

DeMarco took a seat at one of the tables where he could see the motel across the highway. From where he was seated, it would be easy to observe people going in and out of their rooms but it would be difficult to see their faces clearly. DeMarco was also relieved that a "Mexican-looking guy" was in the cooking area behind the counter standing in front of a grill flipping burgers. He picked up the menu and glanced at the offerings, and a moment later the woman who'd been at the cash register came over and said, "What'll you have?"

He figured the woman had to be Harriet, but DeMarco decided not to introduce himself. He wanted to talk to her when she was alone. He said, "I'll have a cheeseburger, fries, and a Coke."

She jotted down his order and turned to leave but he said, "Oh, what time does this place close? I'm staying at the motel over there."

She hesitated then said, "Nine, unless I feel like closing earlier. Or later."

---

Harriet had barely noticed the man walk into the café and take a seat at a window table. After she'd collected the money from the trucker who'd just finished his lunch, she reached for an order pad and started toward his table—and stopped abruptly. Oh, Jesus! The guy was the spitting image of a man she'd known in Chicago, a man she knew had killed half a dozen people.

Shannon must have lied to her!

Then she realized she was being ridiculous. If it had been the man she'd known in Chicago, he would have been in his seventies by now; the guy sitting at the table was in his forties. And except for his nose and the color of his hair and the way it was combed, he really didn't look at all like the man she'd thought he was. She had to get a grip on herself. Shannon had turned her into a basket case.

She walked over and took his order, hoping he didn't notice how her hand was shaking when she wrote it down. She didn't like it, however, when he'd asked when the café closed. It may have been a reasonable question for someone staying at the motel, but it was almost the same as asking: *When will you be alone?*

While waiting for his lunch, DeMarco pulled out his phone and was pleased to see that the café had a wireless network, probably to accommodate the truckers. DeMarco was curious about the Sweetwater County Sheriff.

A website contained a photo of Sheriff Clay Webber and confirmed that Webber had held the position for twenty-five years. The photo showed a narrow-faced man in his sixties with short gray hair and a white-brush mustache. The smile on his face looked forced, as if smiling wasn't something he did very often.

DeMarco learned that the sheriff's office employed seventy-five sworn officers and about twenty-five other people who handled administrative tasks. The main office was in Rock Springs. He also learned about the various functions overseen by the sheriff, which included emergency management, search and rescue, animal control, and management of the county detention center. No information was provided about Deputy Jim Turner, the man leading the investigation into Shannon's death.

The impressive thing was that although the sheriff only served about 45,000 citizens, his jurisdiction was all 10,500 square miles of Sweetwater County. The area of Sweetwater County, Wyoming was almost identical to the area of the entire state of Massachusetts.

DeMarco finished lunch, and as he was paying his bill, he asked Harriet, "Can you tell me where I can find a sheriff's deputy named Jim Turner? I was told he lived here in Waverly."

He could tell Harriet was reluctant to answer the question but finally she said: "He's usually out riding around, but he has an office in the municipal building on McCormick Road. I'm not going to tell you where he lives. I'd suggest you drive over to the municipal building and see if he's there. Or I imagine you could call the sheriff's office in Rock Springs and they could get word to him that you need to see him."

"Thanks," DeMarco said, thinking Harriet wasn't exactly the friendliest person he'd ever met and he wondered how hard it was going to be to get her to talk to him about Shannon.

---

Harriet watched DeMarco walk back to the motel. He may not have been the man she'd thought he was when she first saw him—when he'd almost made her heart stop—but there was something about him that made her leery. He obviously wasn't a trucker or a gas worker; he just didn't have that look about him. And why did he want to talk to Jim Turner? For her own protection, it would be good to know more about him and see what he was doing in Waverly. She picked up the phone and called Turner.

She said, "I thought you'd like to know that a man who just left my place asked me where he could find you. I told him you might be in your office."

"Who is he?" Turner asked.

"I don't know, but he's staying over at the motel."

"What's he look like?"

"Dark hair. Maybe six foot. He was wearing a dark blue golf shirt with the name of some golf course on it."

Harriet hung up, thinking tomorrow she'd find an excuse for calling Turner and see if he'd tell her anything about the guy, whoever he was.

# 9

DeMarco found the municipal building and was pleased to see a dusty, white sedan with a light rack on the roof parked in front of the building. On the sides of the vehicle was the word "Sheriff" in large letters placed over a seven-pointed star that said "Sweetwater County Sheriff's Office." He walked into the building and found a young woman standing in front of a vending machine studying the selection of candy, chips, and cookies. DeMarco asked her if she knew where he could find a deputy named Jim Turner.

She pointed to her left. "End of the hall," she said without looking at him. She appeared to be having an intense, internal debate with herself as to whether or not she should get a snack.

DeMarco walked down the hall and came to an unmarked office with an open door and found a man sitting behind a desk, his black ankle-high boots up on the desk. He was wearing a uniform consisting of hunter green pants, a short-sleeved gray shirt, and a wide belt holding a pistol, handcuffs, a radio, and all the other typical law enforcement paraphernalia. On the desk was a half-eaten sandwich and a can of Coke, and he was holding a catalog from a sporting goods store named Cabela's. On the front cover of the catalog was a deer with an enormous set of antlers. The deer looked glassy-eyed and DeMarco suspected it was dead.

The man stood up when he saw DeMarco standing in the doorway. He was at least six foot four with broad shoulders and a narrow waist and was probably the handsomest son of a bitch that DeMarco had ever seen who wasn't a movie star. He had wavy dark hair, full lips, a blunt chin, and a perfect, straight nose. He reminded DeMarco of Rock Hudson or maybe a young Tom Selleck. In a cowboy hat, Turner could have been one of the models who'd posed as the Marlboro Man.

"Can I help you?" Turner said.

"My name's Joe DeMarco. I wanted to—"

"Yeah, I've been expecting you."

"Expecting me? How did you know—"

"Sam Clarke told me you'd checked into his place and was asking about the Doyle woman's murder. I also got a call from Harriet Robbins who said there was a guy who wanted to see me and she described you."

Talk about jungle drums. Or maybe smoke signals would be a more appropriate analogy.

Turner sat back down and pointed DeMarco to a chair.

"Ol' Sam gave me your address and I looked you up on the Internet. I was surprised to see you were accused of killing some congressman."

"I was proven innocent."

"Yeah, I noticed that, but that's not the only thing that got my attention. One of the articles I read said you're John Mahoney's fixer."

*Fucking Internet.* "The article's wrong. I'm not anyone's fixer. I'm just a lawyer who works for Congress. And the only reason I'm here is because Shannon was a good friend of mine and I want to understand what happened to her. I'm not here in any official capacity."

"You're telling me you flew out here on your own dime?" Turner sounded skeptical.

"Yeah, I did. This is personal for me."

"So you're not here on behalf of Mahoney, a man I have to tell you isn't all that popular in this state."

"Mahoney isn't involved at all. He doesn't even know I'm here."

He could tell Turner didn't believe him.

"So what exactly do you want, Mr. DeMarco?"

"I want to know who killed Shannon Doyle and why. And I'll be frank with you, Deputy. I'm having a hard time believing that some trucker passing through just happened to see her going into her motel room and decided to rob and kill her."

"How do you know that's something we're investigating?"

Whoops. DeMarco couldn't say he knew that because he'd listened in on a call between the sheriff and Congressman Burns. That could be a problem for Burns. He said, "I talked to a reporter who worked on the story and that's what he told me."

"Well, the reporter's right, but if I get my hands on the guy who talked to him, I'll make sure he's fired. But right now that's the best theory we have, that someone passing through town, most likely a trucker or someone who'd stopped late at night at the truck stop, saw Miss Doyle, decided to rob her, and killed her in the process."

"But how do you know it wasn't someone who lives here, someone local?"

"I don't for sure, but that seems pretty unlikely. She was only here in town for a couple of months and didn't make any enemies that I could find. Everyone I spoke to about her liked her, including my wife."

"Did you know Shannon?"

"No. I'd seen her around town and in the Hacienda Grill a few times, but I never spoke to her. But my wife met her when she came to talk to this book club that Carly belongs to. Anyway, Mr. DeMarco, we're doing everything we can to find out who killed her. We collected about a million fingerprints from her motel room but none of them has led to someone with a record. And none of the prints in the room belong to anyone here in Waverly other than Sam Clarke's daughter who cleans the rooms. The slug that was taken from her body was a .22 caliber but we have no way to trace it to a specific weapon. There was no shell casing in the room, so the killer either used a revolver or picked up the casing. And Miss Doyle never told anyone, including the sheriff's office, that anyone was bothering her or harassing her or threatening her or anything like that.

"What we're doing right now is running truckers who passed through that day through law enforcement databases, looking for anyone who stands out. But most long-haul drivers don't have felony records because the trucking companies usually won't employ them if they do. So we're going the extra yard when it comes to Miss Doyle, and a couple of clerks in the office in Rock Springs are contacting law enforcement where these truckers live to see if any of them have had run-ins with the law, like drug issues or beating up their wives or getting into fights with their neighbors, anything that might set off any alarm bells. But that's going to take some time because a lot of trucks roll down that highway every day.

"We also took photos of the slug removed from Miss Doyle's body, you know, photos showing striations from the barrel, and sent them to the FBI to see if the same weapon was used in another crime. So far we haven't heard back from the bureau, but as it's only been a few days, that's not surprising."

DeMarco was surprised that Turner was being so open with him regarding the status of the investigation. And although it sounded as if he was doing a lot, it still bothered DeMarco that Turner didn't appear to be looking at all in the direction of a local who might have had a motive.

DeMarco said, "What about the people who live in the trailers behind the motel?"

"I've checked out all of them. They're all gas workers and most of them have been here for months and have never gotten into any kind of trouble other than drinking too much. They also make decent money and wouldn't have much reason for stealing a woman's purse. Anyway, like I said, I checked them all out and none of them struck me as a likely suspect."

DeMarco said, "Did you think about seeing if anyone here in Waverly owns a .22."

Turner smiled. "Mr. DeMarco, you're in *Wyoming*. Now I don't know if it's true, but I read somewhere that there are more guns per capita in Wyoming than in any other state in the country, and it's the state with the fewest regulations when it comes to owning, buying, or carrying a firearm. There's no central firearms registry. People in this state wouldn't stand for that. If you buy a handgun from a federally licensed dealer there's a little paperwork, but if you buy one at a gun show or from your neighbor or inherit one from your daddy, there's basically no paperwork at all. So there's no way I could possibly find out who owns a .22 in this town and if I was to go around asking people if they did, they'd be within their rights to tell me to go to hell."

So much for that bright idea. DeMarco thought for a moment about asking about the BLM agent who was killed then decided not to. According to Gloria, that investigation was being handled by the FBI and he'd rather talk to the FBI than a guy who worked for an outfit that apparently didn't have a problem with Hiram Bunt's cowboys pointing weapons at federal officers.

Turner said, "Now if there's nothing else, I need to finish my lunch and get back to work."

"Just one other thing," DeMarco said. "I know Shannon was interested in an incident that happened here involving a bunch of wild horses that were killed. I know this because she told her sister and her literary agent. Did you ever solve that case?"

"Well, first of all, it wasn't my case to solve. The horses were shot on federal land and the BLM was leading the investigation. But I'm about a hundred percent sure I know who did it, and I told the BLM, but they couldn't prove it any more than I could."

"So who did it?" DeMarco asked. "I read an article that implied that a man named Hiram Bunt might have killed them because of some dispute with the BLM over the horses being on his property."

Turner laughed. "Hiram would never do that. I mean, he might have wanted to but his wife loves horses and she would have killed *him* if he ever did."

"So who killed the horses?"

"A guy named Brodie Miller, who was still living with his mother when he was forty. His father used to beat the hell out of both Brodie and his mom until he broke his neck falling off his own front porch when he was drunk. Anyway, when Brodie was a teenager, he used to go around shooting cats with a bow and arrow until he shot the wrong person's cat and got the crap knocked out of him. He liked to shoot prairie dogs and birds with a shotgun loaded with double-ought shot because he got a kick out of seeing them blown apart. And I'm pretty sure he shot the horses because of the weapon that was used, which is fairly rare, but not unique, and Brodie owned that kind of weapon. Brodie just likes to kill things."

"Jesus. Does this guy live in Waverly?"

"Not anymore. Brodie's currently residing at the state penitentiary in Rawlins. He raped a retarded girl, and because of that, and because the judge knew Brodie was going to end up killing a person someday, he was sentenced to twenty years."

"I see," DeMarco said.

"Anything else, Mr. DeMarco?"

"No, I guess not. And thanks for taking the time to talk to me," DeMarco said.

"So what are you going to do now? Personally, I think the best thing would be for you to fly back to Washington and let me do my job."

"I haven't decided what I'm going to do next. Since I've never been in this part of the country before, I might do a little sightseeing before I leave."

Turner stared at DeMarco for a couple of heartbeats. "Sir, I have to tell you something. As you're not law enforcement and have no jurisdiction when it comes to Miss Doyle's murder, I won't tolerate you doing some sort of independent investigation and going around questioning folks."

"Really," DeMarco said. "You're going to stop me from talking to people?"

Turner's jaw clenched. "You don't want to aggravate me, sir. I've been pretty pleasant towards you but that can change in a hurry."

---

Turner didn't know what to make of DeMarco

The sheriff had sent him to New York once to take an anti-terrorism class put on by Homeland Security and the NYPD. Sweetwater County, Wyoming, wasn't a likely terrorist target, but attending the class was mandatory for the county to get some of those anti-terrorism federal funds.

He met a couple of NYPD detectives at the class named Morelli and Carlucci, and they took him to one of those bars in Manhattan where cops never paid for drinks. Morelli and Carlucci were hard-looking bastards who seemed laid back, but their eyes were constantly in motion studying everyone around them. They wore cheap suits and rubber-soled shoes and carried saps in their back pockets. After a few drinks, they admitted that the way they often dealt with New York's habitual criminals was to take them into an alley and pound the snot out of them.

DeMarco reminded him of the two detectives. He even looked a bit like Carlucci. And he didn't look like some politician's flunky or what Turner thought a political flunky would look like. He didn't have the requisite air of slickness about him. As for him being Mahoney's fixer, he didn't know what that meant or what a fixer did. The only fixer he'd ever heard of was that guy who went to jail for paying off a porn star who'd slept with the president. Whatever the case, Sweetwater

County wasn't Washington, D.C. and DeMarco was completely out of his element.

He wondered if she knew that DeMarco was looking into the writer's death. If she didn't know already, she'd probably know before the day was out, the way news traveled in this town. What he really wanted to do was ask her that if she *had* done it, had she been smart enough to dump the gun and the writer's laptop someplace they couldn't be found. But, of course, she was smart enough—and no good could come from him asking a question like that.

# 10

DeMarco was impatient to talk to Harriet but figured he should wait until tonight and try to catch her just before the café closed. Until then, he'd do a little sightseeing as he'd told handsome Jim Turner, and get the lay of the land.

Before setting out he drove over to the truck stop convenience store to top off his gas tank and buy a couple of bottles of water. While paying for the water, he asked the clerk if he could tell him where Hiram Bunt's ranch was. If the clerk asked why he wanted to know, DeMarco would have said that he wanted to see the place where the famous standoff had occurred—maybe adding that he really admired what Hiram had done—but the clerk never asked. He told DeMarco to head east on I-80 and then take County Road 23 north and look for a big sign saying Bunt Ranch.

The land near Waverly was sprinkled with rocks and sagebrush—and not much else. The vista was mostly the pale-yellow color of dry grass or hay, with the occasional splotch of green. He didn't see a single tree unless it was planted in someone's yard. DeMarco's overall impression was: flat, dusty, dry, and unappealing. Shannon certainly would have found something complimentary and poetic to say about the landscape—capturing in words its vastness and the subtle splendor of the high desert foliage—but to DeMarco, flat and dry was good enough. He didn't see any of the wildlife known to inhabit the area, no pronghorn, mule deer, or wild horses. He didn't even see a rabbit. He did see a lot of barbed wire fencing, a bunch of tanks he assumed were for storing natural gas, a couple of windmills, and a few cows. He tried to imagine the area without signs of human habitation and industry—the way it had looked when millions of buffalo roamed the plains—but couldn't. Mankind had made too much of a negative impact. It just struck him as a stark, wind-whipped place to live. He suspected that the natives would take exception to his opinion and wouldn't appreciate an east coaster's view of their habitat, but the truth was that it wasn't Chesapeake Bay.

About fifteen miles from Waverly, he saw a sixteen-foot wide metal gate and on the gate was a wooden sign that said "Bunt Ranch." Below the words, burned into the sign, was the letter B inside a circle. He figured that was Bunt's brand, which made him wonder, in an era of GPS tracking devices and barcoding, if ranchers still branded their cattle. Off in the distance was a brick three-story house with white columns supporting a second-story balcony. It looked a bit like a Southern plantation house transplanted from Georgia.

There were several outbuildings, which he guessed were stables or barns or equipment sheds. He also noticed a couple of fenced-off areas containing a complex assembly of gauges and valves and red-painted pipes, which were possibly associated with natural gas collection or distribution, but he didn't know for sure.

He tried to imagine Hiram Bunt standing defiantly in front of the gate alongside a bunch of guys in cowboy hats carrying rifles, facing off federal agents dressed in tactical gear. The feds should have never let the arrogant asshole get away with it.

About three miles south of Hiram's place, DeMarco saw a black, lockable mailbox with the word *Bunt* on it. A closer look revealed the names Steven and Elaine Bunt, who he assumed were people related to Hiram.

After driving around aimlessly for a couple of hours, he headed back to Waverly. As he was entering the town, he spotted a restaurant called the Hacienda Grill. The parking lot was about half full. He decided to stop for a beer.

The dining room had a Mexican motif—sombreros hanging on the walls; bright, multicolored placemats on the tables; a couple of small, artificial Saguaro cacti in the corners. At the back of the place was a bar with a small dance floor.

He remembered Gloria Brunson telling him how Shannon had danced with some of the cowboys and had a momentary twinge of jealousy. He had never taken Shannon dancing because he always felt like an uncoordinated doofus trying to dance to the fast songs. Now he regretted that.

Walking into the bar he had the feeling of being in an old western movie, the one where the gunslinger walks into the saloon and everyone in the place turns to stare. At the bar were four men dressed in smudged jeans and T-shirts, as if they'd just come from work. There were only three women in the place, one behind the bar pouring the drinks and two others sitting with men at tables near the empty dance floor.

DeMarco went up to the bar and ordered a bottle of Bud and took it over to a table where he could see a baseball game playing on a television over the bar. The Rockies—the closest major league baseball team to this part of Wyoming—were playing the LA Dodgers. DeMarco didn't care which team won. He normally rooted for the Nationals and booed the New York Yankees just because they were the Yankees.

He'd only been there about ten minutes when a group of four men entered the bar, all of them wearing cowboy boots, two of them wearing cowboy hats. They took a seat at a table a few feet from DeMarco and one of the men walked up to the bar to order drinks.

The man was about six feet tall with a lanky build. He would have been handsome if he'd had a bit more chin. His hair was a dirty blond color and long, touching his collar. He went to the end of the bar and crooked a finger at the bartender, a pretty Hispanic woman wearing a frilly white blouse that left her shoulders bare. She walked down to the end of the bar and they put their heads close together. The man must have said something funny because the bartender tipped back her head and laughed. She had a long, graceful neck.

Four beers in hand, he walked back to the table where his friends were sitting and one of them said, "You keep messing with that, Sonny, you're gonna wake up some night like that one guy did and find your wife holding a knife in one hand and your little dick in the other."

The man sounded serious but Sonny laughed.

---

DeMarco returned to his room; he still had a couple of hours to kill before going to see Harriet. He flopped down on the bed and turned on the television and saw it was tuned to CNN—and there was Mahoney's white-haired head and large red face filling the screen. The story was about Mahoney's so-called trade mission to China, and he was sitting at a banquet table with Chinese president Xi Jinping, smiling, a glass of some brownish liquid in front of him that DeMarco suspected was bourbon. The picture changed to the grinning face of Anderson Cooper, who had apparently decided to make Mahoney his bitch after the merger story. Cooper was saying how Mahoney was supposed to be in China giving Jinping a hard time about Chinese trade practices but had spent the day touring Chinese distilleries. DeMarco hoped that Mahoney didn't see the story and decide to call and ask him what he was doing to find the leaker. He tapped buttons on the television remote until he found the golf channel.

At eight, he headed over to the café. There were only two other men in the place. He again sat at a table by himself and ordered meatloaf and mashed potatoes for dinner. Billy, the guy who'd cooked his lunch, wasn't in the kitchen and Harriet was functioning as cook, waitress, and cashier. The meatloaf was mediocre.

By eight forty-five, DeMarco was the only customer in the café. Harriet was in the kitchen, cleaning up in there, and DeMarco walked over to the counter and said, "Could I get another Coke?" The café didn't serve alcohol.

"No, I'm closing up. You ready to settle your bill?"

"Why'd you rat me out to the deputy, Harriet?"

She turned and scowled at DeMarco. The lady had a first-class scowl. "What did you say?"

"I went over to see Turner after I had lunch here today, and when I got to his office he told me that you'd called and told him I was looking for him. I'm just curious as to why you did that."

Harriet didn't answer him immediately, then said, "Like I told you, I'm closing and it's time for you to settle up."

"Harriet, my name's Joe DeMarco. I was a friend of Shannon Doyle's."

Harriet raised a white eyebrow. She said, "Huh. So you're DeMarco. Shannon told me about you. Made it sound like you were the one who got away." This was the same thing Shannon's sister had said, although the way Harriet said it, it was as if she couldn't imagine DeMarco being a catch worth keeping.

DeMarco said, "I didn't get away, Harriet. I was in love with Shannon but when her book hit it big, she moved out to Hollywood and left me behind. It wasn't my choice."

"Shannon told me you work for that blowhard, John Mahoney."

"I do work for Mahoney in a way, but Mahoney isn't the reason I'm here in your lovely little town."

"Then why are you here?"

"Because I want to know what happened to Shannon. I want to know who killed her and I'm not buying the story being peddled by the sheriff that some trucker did it. So talk to me. Tell me what you know about what she was doing here. Tell me if she could have gotten cross-wired with someone local who might have killed her."

Harriet shook her head.

"Harriet, I was told that you spent a lot of time talking to Shannon and that you were close to her."

"Who told you that?" To DeMarco that didn't sound like a casual question. It was as if Harriet was seriously concerned that someone knew she'd been talking to Shannon.

"A writer named Gloria Brunson who lives in Rock Springs. She was the one who introduced Shannon to the Waverly book club. And if what Gloria said is true, I figure you might have a better idea than anyone about something that Shannon might have done that would have given someone a motive for murdering her."

Again Harriet shook her head.

"Did you like Shannon, Harriet?"

Surprisingly, Harriet's eyes welled up with tears. "I loved that girl. But I don't know you and I'm not talking to you."

DeMarco studied her for a moment then said, "What are you afraid of, Harriet?"

"I'm not afraid of a damn thing. Now you have to leave."

---

Harriet flipped the sign on the door to CLOSED after DeMarco left, then stood watching as he headed over to the truck stop convenience store and then back to the motel. She finished cleaning the kitchen, started the dishwasher, and got the coffee ready to go so all she'd have to do in the morning was turn on the coffee pots.

She took the bottle of Jim Beam out of the cabinet under the cash register, splashed two fingers of bourbon into a water glass, and added a cube of ice. She then turned off all the lights in the café and went to sit in the dark at a table near a window. She knew she wouldn't be able to sleep tonight.

She sat there watching the trucks roaring down the highway, thinking about Shannon. She'd only known her for two months, but as she'd told DeMarco, she'd just loved her. She'd never met anyone so bright, so full of life, so insightful. In fact, her being so insightful was what had probably gotten her killed. But Shannon saw the world in ways that Harriet couldn't, observing things about the land and the people that Harriet never would have noticed, much less been able to write about. She'd read *Lighthouse* twice, once before she met Shannon and once afterward, and she couldn't ever match the woman who talked like an ordinary person to the person who had written such a beautiful story. Harriet had never considered herself an emotional person, but that book had made her cry and at the same time, soar with joy. No other book she'd read had ever affected her that way, and now the brilliant woman who'd written it would never write another one—and there was nothing DeMarco or anyone else could do to bring her back.

DeMarco scared her—but these days it seemed as if everything scared her, and nothing scared her more than the future and the possibility of her secret getting out. When on earth had she become such a coward? She supposed it wasn't long after Gene died and left her all on her own. With her mannish haircut and her brusque attitude and the way she talked to the truckers, people would never guess how frightened she was of what lay ahead. If Gene were still alive she knew she wouldn't have felt so insecure.

Unlike her, Gene had been skinny as a rail and then he goes and drops dead one morning of a heart attack neither one of them had seen coming. Gene had always been the optimist, even in the worst of times—and there'd been some really bad times—but he'd always allayed her fears and told her they had nothing to worry about, that everything would be all right. And maybe if he'd still been alive she wouldn't have been so lonely and spent as much time talking to Shannon as she did. But Gene was gone and now she had no one. No kids and no relatives, at least none that she could call upon to help her. She didn't even have any close friends in Waverly, which in a way was surprising considering how long she and Gene had lived there. Gene had always said they couldn't afford to have close friends, and she knew he'd been right, but with him gone, she now regretted that. What was going to happen to her when she was too feeble to work? She had hardly any savings; she barely scraped by with Social Security and the little she made off the café. She didn't have the money to move into some assisted living place, not that there was such a place in Waverly. All she knew was that the last thing she could afford to do was alienate the people in this town and she wasn't going to tell DeMarco anything.

DeMarco. He was a good-looking man and she could see why Shannon might have been attracted to him, but Harriet sensed that there was a hard side to him that he usually kept under wraps. Shannon had told her how she met him when she was living in Boston, while she was still tending bar there, before *Lighthouse* was published. She said DeMarco had gotten involved in a case in Boston involving a devious female lawyer who'd embezzled from a young girl's trust fund and tried to kill her and then fled to Montenegro to avoid being arrested. According to Shannon, DeMarco had gone to Montenegro and literally kidnapped the lawyer and brought her back to the United States to stand trial. Yeah, no doubt DeMarco was a ruthless, tricky son of a bitch—but was he as good as Shannon seemed to think he was?

She wondered if maybe there was a way to steer DeMarco—just give him a little nudge to point the way—but in a manner that he wouldn't know she was the one doing the nudging. She sipped her bourbon and thought about that.

No, forget it. She didn't have the guile or the subtlety. Gene could have done it; he'd misled people for thirty years before he died, but she didn't have that ability. No, she wasn't going to point DeMarco anywhere. She was going to keep her head down, her mouth shut, and hope for the best.

And pray that Shannon hadn't lied to her.

# 11

DeMarco bought a couple of cold beers from the convenience store at the truck stop and walked back to his motel, where he filled a bucket with ice and put one of the beers in the bucket.

Something was going on with Harriet, but he didn't know what. All he was certain of was that she knew more than she was willing to talk about and his presence in Waverly frightened her, but he couldn't imagine why. Rather than waste his time thinking about Harriet, he decided to find out more about the death of the BLM agent.

He placed his laptop on the small desk in the room, took a seat, opened the beer he hadn't put in the ice bucket, and booted up the computer. He googled the BLM agent's death and found an article posted by a Wyoming newspaper.

The agent's name was Jeff Hunter. He was twenty-four years old when he died. He'd been an army veteran, earned a Purple Heart in Iraq, and was survived by a wife and a two-year-old daughter. As DeMarco continued to read the article, he reached for his beer without looking—and almost knocked the bottle over. Luckily, he caught the bottle before it tipped and spilled twelve ounces of Bud into his laptop—which made him remember an incident that had happened when he'd been dating Shannon.

He'd been at her apartment in Boston and she'd been preparing dinner, having warned him in advance that she was a lousy cook. (It turned out she really was.) While she was cooking, DeMarco had opened a bottle of wine and poured each of them a glass. At some point, DeMarco wandered over to the table where she worked. Her laptop was on the table, next to a stack of photographs that he learned were photos of the coast of Nova Scotia. Anyway, when he'd placed his wine glass on the table to reach for one of the photos, Shannon had shrieked: "Don't put your glass there!"

"What?" he'd said, wondering if she meant he was supposed to put his glass on a coaster, although the table was so battered he couldn't imagine why she would have cared.

She'd rushed over and picked up his glass, put in on the kitchen counter, then picked up her laptop and moved it away from the table. She said, "Sorry, I freaked out. Six months ago, I was drinking a can of Coke while I was working on my book and the can slipped out of my hand and almost all the Coke ended up on the keyboard of my laptop. It destroyed the damn computer and the geeks at the Apple Store were only able to save about a dozen files. One of the files they couldn't save was my book, and because I hadn't backed up the file for a couple of days, I lost an entire chapter that I had to completely recreate. Since then, I don't put any kind of liquid near my computer." Fortunately, after that, the evening proceeded to more pleasant things and he ended up in Shannon's bed.

DeMarco took out his cell phone and called Gloria Brunson. It was only nine p.m. and he figured the writer would still be awake.

When she answered he said, "Hi, this is Joe DeMarco. I'm sorry to bother you so late—"

"It's fine. I don't usually go to bed until midnight. What's going on?"

"I want to know how Shannon would have backed up her computer files." He went on to tell the story of how Shannon had reacted when he'd put the glass of wine near her laptop. He concluded with, "If I could find the backup files, it might give me a clue as to what she was doing out here."

"I see," Gloria said. "Well, I'm pretty old-fashioned, not to mention practically broke, so I back up my work to a flash drive. Other writers get more sophisticated. Some of them attach an external hard drive directly to their computer and files are backed up continuously to the hard drive as the writer works. I've heard other writers back up their files to the cloud but I don't know anything about that."

He chatted with Gloria a bit longer then disconnected the call and sat back to think. If Shannon had backed up her files to a flash drive or an external hard drive, those items should have been in her room when she was killed and might now be in the possession of the sheriff's office. Tomorrow he'd call Jim Turner and ask if he'd found a flash drive or a hard drive. If Turner had, however, DeMarco doubted that Turner would give him access to the device. Then something else occurred to him, but he realized it was almost midnight on the east coast. He'd make the call tomorrow morning.

He went back to reading the article on the BLM agent and concluded there wasn't anything in the article that was useful. It didn't say what Hunter was doing when he was shot or even exactly where he'd been shot, just that it was on public land somewhere northeast of Waverly. The article did mention the standoff between Hiram Bunt and the BLM, and while making it clear that there was no indication that Bunt had been involved at all in Hunter's death, made the point that tensions were known to run high between local ranchers and the agency. The story concluded by saying that the FBI was pursuing all avenues of investigation and if any good citizen had any information, they should contact the FBI's office in Casper.

DeMarco woke up at eight the following morning, and after showering and shaving, moseyed on over to Harriet's café for pancakes and sausage. Harriet took his order but acted as if he was a complete stranger. After breakfast, he called the Sweetwater County Sheriff's general number and said he needed to speak to Jim Turner regarding an ongoing investigation in Waverly. Turner called him back half an hour later while DeMarco was taking a stroll through the town to work off some of the calories from his breakfast.

DeMarco said, "I wanted to know if you found a flash drive or an external hard drive in Shannon's room?"

"Why are you asking?"

"Because writers tend to back up their files to devices like those."

"Okay, but I still don't see why you're asking."

DeMarco decided a lie might be appropriate. "Because Shannon's sister asked me to ask. Her sister is the beneficiary of Shannon's estate and because Shannon was famous, even a partially completed novel could be valuable." Before Turner could say anything else, DeMarco added, "Now I imagine Shannon's sister's lawyer could make a request that you turn over anything you found in Shannon's room, but the only thing she wants are the backup files if they exist. I thought the simplest thing would be to ask if you found a flash drive or something like that, and if you didn't, the matter would be closed. If you did find something, I'll pass the information on to her sister and let her, or her lawyer, proceed from there."

Turner, without hesitating, said, "We didn't find a flash drive or an external hard drive in the room. If we had, it would have been collected as evidence in the investigation. But the only things in the room were her clothes, a suitcase, and a knapsack. There wasn't anything in the suitcase and the only things in the knapsack were sunscreen lotion, sunglasses, and a cheap pair of binoculars."

"Well, then that settles that," DeMarco said.

"Mr. DeMarco, how much longer do you intend to be here?"

"I don't know, Deputy. Like I told you yesterday, I've never been to this part of the country before and I was thinking about doing some exploring. Maybe I'll see if I can spot some of those wild horses. You got any suggestions for where I should go?"

Turner said, "Don't call me again."

---

Turner disconnected the call. He'd never even thought about there being a backup copy of whatever Doyle had been working on. If there had been, God knows what could be in it. The good news was that he'd told DeMarco the truth. The forensic people hadn't found a backup drive in the writer's room. If they had, he would have known. He also would have been powerless to stop them from reading whatever was on the drive. So if Doyle had some sort of device for backing up her files, maybe it had been in her laptop case, which had been stolen along with her computer. And if she was the one who'd killed Doyle, she certainly would have gotten rid of any evidence tying her to the crime. He could just see her going for her morning horseback ride on that black mare she liked, taking a small folding shovel with her, and burying everything she'd taken from the writer's room. *If* she killed the writer. God, he hoped he was wrong.

---

DeMarco continued on his stroll through Waverly, stopping once to call Shannon's literary agent in New York. The agent's secretary said he wasn't available, that he was meeting with Martin Scorsese to discuss the sale of the film rights to one of his client's books. She said this in a breathless tone, as if a meeting with Scorsese was only one step down from a meeting with God Almighty. DeMarco asked her to have the agent call him as soon as he could.

He noticed a barbershop across the street and walked over to it. He'd needed a haircut before he left D.C. and the situation when it came to his hair hadn't improved. There was no one in the barbershop but one man sitting in one of the shop's two barber chairs reading a newspaper. The man had a shaved head but compensated for his baldness with an impressive waxed, white handlebar mustache. DeMarco figured the man had to be the barber, and thinking it might be a while before Shannon's agent concluded his meeting with Scorsese, decided to get his hair cut.

About halfway through the process, the barber asked what DeMarco was doing in Waverly; he apparently knew all his customers and knew DeMarco was an outsider. When DeMarco said he was looking into the death of the writer, Shannon Doyle, the barber said, "Never met the woman. Never read her book either, although my girlfriend tried to make me."

He paused then added, "The last book I read was some stupid thing called *Vanity Fair* by a writer named Wackery, or something like that. This English teacher in high school wouldn't give me a passing grade til I finished it and wrote a report on it. That damn book was more than seven hundred pages long and I couldn't understand what the hell the guy was talking about. Fortunately, my buddy Harley—he's dead now, killed himself on a snowmobile—told me a guy named Cliff had boiled the whole damn book down to about seventy pages, so I read Cliff's book and wrote the report based on it. Now if you ask me, the man who can tell a story in seventy pages instead of seven hundred is the better writer."

DeMarco was just admiring his haircut in the mirror, waiting for his change from the barber, when David, Shannon's agent, returned his call. He stepped outside the barbershop and explained that he was trying to find out how Shannon backed up her work, and once again told the story of how Shannon had reacted when he'd put a glass of wine near her laptop.

David said, "Do you think her backup files might tell you something about why she was killed?"

"I don't know, but I'd like to look at them."

"Well, she told me the story about spilling the can of Coke into her laptop—that's pretty traumatic for a writer—and after that she started backing up her files to the cloud. She had an Apple laptop and she used the iCloud feature on the machine. But since she stored them in the cloud, I don't know how you'd get access to the files."

"I couldn't," DeMarco said. "But I know someone who can."

---

DeMarco called Neil.

Neil answered, saying, "Oh, yeah, I forgot to call you back. Sorry about that. Anyway, that gal, Candy, never called Anderson Cooper or anyone else over at CNN."

"Thanks, but that's not why I'm calling," DeMarco said. The last thing on DeMarco's mind was Mahoney's leaker.

DeMarco explained that he was calling because he needed Shannon Doyle's backup files, which were stored in the cloud. "Do you think you can find them and get them for me?" he asked.

"Maybe, if you can provide some basic information," Neil said.

"You mean the cloud isn't secure enough to stop you?"

"The cloud isn't secure at all. Google the subject and you'll see what I mean. But you need to get me as much information on Shannon as you can. Social security number, credit card numbers, home addresses, email addresses, phone numbers, everything that folks tend to put down when setting up accounts. And if you can get me the password she used for her iCloud account that would make things even easier."

"Her password? How the hell would I get that?"

"I was mostly joking, but people tend to put their passwords into their phones or they put them on Post-It notes under a desk blotter or some other place they can get to easily. I know one idiot who had a file in his computer titled Passwords, which I found when I got into his machine. Anyway, get me as much information as you can and I'll see what I can do. Expect my bill in the mail whether I get anything or not."

"This is urgent, Neil," DeMarco said.

"Yeah, well, urgent will cost you more."

---

DeMarco called Shannon's sister, Leah, and told her what he needed.

"What are you doing, Joe?"

"I'm trying to find out why she was killed."

Leah was silent for a moment then said, "They cleaned out Shannon's apartment in California and boxed up everything and sent it to me. A couple of the boxes contain files like bills and tax returns, stuff like that. I can probably get everything you need from the files."

"See if you can find anything that looks like a password she might use on a computer. You know, a string of weird letters and numbers."

Leah laughed. "I can already tell you what her password most likely was because she used the same password for everything. It's CoryJudy. That's all one word, capital C, small case o, r, y, capital J, small case u, d, y. Sometimes, if she had to, she'd put numbers after it, like 1, 2, 3, or she'd put an exclamation point or a dollar sign. But the basic password was always CoryJudy."

"CoryJudy?"

"Yeah, those are my kids' names. I told her she was a fool to use the same password for everything but that's what she did."

Two hours later, Leah emailed him the information he'd asked for and he forwarded the email to Neil, adding that Shannon's password might be some variation of CoryJudy, the names of Shannon's niece and nephew.

---

That evening, DeMarco had dinner again at Harriet's, this time trying the pot roast. He was hoping that his presence might shame Harriet into talking to him. It didn't. While he was polishing off a piece of apple pie for dessert, Neil called him.

"Okay, I got her files from the cloud. There're about five hundred of them. What do you want me to do with them?"

"I want you to send me every file she added or updated in the last two months."

"Hang on a minute. There's only one file, a Word file, that was saved in the last two months. It's about eighty thousand words, maybe three hundred pages double-spaced."

"Email it to me but also print it out and overnight it to me. I'm not sure I can find any place near where I'm staying to print out a file and I'd rather read a paper copy than try to read it on my computer."

"Where are you?"

"Waverly, Wyoming."

"Where the hell's that?"

DeMarco gave Neil the address of his motel. "And thanks, Neil."

DeMarco dropped by Sam Clarke's office before going back to his room to let Sam know that he was expecting a FedEx package tomorrow. He asked Sam to call him as soon as it arrived.

---

Sam called Jim Turner at ten the next morning. "Just thought you might want to know that DeMarco got a FedEx package this morning."

"What's in it?"

"Hell, I don't know. I wasn't going to open the man's mail. But it felt like a bunch of paper and right now DeMarco's sitting outside his room in a chair reading something."

Goddamnit, Turner thought. Had that son of a bitch managed to get those backup files he'd been asking about? But how could he have done that? And if he had gotten the files, what was in them? DeMarco had indicated that Doyle's sister wanted the files because one of them could be a partly completed novel—a novel based on whatever Doyle had seen and learned in Waverly. Could there be anything in the novel that pointed to whoever killed her? Jesus, he had to find out.

# 12

DeMarco opened the package Neil had sent him and saw it contained about three hundred pages, just as Neil had said. It was warm in the motel room and the small, stuffy space was making him claustrophobic. He bought a Coke from a vending machine, then took the chair from his room and put it outside on the walkway in front of the door. It was a pleasant early summer morning made somewhat less pleasant by the eighteen-wheelers noisily streaming down I-80.

He flipped through the pages quickly to see what he had. It appeared to be part journal and part sections of the novel that Shannon had been planning to write and it revealed the two distinct aspects of Shannon's character: Shannon the person that other people saw and Shannon the writer. The journal material wasn't dated but appeared to have been written in chronological order from the time she'd arrived in Wyoming, starting with a visit to Gloria Brunson. In these entries, Shannon wrote in a lighthearted, conversational style, similar to the way she spoke, many of her comments humorous and most likely not intended for anyone else to read. Like a remark about a cowboy who'd helped her change a tire when she got a flat.

She wrote: *The kid looked strong enough to have lifted the back end of the car without a jack, but he was so shy he could barely look me in the eye. He kept calling me 'ma'am' like I was his grade school teacher, even though I wasn't more than ten years older than him. Cute guy with a rip in the back of his jeans he probably wasn't aware of. He was wearing red jockey shorts which made me smile."*

But with other entries in the journal, the style was completely different, as if Shannon had been looking through a different pair of eyes. There was one section that went on for a page describing a thunderstorm coming across the grasslands, toward an isolated ranch house. It was lyrical, poetic, each word carefully selected for maximum impact and DeMarco could not only see the approaching storm, he could practically smell the ozone in the air. This was the voice of the woman who'd written *Lighthouse.*

He'd read the novel entries later. What he wanted now were facts; he wanted to know what she had to say about the people she'd talked to and to see if any of them had frightened her or threatened her or if she'd seen anything that could have put her in danger.

He kept skimming the document and at one point he read:

*Harriet told me that a man who worked for the BLM was killed today. He was shot in the back. I knew him. I'd never spoken to him but I'd seen him at the Hacienda Grill. He couldn't have been more than twenty-five, a short, wiry guy, trying to grow a mustache, probably to make himself appear older. He was wearing a khaki-colored shirt, like a forest ranger might wear, with a triangular patch on one sleeve. What struck me was that everybody in the place seemed to be making a point of ignoring him. I asked the waitress who he was and she said, "Oh, he's the local BLM dick." "Dick?" I said." You mean like detective?" and she said, "No, dick like in pecker." I'd already learned that people around here didn't care much for the BLM but it seemed a shame they'd ostracize a guy, basically just a kid, for doing his job. Whatever the case, I was shocked to hear he'd been shot but Harriet had no idea what had happened.*

A few pages later, the BLM agent came up again.

*My God, I wonder if the FBI knows what Harriet told me tonight. Harriet said that about a week before the BLM agent was killed, he got into a fight with Sonny Bunt. Harriet said Sonny's real name is Steven but everybody calls him Sonny. Sonny Bunt. That sounds comical but I guess there's nothing comical about Sonny. Harriet said Sonny was in the Grill drinking with a couple of his pals and he started lipping off to Jeff. According to the story she'd heard, Jeff was in there having a beer, working on some kind of report, and Sonny starts giving him a hard time, but Jeff ignores him. That apparently pisses Sonny off, so he goes over and does the I'm-talking-to-you routine. Jeff stands up, says something to Sonny that no one heard, and Sonny takes a swing at him—after which Jeff just cleans his clock, hits him half a dozen times, and doesn't stop until Sonny's buddies pulled Jeff off him.*

*I've seen Sonny several times. He's four inches taller than Jeff and outweighed him by thirty or forty pounds. He was probably humiliated to get his ass kicked with everybody in the bar watching. But I wonder if the FBI knows about this? In this town, it seems unlikely that anyone would say that Hiram Bunt's son might have had a reason for shooting Jeff, but I'm sure they must know. They're the FBI.*

A couple of pages later, there was another entry about Sonny Bunt.

*I saw Sonny down at the Grill tonight while I was having dinner with Joanne and Linda, these twin sisters who belong to the book club. They're a hoot. It occurred to me that the kind of face Sonny has he'd never be the big villain in a movie. His face just lacks character. Most likely he'd be cast as the villain's sneaky sidekick, the one who would rat out the villain when the cops start to squeeze him. When I saw him at the Grill, he was down at the end of the bar talking to Angela, the pretty Hispanic bartender. Linda saw me looking and said, "Sonny better watch his ass. Everybody knows he's fooling around with her, which means by now someone must have told his wife." I asked if they'd heard about the fight Sonny got into with the BLM agent and they both had. They said the whole town had heard about it and that Sonny couldn't show his face until the black eye Jeff had given him had faded. I said, "Do you think he might have killed that agent because of the fight?" Joanne said, "Oh, no, he'd never do that," but Linda said, "He's a sneaky shit and I wouldn't be totally surprised if he did.'*

DeMarco flipped the pages looking for more entries about Sonny and the BLM agent, but didn't see anything else.

He'd also noticed that he hadn't seen anything written yet about the standoff between Hiram Bunt and the feds. It appeared as if Gloria Brunson was right and the standoff didn't particularly interest Shannon. What interested her were the personalities of the people involved. There were a lot of short entries about men she'd encountered where she described them as being fiercely independent characters who looked on the federal government as some sort of occupying army. She said she could imagine them standing in a line, willing to die to protect what they considered to be their rights. It was almost as if she admired them.

DeMarco still had a couple of hundred pages to read in the journal but he decided to put it aside for a bit. He wanted to talk to the FBI.

# 13

The Federal Bureau of Investigation has four field offices in Wyoming: in Cheyenne, Jackson Hole, Casper, and Lander. According to what DeMarco had read online, the BLM agent's murder was being handled by the FBI office in Casper, which was about a hundred and sixty miles from Waverly.

DeMarco made the two-and-a-half-hour drive north on a day when the sun beat down without mercy on the land. At one point he saw a dust devil, like a small tornado, whirling toward five or six cows that had their heads down eating whatever it is they ate on the sagebrush plain. If the cows noticed the dust devil, it didn't seem to bother them as they just kept on placidly grazing. DeMarco hoped that if reincarnation was actually a possibility that he wouldn't be reincarnated as a cow.

He arrived in Casper mid-afternoon. He figured he was probably wasting his time, but talking to the FBI was better than doing nothing. That is, it was better than doing nothing if the FBI would talk to him.

The FBI's office was located in the Dick Cheney Federal Building on East B Street, a four-story, grayish-white concrete box with slits cut into it for windows. DeMarco started to park his car then a thought occurred to him, and he used his phone to find a place nearby where he could have copies made. He drove over to a Staples and used one of their machines to make a copy of Shannon's journal. He also bought two brown accordion file folders and put the copy in one and the original in the other.

Back at the federal building, he told the security guards manning the metal detectors that he had information for the FBI agent handling the case of the BLM agent murdered near Waverly. He was told to plant his ass in an uncomfortable plastic chair and fifteen minutes later a woman wearing jeans and a white polo shirt, and with a Glock in a holster on her hip, approached him.

She said, "I'm Special Agent C.J. McCord. Who are you?"

McCord had short blonde hair, a pug nose, and a square jaw. She was what his mother would have called "a big-boned girl." She wasn't fat, just solid, about five nine, with a thick waist, substantial hips, and muscular arms and thighs. DeMarco had always gotten a kick out of female cops in movies, those size-two starlets that weigh a hundred and two pounds, karate-kicking six-foot-four bad guys into submission. But McCord . . . He could see her doing that.

DeMarco told her his name and figuring it couldn't hurt, told her he worked for Congress. He showed her his congressional ID and his driver's license.

"What are you doing here in Wyoming, Mr. DeMarco?" McCord asked.

DeMarco said, "Do you think we could go to your office to have this discussion." Then he held up the accordion folder containing the copy of Shannon's journal and added, "I have some information here that might be useful to you regarding Jeff Hunter's murder."

McCord hesitated briefly, then obtained a badge from the security guards that said VISITOR on it. She gave the badge to DeMarco, he affixed it to his shirt, and she escorted him to a windowless room on the second floor containing a small table and four wooden chairs.

DeMarco suspected it was an interrogation room, which made him feel as if he was being treated like a criminal.

McCord said, "I'll be back in a few minutes. Don't leave this room."

---

McCord returned to her desk and in five minutes learned that DeMarco didn't have a criminal record or any outstanding warrants. Then, because she was curious, she googled him.

The all-knowing Internet informed her that DeMarco had been arrested for killing a congressman named Lyle Canton, who, at the time, had been the House Majority Whip. Once she had read the article she remembered the case because the death of the congressman had been a big deal, but she hadn't paid any attention to it as she'd been in Afghanistan at the time chasing a homegrown terrorist. She continued reading and learned that DeMarco was never tried for Canton's murder because the FBI field office in Washington eventually learned that DeMarco had been framed for the crime and then learned who the real killer was. The other thing she learned was that according to several articles posted online, DeMarco was John Mahoney's fixer, although exactly what he did to earn that title was never specified. McCord was absolutely certain that John Mahoney was a criminal—just one who'd been devious enough to never get caught. As for DeMarco, she wasn't sure.

Now knowing who she was talking to, McCord returned to the interrogation room to see what DeMarco had to say.

---

The door to the room opened and McCord walked in and took a seat across from DeMarco.

"So," she said. "What information do you have for me?"

"You know about the murder of the writer Shannon Doyle?

"Yeah. Of course."

"Well, Shannon was a good friend of mine and I'm not buying the story that she was the victim of some random robbery committed by a trucker passing through Waverly, which is the theory that the Sweetwater County sheriff is currently pursuing."

"How do you know what the sheriff is pursuing?"

"Because I've talked to the deputy heading up the investigation. I came to Wyoming because I wanted to learn more about Shannon's murder."

"Did Congress authorize your visit?" McCord asked.

"No. I'm out here on my own."

"You're saying that John Mahoney didn't send you."

"That's right. Mahoney doesn't even know I'm here."

"Huh," McCord said, seeming skeptical. But then skepticism was a trait common to most folks in law enforcement.

"So you came to Wyoming to do your own investigation? Is that what you're telling me?"

"I didn't come here to do an investigation," DeMarco said. "I came out here to see what the local cops were doing to find Shannon's murderer and so far, I'm not impressed."

"Shannon Doyle must have been a pretty good friend."

"She was," DeMarco said.

"Okay, but why are you talking to me? The FBI isn't investigating Miss Doyle's murder. And what does her death have to do with Jeff Hunter?"

DeMarco said, "I think there's a possibility that Shannon might have learned something that posed a threat to the person who killed Hunter and maybe that's why she was murdered."

"What makes you think that?"

DeMarco pointed to the folder that he'd placed on the table. "That contains a copy of a journal that Shannon kept while she was in Wyoming researching her next book. The copy's for you. In the journal, she talks about Hiram Bunt's son, a guy named Sonny, getting into a fight with Hunter and Hunter beating the shit out of Sonny and embarrassing him in front of his friends. I didn't know if you were aware of the confrontation between Sonny Bunt and Hunter."

"Yeah, I'm aware of it, but only because some citizen in Waverly decided to grow a conscience." She shook her head and said, "That goddamn Bunt—I'm talking about Hiram, not his son—has everyone in that town afraid of him. But somebody there made an anonymous phone call to the FBI and told us about the fight that Jeff had with Sonny. After I learned that, I questioned a bunch of people who were in the restaurant when it happened and they confirmed it.

"So is Sonny a suspect?"

McCord didn't say anything. She appeared to be studying DeMarco. The look she gave was calculating.

---

McCord was thinking that DeMarco was abnormally motivated to find out what had happened to Shannon Doyle and that Doyle had most likely been DeMarco's lover at one point. She'd certainly been more than just a friend. She was also thinking that if the guy worked for a political heavyweight like John Mahoney, he was probably a tricky bastard who got things done in unorthodox and maybe even underhanded ways. *Fixer* wasn't a label you put on a guy who played by the book. She'd been stonewalled by practically everyone in fucking Waverly when it came to Hunter's murder, so maybe a motivated, tricky bastard poking into things might turn out to be useful.

---

McCord finally said, "Of course, Sonny's a suspect. There are a lot of people in this state who don't like the BLM but no one's ever killed an agent before and murder's usually personal. The only one I've been able to find who had a personal reason for killing Jeff was Sonny Bunt."

"Was Jeff killed on Bunt's property?"

"No. He was killed near it, but not on it. Jeff's boss didn't know exactly what Jeff was doing that day—the guy had a lot of latitude when it came to his job—but he might have been counting wild horses or looking at the damage caused by overgrazing, though his boss didn't know for sure. Whatever he was doing, someone got behind him on a small hill that overlooks the place where Jeff was standing. You can drive right up to the hill if you have a four-wheel-drive vehicle, which almost everybody who lives out there does. I suspect his killer followed him that day or maybe he just saw him standing out there on the prairie, and then took up a position on the hill and sniped him. The shot would have been about three hundred yards, not a long distance for a guy with a scoped hunting rifle, which again, almost every male in Wyoming has. But we didn't find a shell casing on the hill and if there were tire tracks or footprints, the wind erased them."

"Do you know if Sonny owns the kind of rifle that was used."

"Yes, he does. Jeff Hunter was killed with a .308 caliber bullet. We have the slug and we can match it to the weapon that was used if I can get my hands on it. Anyway, Sonny owns a Remington 700 that he uses for hunting deer and elk, and that model Remington is bored for a .308. I found out about the rifle from a guy who used to hunt with Sonny. The problem is, I don't have justification to get a warrant to get his rifle and test-fire it. You see, the day Jeff was shot Sonny claims he was in Cheyenne attending a gun show at the Laramie County Fairgrounds, and this was confirmed by a pal of Sonny's who I suspect lied to me. I tried to determine if Sonny actually attended the show but couldn't. None of the dealers I talked to remembered him and this particular gun show doesn't have a lot of cameras because cameras make their customers nervous. So I can't prove he was there and I can't prove he wasn't, and since his pal backs up his alibi, I can't get a warrant."

DeMarco said, "Even if you could get a warrant, don't you think Sonny would have gotten rid of the rifle if he killed Hunter?"

"No, I don't think he would have done that, in part because it's a three-thousand-dollar rifle if you include the Leupold scope. But the main reason he wouldn't have tossed the gun is that Sonny is about a hundred percent certain that I won't be able to touch him because of who his old man is. Hiram Bunt's an asshole and if I had my way, he'd be rotting in a jail cell right now for that bullshit he pulled over the grazing fees. But Hiram's a man. He's not someone who would backshoot an enemy. Sonny, on the other hand, is exactly the kind of guy who would do that, and his daddy has been protecting him his entire life."

McCord stopped speaking to move her Glock a bit, which appeared to be digging into her side. "Sonny's gotten into trouble with the law before. When he was in college down in Laramie, before he flunked out, he was accused of getting a girl drunk and raping her. Hiram's lawyer got the charges dismissed. Another time, he was accused of assaulting a man in Rock Springs. According to witnesses, some guy in the bar pissed Sonny off and Sonny came up behind the guy and hit him with a beer bottle. Once again, Daddy's lawyer got the charges dismissed because the guy Sonny hit refused to press charges, and most likely because someone gave him a wad of cash. I'm guessing Hiram Bunt probably can't stand his own son, but he's not going to let him go to jail."

DeMarco was frankly surprised that McCord was being so open with him. He suspected that she was frustrated by the whole situation with the Bunts and was just letting off steam. Or maybe she was under the illusion that DeMarco had some sort of congressional clout and could be useful to her. Whatever the case, he was grateful.

McCord said, "But what makes you think Shannon Doyle's death could be connected to Jeff's murder?"

"I don't know that it is. But she knew about the bar fight and if you read her journal, you'll see she was thinking about telling the FBI about it. Although I think if Shannon had called you, she would have given her name. She wasn't the type to make an anonymous call. But the main thing is, Shannon was all over that town, talking to people, observing things, and maybe she stumbled onto something. And I have to tell you that I don't have a lot of confidence in the Sweetwater County Sheriff solving her murder, particularly if Hiram Bunt's kid is involved."

McCord said, "The sheriff, in general, has a good reputation but you might be right about him when it comes to Bunt. I know he was on Hiram's side of things when the standoff happened."

"I have to know something," DeMarco said. "How could you guys let Bunt get away with what he did?"

"Because, as the papers all said, the FBI didn't want to get into a situation where we ended up killing a bunch of civilians to confiscate a herd of cows. And although I wasn't the agent in charge that day, I agreed with his decision. But what I would have done is waited until Bunt was alone someplace and arrested his ass and tossed him in jail."

"So why didn't that happen?"

"Because there are senators and a congressman in D.C. essentially backing Bunt, arguing that the federal government is overreaching when it comes to public lands, and the big shots in the Hoover Building said to back off."

McCord shook her head. "I just hate these goddamn people who are always bitching about the federal government until they have some kind of disaster, like a forest fire or a flood or some financial scam that wipes out their savings, after which they all start bitching because the government didn't do enough."

DeMarco said, "Well, I just wanted to give you a copy of Shannon's journal. I haven't finished reading the whole thing, but maybe there's something in there that will be helpful. And what I'm hoping is that you'll find a way to connect Shannon's murder to Jeff's and take over the case."

McCord said, "That's probably not going to happen but thanks for dropping by. And if you hear anything while you're in Waverly let me know, but I'd suggest you be careful. It's not beyond the realm of possibility that more than one person could get shot in the back over there."

# 14

By the time DeMarco got back to Waverly, it was almost dark and he was hungry. He decided to give Harriet a break and have dinner at the Hacienda Grill. He also wanted a place where he could get a drink before dinner.

He was surprised to find the front parking lot of the restaurant full, but then the Grill was the best of the two dining establishments in Waverly, so maybe he shouldn't have been. He pulled over to the side of the building and found a parking space between a couple of big Dodge pickups with king cabs and oversized tires. He took Shannon's journal into the restaurant with him.

He was seated at a table for two and ordered a vodka martini. By the look the server gave him, he guessed folks here didn't often order martinis. Several couples were enjoying the place, the women looking as if they'd put some thought into their hair, makeup, and apparel. As for the men, well, their jeans looked clean and they weren't wearing baseball caps. He noticed Sam Clarke sitting at a table with a young woman who appeared to be Native American. Her dark braids were almost as long as Sam's gray ones. Then DeMarco realized the woman was the maid at the motel; he'd seen her this morning outside his room pushing a cleaning cart stacked with bedsheets and toilet paper. He remembered

Sam saying his daughter was the one who cleaned the rooms, and the young woman did bear some resemblance to Sam, although she was taller and thinner.

---

Sam said, "You gotta be straight with me, Lola. Are you using again? I can't have you showing up late every day. You didn't finish cleaning the rooms yesterday until seven and a couple of the guys complained about it."

"Is that why you asked me to dinner tonight, to give me a hard time?"

"I'm not trying to give you a hard time. I want to help you if you need help."

"I'm going to those NA meetings in Rock Springs three times a week. What more do you want? And I don't need help. I need money."

He suspected she was lying about the NA meetings. That was the problem with junkies: they lied about everything. She was probably getting together with her loser friends when she was supposedly in Rock Springs at the meetings. As for the money she claimed she needed, he could understand that because he didn't pay her a regular salary. Instead, he bought groceries for her and stocked her refrigerator. Lola lived rent-free in the house that Sam and his late wife had owned, and Sam had moved into the motel. He filled up her car with gas. He bought her a carton of cigarettes every week. He paid for her cell phone and he'd paid for her TV cable before she'd hocked the TV. He'd told her that if she needed something, all she had to do was ask, and he'd get it for her or go shopping with her if she needed clothes. Naturally, all this pissed her off, but pissing her off was better than giving her a bunch of money she'd spend on shit to snort up her nose or shoot into her arm. He also had to wonder how she was paying for the drugs if she was still using since he wasn't paying her. She'd hocked everything hockable but her car. He wondered if she could be selling herself, something he didn't even want to think about.

She used to be such a beautiful girl. Now she was underweight, her face haggard, her eyes haunted; she looked ten years older than she was. She also used to be a happy girl, always smiling and joking. Now she was angry all the time. But he didn't think she was angry enough or desperate enough to kill. To steal maybe—but not to kill.

He tried to find a subtle way to broach the subject and when he couldn't, he just spit it out.

"You still got that little popgun Cinda Whitehorse's mom gave you?"

Cinda was a girl Lola had known since grade school, although they weren't friendly anymore. Cinda got tired of Lola constantly begging her for money. But at one point, when Lola was having a problem with one of her shithead boyfriends, this drunk who smacked her around, Cinda's mother had loaned her a little .22 to protect herself.

"No," Lola said. "I gave it back to Cinda. Why are you asking?"

He suspected she was lying but he was afraid to ask Cinda or her mother if Lola had really returned the gun. He didn't want to call any attention to the fact that she had—or once had—a gun. Most likely she didn't have it anymore as she'd probably pawned it to support her habit, just the way she'd probably pawned the writer's earrings. And most likely a pawn shop had a record of her selling the stuff.

"When did you give it back?" What he really wanted to ask was: *Did you give it back before the writer was killed?*

"What the hell difference does it make?" Lola said. "Look, I'm splitting. I don't need this shit, you sitting here grilling me. I thought you were going to buy me a nice dinner."

"Aw, calm down. I am going to buy you a nice dinner. I'm just worried about you, Lola."

He wasn't worried about her. He was terrified for her. If she'd done it, she was too fucked up in the head to get away with it.

After his martini arrived, DeMarco took the journal out of the file folder and flipped through it until he arrived at the point where he'd stopped reading before going to Casper to speak to the FBI. The journal was more of the same: descriptions of the area, humorous observations about some of the people Shannon had encountered, a lot of musings about the relationship between the land and the people.

Most of these DeMarco skipped over, but there was one entry where she described a house on the edge of a prairie and a woman looking out a kitchen window, and then Shannon went on a . . . DeMarco didn't know what to call it—a *riff*, like a jazz musician would do?—where she went on for two pages describing the woman's feelings of loneliness, isolation, and desperation. It was impressive—DeMarco could practically hear the woman's heart breaking—and he wondered if the woman in the house was someone Shannon had met in Waverly or a character she'd created.

A few pages later, DeMarco stopped at a paragraph that started with: *I was invited to a dinner party last night at Hiram Bunt's ranch. That was an interesting experience. Attending were the hosts, Hiram and his wife; Hiram's son, Sonny, and Sonny's wife whose name I can't remember; the sheriff's deputy, Jim Turner—who I swear is the most beautiful man I've ever seen—and his wife; and another rancher and his daughter who were Hiram's neighbors, neighbors who lived thirty miles away due to the size of Hiram's ranch.*

When DeMarco read this the first thought he had was that Jim Turner had lied to him. Turner had said that he'd never met Shannon. Why would the guy lie about that?

He continued reading: *The biggest surprise was that Hiram's wife has to be forty years younger than he is; she appears to be about the same age as Hiram's son, maybe thirty-five or so. She's obviously not his first wife. I didn't hear anything that gave me any clues to Lisa Bunt's background or how she came to be married to Hiram, but she looked as if she could have been a cheerleader for the Dallas Cowboys. Beautiful woman, and also very likable. At least I liked her.*

*Hiram didn't speak much during the dinner—as if he was aloof from the whole thing and only hosting the dinner to please his wife. When he did speak, he came across as arrogant and condescending, particularly toward his son and his daughter-in-law. When his son made some observation about a business opportunity, Hiram's response was: "Aw, you don't know what you're talking about." He obviously doesn't hold Sonny in high esteem. There's also something seriously wrong with Hiram's back. He moves stiffly when he walks and I could see that getting up after he'd been sitting for a while was painful for him. I just have to find out from Harriet the backstory on Hiram and Lisa's marriage.*

*The most interesting person at the dinner was Jim Turner's wife, Carly. She's pretty, although not as pretty as Lisa Bunt; no one in Waverly is as pretty as Lisa. I got the sense that she has a wild streak in her, or did at one time. She was the only woman there who has kids, in her case, two teenage boys. I never learned if she works outside the home or has a profession but she sounded educated and well-informed. She was also the only person there who didn't appear to be intimidated by Hiram, openly disagreeing with him when the conversation veered briefly into politics. It was clear from a couple of the remarks made that she was the only Democrat in the room and I wonder how well that sits with her husband, who clearly isn't. She drank quite a bit, a lot more than anyone else, and I could tell Hiram didn't approve, but I thought she was funny. I wouldn't mind talking to her again.*

*Sonny Bunt is a watered-down version of Hiram. He resembles Hiram physically, although Hiram's a couple of inches taller and was probably better looking than Sonny when he was young. His wife is a timid creature, a high school teacher in Rock Springs, and she didn't say more than half a dozen words. In general, the evening was rather boring but I found the dynamics between the couples interesting. Lisa fawning over Hiram; Sonny Bunt ignoring his wife, resentful of his father; Jim Turner, who had very little to say, but was obviously worried about his wife embarrassing him; the rancher neighbor who didn't appear to be a friend of Hiram's and only came because his daughter wanted to meet me. It really wasn't a fun evening, except for some of Carly Turner's comments.*

*I'm starting to think that some version of Carly Turner is going to have the female lead in my book: an outsider, trapped in a dull marriage, someone who fell far short of her own ambitions. I need to find out more about her.*

DeMarco wondered if the lonely woman Shannon had written about looking out the kitchen window could have been Carly Turner, although that section appeared to have been written before Shannon met Carly. He looked down at the journal again, but his reading was interrupted when a man stopped next to his table.

The man was in his seventies, tall, at least six four, thin, gray haired, wearing stiff blue jeans and what appeared to be expensive cowboy boots. Standing next to him was the best looking woman DeMarco had seen since arriving in Wyoming. She was wearing a tight-fitting, cobalt blue blouse, matching cowboy boots, and a short skirt. It was Hiram Bunt—DeMarco recognized him from articles he'd seen online discussing the standoff—and the woman had to be Lisa.

Bunt said, "You that fella from D.C.?"

DeMarco stared up at him for a moment, not responding immediately, then said, "Yeah."

"What exactly are you doing here in Waverly?"

DeMarco, who hadn't been in a decent mood since he'd heard about Shannon's death said, "What I'm doing is none of your business."

Hiram's face flushed and it looked as if his eyes were about to come out of his head. He pointed a finger at DeMarco and started to say something, but then turned and walked away. As Shannon had written, he moved stiffly, like a man with major back or hip issues. DeMarco expected Lisa Bunt to follow her husband but instead she smiled at DeMarco; she seemed amused by the way he'd spoken to her husband. She gestured toward the stack of paper on DeMarco's table and said, "What are you reading there?"

Before DeMarco could answer, Hiram looked back at his wife and snapped, "Come on, Lisa." Lisa smiled at DeMarco again and turned and followed her husband. DeMarco couldn't help but enjoy the sway of her hips as she walked. He noticed, as he was watching her, Jim Turner standing at the bar, dressed in civilian clothes, having a beer. He was also watching Lisa Bunt—but then so was every other man in the room.

DeMarco didn't see Sonny Bunt. He was at a table with another man and the table was partly hidden by a support column. Sonny saw DeMarco, however. He was glaring at him.

# 15

The man watched DeMarco sip his martini as he flipped the pages of whatever he was reading. He was about ninety percent sure it was a hardcopy of the backup file of Shannon Doyle's work.

He knew it wouldn't do him any good to destroy the copy. If the file was in an electronic format, which it almost certainly was, all DeMarco would do was have another copy printed.

But he had to know what Doyle had written. He had to.

When DeMarco was served his dinner, he left the restaurant and walked around the parking lot until he found DeMarco's rental car. It was sandwiched between a couple of big trucks that provided some concealment, but the spot wasn't ideal. If DeMarco had been parked near the dumpsters behind the restaurant it might have been okay, but he was parked too close to the main entrance and people would be constantly going in and out of the parking lot.

He stood there thinking for a moment, then got into his car and drove to DeMarco's motel. The sun had set and the parking lot was poorly illuminated and filled with shadows. He immediately noticed that someone had parked a U-Haul moving van right in front of DeMarco's room. There was an empty parking space next to the U-Haul where DeMarco would most likely park when he returned from the restaurant unless someone else arrived first and got the space.

Coming from the restaurant, DeMarco would enter the parking lot at the east end and if he stood on the driver's side of the U-Haul, DeMarco wouldn't be able to see him but he'd be able to see DeMarco's car by looking through the U-Haul's driver's side window. And when DeMarco entered the lot, he'd be able to duck down and hide behind the cargo box. If somebody else parked in the empty parking space next to the U-Haul before DeMarco returned . . . Well, then he'd have to forget it or come up with a different plan.

He parked his car around the back of the motel where it wouldn't be visible from the highway and pulled the sap from the glove compartment. The sap was about six inches long and was basically a molded chunk of lead inside a leather casing and had a leather loop that could be slipped over his hand. He put the sap in a back pocket then pulled the lever that opened the trunk. In the trunk was a winter-weather bag containing a snowsuit, thermal boots, thick gloves, goggles, and a black ski mask—the sort of outfit a man riding a snowmobile or hunting in the winter might wear. He grabbed the ski mask and walked over to the U-Haul.

He hoped DeMarco would return to his room soon but there was nothing he could do but wait. As he waited, he thought about what he'd do if someone saw him standing—hiding—behind the U-Haul, and concluded that wouldn't be a problem. He could easily come up with a reason for why he was there that no one would question. But if someone did see him standing there, then he'd have to leave before DeMarco arrived and just hope that he could find another opportunity to get the copy.

A long twenty minutes later, he saw DeMarco's car turn into the parking lot. He ducked down, moved to the back end of the U-Haul, staying on the driver's side. As he'd expected, DeMarco pulled into the parking space on the passenger side of the U-Haul. He pulled the ski mask down over his head to cover his face and took the sap from his back pocket. The sap only weighed about ten ounces but it was a potentially lethal weapon. He waited until he heard DeMarco's car door slam and the little beep when DeMarco punched the remote to lock the car, then he quickly moved around to the passenger side of the U-Haul where he could come up on DeMarco from behind. DeMarco was at the door to his room, holding a brown folder in one hand and putting his key card into the motel room door with his other hand.

He rushed DeMarco. DeMarco heard him but before he could turn his head to see who was behind him, he swung the sap, hitting DeMarco on the back of the head, just above his right ear. DeMarco immediately collapsed to the ground unconscious. At least he hoped he was unconscious and that the blow hadn't killed him. He'd had so much adrenalin running through him that he'd swung the sap harder than he'd intended. He picked up the file folder and jogged back to his car, looking around to see if anyone had spotted him. He didn't see anyone. His luck had held.

He wondered how lucky he'd feel after he'd read what Shannon had written.

---

DeMarco came to to the sight of Sam Clarke's brown, seamed face staring down at him from about six inches away. He was lying on his back on the sidewalk in front of his motel room and for a moment couldn't understand why.

Sam said, "Are you all right?"

DeMarco didn't know the answer to that question. His head hurt. Badly. He tried to move his hands and feet. Thank God, they moved.

Sam said, "I was walking down to see why the TV in a guy's room wasn't working when I saw you lying here. Did you drink too much and pass out?"

"No," DeMarco said. "Someone mugged me. Hit me on the head with something."

"Mugged you? Did he steal your wallet?"

DeMarco didn't know. He reached back and touched the left rear pocket of his jeans. His wallet was still there. He touched the right front pocket of his jeans. He still had his cell phone. Then he remembered Shannon's journal. He moved slowly to a sitting position and looked around for the brown file folder. He didn't see it.

When he sat up, Sam said, "You shouldn't move. You might have a concussion or something."

DeMarco figured there was probably a very good chance that he did have a concussion, but he wasn't feeling nauseous and his vision wasn't blurred. Sam said, "You want me to call for an ambulance?"

"No. Help me up," DeMarco said. Sam helped him to his feet and for a moment he felt light-headed and he closed his eyes and leaned against the motel room door. He looked down at the ground again to see if maybe the file folder containing Shannon's journal was near his car or somewhere else nearby. Nope. It was gone.

Sam said, "Let's get you into your room and you can lie down on the bed. I'm going to call for an ambulance and the sheriff."

"I told you, I don't need an ambulance," DeMarco said.

Sam picked up the key card for the motel room door which DeMarco hadn't noticed lying on the ground at his feet. Sam opened the door, and grasping DeMarco's elbow, led him over to the bed. "I'm going to go call the sheriff. I have to do that, whether you like it or not. I'll be right back and if you're out cold when I get back, I'm calling for an ambulance."

DeMarco lay on the bed for several minutes with his eyes closed, trying to tell if he was seriously injured. After about five minutes, he swung his feet off the bed and sat on the edge of the bed, waiting to see if he got dizzy again. He didn't. Other than a painful lump on the back of his head, he seemed to be all right. He walked to the bathroom, moving slowly, looked into the mirror—he looked like hell—and splashed cold water on his face.

He heard a rap on the door, which Sam had left open, and turned to see Sam and Deputy Jim Turner standing there. One good thing about a small town was that the police response was fast. Turner wasn't dressed in his uniform; he was wearing khaki pants and a polo shirt—and then DeMarco remembered seeing him down at the Hacienda Grill, at the bar, and he'd been dressed the same way. It appeared as if Turner might have come directly from the restaurant.

"Sam said you were mugged," Turner said.

"Yeah," DeMarco said. "Someone hit me on the head. Knocked me out."

"Were you robbed?" Turner asked.

DeMarco immediately decided to lie. He'd told Turner that he was looking for a backup flash drive or an external hard drive containing whatever Shannon had written while she'd been in Waverly. What he didn't want to do was tell Turner that he'd obtained a copy of the journal by asking Neil to hack into the cloud. Nor did he want Turner to ask for a copy of the journal. He told him, "No, nothing was stolen. I still have my wallet, my phone, and my car keys. I'm wondering if someone who lives in this shithole decided to send me a message."

"What kind of message?" Turner said.

"A message to quit looking into Shannon Doyle's death."

"Well, I have a hard time believing that anyone who lives here would do that. And I resent you calling Waverly a shithole. It's a nice town." Before DeMarco could say that he didn't give a damn what Turner resented, Turner asked, "Have you pissed anyone off since you've been here? Did you smart off to one of the gas workers or a truck driver or anyone else?"

DeMarco thought about the question briefly—it wasn't an unreasonable question—but he couldn't think of anyone he'd angered. About the only people he'd spoken to since he'd been in Waverly were Harriet,

Sam Clarke, and Jim Turner. Then another thought occurred to him and he said, "Yeah, I did piss someone off. Hiram Bunt stopped by my table as I was having dinner tonight and asked me what I was doing in Waverly. I told him to mind his own business."

"You said that to Mr. Bunt?" Turner said. He said this as if he couldn't imagine anyone having the balls to do that.

"That's right. Maybe he sent one of his ranch hands over to tune me up." DeMarco was sure Bunt hadn't attacked him. The man could barely walk and he'd still been in the restaurant when DeMarco left.

"Mr. Bunt wouldn't do something like that," Turner said.

"Does that mean you're not going to question him?"

"That's right, I'm not. And I think you're lying to me. I think there's probably a reason someone hit you and you know what it is." DeMarco didn't respond. Turner shook his head and said, "Are you sure you don't want me to call an ambulance?"

"Yes," DeMarco said.

"Then I'm leaving, but if you decide later to tell me why this happened, give me a call."

# 16

DeMarco took a shower, threw on sweat pants and a T-shirt, then laid down on the bed again, not to sleep, but to think.

The fact that someone had been willing to attack him to steal a copy of Shannon's journal meant that someone local was seriously worried about something Shannon might have learned in Waverly. The attack also meant that the sheriff's dumbass theory that some trucker had killed Shannon was almost certainly wrong. No trucker had known that he had a copy of the journal.

But who had known that he had a copy? The only person he'd told was the FBI agent in Casper and he'd never told McCord how he'd obtained it. Sam Clarke knew that he'd gotten a FedEx package, but Sam wouldn't have known what was in the package unless he opened it and DeMarco didn't think the package had been tampered with. Jim Turner had known he was looking for Shannon's backup files but Turner wouldn't have known that Neil had FedExed him a paper copy of a file. Well, come to think of it, that wasn't necessarily true.

Sam Clarke had ratted him out to Turner before, telling Turner who he was when he'd checked into the motel. Maybe Sam had told Turner that he'd received a package and then Sam later saw DeMarco sitting outside his room, reading a stack of unbound pages, and he also passed this on to Turner. So maybe Turner had deduced that he'd received a copy of something related to Shannon's work, but it seemed pretty unlikely that a deputy sheriff would bash him over the head to get a look at what he was reading. If Turner thought he'd obtained Shannon's backup files all the guy had to do was ask, saying he had a right to look at the files as they might help him solve Shannon's murder.

So who else knew he had the journal? There were a lot of people in the Hacienda Grill who saw him reading it while he was having dinner, including Hiram Bunt, but how would they have known *what* he was reading? One possibility, although DeMarco thought it was pretty unlikely, was that Agent McCord had told someone that he had given her a copy of Shannon's journal and she passed this information on, either intentionally or inadvertently, to the person who'd attacked him. Yeah, maybe, but doubtful.

But whoever had stolen his copy of the journal should have known it was printed from an electronic file, meaning this person should have known that stealing DeMarco's copy and destroying it wasn't going to prevent him from getting another one. The objective of stealing the copy had not been to destroy it or even to prevent DeMarco from learning something that might identify Shannon's killer. Most likely the person who had hit him on the head was the same person who'd killed Shannon and he was desperate to learn what was in the journal so he could better protect himself. Forewarned is forearmed as they say.

DeMarco thought for a moment about calling Neil and telling him to FedEx him another copy of the journal then decided not to do that. The copy would have to be FedExed to the motel and he'd just as soon not have Sam Clarke or anyone else see him getting another package. He couldn't trust old Sam. Neil had said that he'd emailed him a copy of the journal. DeMarco got off the bed and turned on his laptop. Yep, Neil had sent him an email with an attachment. He needed to finish reading the journal, which he hadn't yet, and he needed to read everything he'd already read more slowly. The first time he'd pretty much just skimmed the journal looking for anything connected to the BLM agent's death. Maybe tomorrow he'd go into Rock Springs, which was big enough to have a FedEx or a Staples. He'd move the email attachment to a flash drive and have it printed out again.

Knowing he would have a hard time falling asleep, DeMarco stepped outside to breathe in some fresh air before going to bed. The night was clear and a million stars were blinking in the heavens; a full moon sat low over the sagebrush landscape. The place was definitely more attractive in moonlight than it was in the harsh light of day.

He looked across the highway and at that moment saw a single light come on in the darkened café and watched someone—it had to be Harriet—take a seat at a table near a window. He glanced at his watch and saw it was about eleven and wondered why she was sitting there. He thought for a moment about going over and rapping on the café window and asking if she would talk to him. Then he decided: screw it. He'd talk to Harriet later.

But he needed to do *something.* He needed to change the status quo.

Right now, nothing was really happening when it came to finding out who'd killed Shannon. All Turner was currently doing was waiting to hear if some trucker who'd passed through town might be a viable suspect, but he wasn't investigating to see if anyone local could have killed her. The FBI wasn't looking into Shannon's murder because it wasn't under its jurisdiction, nor was the FBI buying his theory that Sonny Bunt might have killed Shannon because she'd learned something connecting Sonny to Jeff Hunter's murder. As far as DeMarco was concerned, Sonny Bunt should have been at the top of everyone's suspect list. C.J. McCord clearly thought Sonny might have killed Hunter, and based on what McCord had told him about Sonny's character, DeMarco could see Sonny killing Shannon if she had any information that tied him to Hunter's death. Which also placed Sonny at the top of DeMarco's list as the person who might have mugged him. The problem when it came to Sonny was that the FBI was powerless to get a search warrant to see if his rifle had been used to kill the agent or if he owned the pistol that had killed Shannon.

Well, the FBI may have been powerless because they were following the law—but when it came to catching Shannon's killer, DeMarco didn't give a damn about the law.

# 17

Sonny Bunt lived in an unimpressive, single-story, ranch-style home about three miles from his father's much grander home. The house had an attached two-car garage, and on one side of the house was a vegetable garden and on the other side was an open shed, like a carport, containing a trailer on which an ATV sat. In front of the house was a small patch of lawn so green that DeMarco wondered if it was Astroturf, and a few yellow flowers—daffodils?—were planted near a small front porch.

DeMarco had parked on the road that ran in front of the house at five a.m. It was now six. He felt groggy from only getting a few hours of restless sleep and his head ached dully. He sat watching the house drinking coffee he'd purchased at the truck stop. He was a bit concerned that some early riser, like maybe the cowboys who worked for Hiram, might pass by on their way to work and see him parked near Sonny's place. Considering what he was about to do, he should have been more concerned about that possibility, but oddly enough, he wasn't. He was already committed and wasn't going to change his mind.

He knew from Shannon's journal that Sonny's wife was a teacher in Rock Springs, forty minutes away. He also knew schools were still in session because he'd checked online. The school year had been extended because of winter snows. At about six o'clock, as DeMarco had been hoping, a sedan with a woman driving pulled out of the garage, turned out of the driveway, and headed in his direction. Since he didn't want Sonny's wife to see him parked on the side of the road, he started his car and began driving, heading in the opposite direction Sonny's wife was going and they passed each other. He didn't know if Sonny's wife knew who he was, but he turned his head away as she went by him so she wouldn't get a clear look at his face.

After Sonny's wife's car disappeared in his rearview mirror, DeMarco made a U-turn and drove back and parked where he'd been before. All DeMarco knew about Sonny was that he worked for his father, but he didn't know what time he went to work and or exactly where he worked. He'd just have to play it by ear.

At seven, DeMarco was pleased to see the garage door open and a black Ford F-150 pickup pull out of the garage. The pickup turned out of the driveway and headed in the direction of Hiram's house, going away from DeMarco and not toward him. DeMarco didn't know if Sonny had noticed DeMarco's car parked on the side of the road; if he did, he didn't do anything about it, such as coming back to see who was sitting in the car.

DeMarco figured that hesitating wasn't to his advantage; if he was going to do what he was planning, he needed to move quickly and decisively. There was always the chance that Sonny might return home if he'd forgotten something or that he might have gone on a short errand and would be back soon. If that were the case . . . Well, the best scenario was that DeMarco would be arrested. The worst was that he'd be shot and killed. He couldn't help but recall Jim Turner saying that there were more guns per capita in Wyoming than any other state in the Union and the likelihood of Sonny walking around with a gun was probably higher than average.

DeMarco pulled into Sonny's driveway. An unpaved road ran next to the house, passing between the shed containing the ATV and the house, and DeMarco followed the road to the rear of the house where he saw a small corral containing two horses and a shed that probably held oats or hay or whatever it was that horses ate.

Satisfied that his car wouldn't be visible from the road in front of Sonny's house, DeMarco got out of the car and approached the back-door of the house. He didn't see any signs advertising that the house had a security system. Nor, thankfully, did he hear a dog inside the house barking. A dog would have really complicated things.

The backdoor to the house was a sliding door that opened onto a small concrete patio where there was a barbeque and a couple of folding lawn chairs. DeMarco tried the patio door but it was locked. He moved along the back wall of the house and came to a window and tried to open it, but it too was locked. Shit, he really didn't want to break a window or the sliding door to get in, but he might have to. He wished he knew how to pick a lock.

He reached the corner of the house and turned to try the windows on the side of the house that faced the vegetable garden. Near the corner was a rain barrel that was slightly elevated, sitting on concrete blocks. A hose ran from the rain barrel to the garden. DeMarco hadn't counted on the rain barrel but it was perfect for what he had in mind. He proceeded to the next window, placed his hands against the glass, and tried to slide it upward—and the window moved. He slid the window all the way up, pushed a curtain aside, and saw he was looking into a small bedroom.

He crawled through the window and began walking rapidly through the house, looking into closets as he walked. He passed through a kitchen, the breakfast dishes still sitting on the table, and into a living room. He didn't see what he was looking for there. He proceeded down a hallway, came to what looked like the master bedroom, one containing an unmade queen size bed. The bedroom had a walk-in closet. He looked in there and didn't see anything but clothes. He looked under the bed—nothing but dust bunnies—then checked a nightstand on the right-hand side of the bed. In the nightstand he found a large revolver with a chrome-plated barrel and a walnut handle. DeMarco didn't know much about guns but he thought the pistol might be a .45 or .357 caliber. It was a big bore weapon, not the .22 that had killed Shannon. He put the pistol back where he found it and checked the nightstand on the other side of the bed. There was nothing in it but reading glasses, cough drops, a romance novel, and a pair of earplugs.

He walked to the next room down the hallway. It appeared to be Sonny's den. There was a large screen television set, a recliner facing the TV, a controller for playing video games, and a low bookshelf that contained mostly magazines. A trout, over two feet long, was mounted on one wall and there was a photo of Sonny posed standing over a dead Grizzly bear, holding a rifle and smiling broadly. Lastly, there was the object DeMarco had been looking for: a gun cabinet. It was a cabinet with double glass doors, not a metal gun safe. Visible inside the cabinet were two shotguns and two rifles. One of the rifles had a scope. DeMarco tugged on a handle and one of the doors opened. He would have definitely broken the glass if it had been locked.

He pulled out the rifle with the scope. It was a Remington and had a Leupold scope. It was the hunting rifle that Agent McCord said that Sonny owned and the weapon that might have been used to shoot the BLM agent. DeMarco opened the breach to see if the rifle was loaded. It wasn't.

Beneath the upper, glass-enclosed section of the cabinet, was a lower section that had drawers. DeMarco opened one of the drawers and found two pistols, both semi-automatics. One was a large-caliber weapon, the bore similar to the bore of the revolver he'd found in the bedroom. The other was a small gun, small enough to fit in a woman's purse or in someone's back pocket. A .22? He didn't know. He checked the gun's magazine and saw it was full.

In a drawer next to the drawer with the pistols, were boxes of ammunition. One of the boxes contained .308 caliber bullets. He took one of the bullets from the box and loaded it into the Remington rifle. Carrying the rifle and the small-caliber pistol he started to leave Sonny's den, then stopped and walked over to the bookcase and grabbed about a dozen magazines. He noticed that the magazines were about guns, hunting, fishing, snowmobiles, and ATVs.

He walked to the sliding backdoor of the house, unlocked the door, stepped outside, and walked over to the rain barrel he'd seen on the side of the house near the garden. The rain barrel was about half full. He didn't know if that was enough water or not. He saw an outside faucet that had a hose attached to it. He pulled the hose over to the rain barrel and filled the barrel almost to the top. He'd now been at the house for almost ten minutes; he needed to speed things up.

He dropped the stack of magazines he'd taken from Sonny's den into the rain barrel, letting the magazines settle to the bottom. He then took the small-caliber pistol, put the barrel of the pistol under the surface of the water to hopefully reduce the sound of a shot and pulled the trigger. The pistol emitted a small *crack*; hardly any noise at all. He then did the same thing with the rifle: shoved the barrel of the rifle into the water and pulled the trigger. He didn't care if the water might fuck up Sonny's guns. The sound of the rifle shot was louder than the pistol, but there was nothing he could do about that. Thankfully, Sonny's closest neighbor was his father, three miles away.

He placed both weapons on the ground a few feet away from the rain barrel, tipped over the barrel, the water pouring onto the concrete patio. He reached inside the barrel and pulled out the magazines and after a brief search found the two slugs embedded in the magazines.

He put the slugs into a pocket, righted the rain barrel, tossed the wet magazines into it, put the hose back where he'd found it, then picked up the rifle and the pistol and went back into the house. Using a towel he found lying on the floor in the master bathroom, he quickly wiped the moisture off both weapons and put them back in the gun cabinet. Before he left the house, he closed the bedroom window he'd opened to enter the house and then walked out the backdoor, leaving the door unlocked.

The whole operation had taken less than half an hour.

Next stop, Casper, Wyoming, office of the Federal Bureau of Investigation.

Fuck a bunch of search warrants.

# 18

DeMarco called Agent C.J. McCord when he was about an hour away from Casper, telling her that he was on his way to her office with something that might solve the murders of Jeff Hunter and Shannon Doyle.

"What are you talking about?" McCord said.

"I'll tell you when I see you. Will you be available around eleven? I'll be in Casper by then."

"No. I have a meeting that starts at ten and won't wrap up until noon."

"So meet me someplace for lunch. Give me the name of a restaurant near your office."

DeMarco arrived in Casper about eleven as he'd predicted and found the restaurant where McCord said she'd meet him, a diner called Peaches', a few blocks from the federal building. He was hungry as he'd been up since the crack of dawn and hadn't eaten, but he didn't order any food as he'd be having lunch with McCord. That turned out to be a mistake.

He ordered a Coke from a slow-moving waitress then turned his attention to the television mounted on a wall near his table. The television was tuned to FOX News. The anchorman could have gotten a job as a young George Clooney's stunt double and his female co-anchor probably had a trophy case filled with tiaras from beauty pageants. DeMarco couldn't remember the last time he'd seen an old, homely commentator on television; he figured the TV executives must jettison their newscasters when the first wrinkle appears. He wasn't able to hear what the fetching couple was saying as the TV was muted, but he could follow the story with the closed captions on the bottom of the screen.

The anchorwoman laughed about something and pointed to a graph that magically appeared on the screen. The graph showed the stock price of a company that made hardware for the military and that was in competition with a similar company for a Pentagon contract. Per the graph, the company's stock had risen significantly after the president was caught on a hot mic saying that he played golf with the CEO of the company and thought he was a much better manager than the female CEO of the competing company. And that's all it took—a casual remark from the president, not intended for public consumption—to make the company's stock price take off like a North Korean missile.

And DeMarco thought: *Hmmm.*

He'd never given any thought to Mahoney's leaker in the context of the stock market. Mahoney's only concern had been the political fallout resulting from the leak, namely that it made Mahoney look bad to the Democrats who were opposed to the merger. DeMarco took out his phone, and because he didn't know what he was doing, it took him half an hour to confirm what he'd expected: The stock prices of the two telecommunication companies that had been planning to merge shot up by about twenty points after Mahoney's meeting with the CEOs was leaked, then dropped by about twenty points after Mahoney denied that he supported the merger.

And DeMarco thought: *Hmmm.*

At ten after twelve, McCord walked into the restaurant and saw DeMarco seated at a table for two near a window. She was wearing a blue blazer over a white T-shirt that only partially concealed the Glock on her hip.

She sat down across from him and said, "So. What's this all about?"

"You want to order some lunch?"

"No, I don't have time for lunch."

Well, shit, DeMarco thought. He was going to faint if he didn't get some food in his belly soon. At that moment the waitress who'd served DeMarco a Coke walked over to the table and asked McCord if she wanted anything. McCord said no. DeMarco told the waitress, "Give me a few minutes. I'll order lunch after my friend leaves."

It occurred to him only then that he might be having lunch in the closest jail if McCord decided to place him under arrest after she'd heard what he had to say.

The waitress left and DeMarco reached into a pocket and dropped two slugs on the table between him and McCord.

"What the hell?" McCord said.

DeMarco pointed at the slugs. "One of those came from Sonny Bunt's hunting rifle. The other came from a small-caliber weapon I found in a gun cabinet in Sonny's den. I brought them to you so you can see if they came from the weapons used to kill Jeff Hunter and Shannon Doyle."

"What! How in the hell did you get these?" McCord asked.

"I walked into Sonny's house when he and his wife weren't there, found the weapons, then went outside and fired them into a rain barrel. I did a little reading online about how the CSI guys do ballistics tests and figured the rain barrel would work. Isn't the Internet marvelous?"

"Are you shitting me!" McCord said. "You broke into Sonny's house?"

"I didn't *break* in. I went in through an unlocked backdoor." DeMarco figured that sounded a little better than creeping in through an unlocked window.

McCord said, "Jesus Christ, DeMarco. I'm going to have to report you to the sheriff and he's going to arrest you."

"Arrest me for what? As best I can tell, the only crime I've committed is trespassing. I didn't break into the house, I didn't damage any property, and I didn't steal anything. All I did was fire two bullets into a rain barrel and then I put the guns back where I found them."

"You stole two bullets."

"Okay, you got me there. I trespassed and stole two bullets. Since I'm guessing the value of the bullets is less than ten bucks, I'm guilty of two misdemeanors. And I don't give a damn if you report me to the sheriff and he arrests me. But I'd suggest you wait until you've compared the bullets to the ones used to kill Shannon and Hunter before you turn me in. The way the sheriff's office is wired into the Bunt family, someone is liable to tell Sonny what I've done and he may split before you have a chance to arrest him."

"Goddamnit, DeMarco. I don't know if I can even use those slugs as evidence because of the way you obtained them."

"Sure, you can. I'm not law enforcement. I didn't need a warrant to get the bullets. I'm just a guy who trespassed then passed the evidence on to you. And I'm willing to give you a statement saying exactly what I did so you have something to show when it comes to chain of evidence. So go talk to the lawyers and see what they have to say. But I'm guessing that what I did is no different than if you used a confidential informant to provide evidence related to a crime."

McCord shook her head.

DeMarco kept talking. "While you're waiting to hear what the lawyers have to say, go compare those bullets to the ones used to kill Shannon and Hunter. If the results show they were used in a crime, then you should have a basis for getting a search warrant to obtain the guns legally and test-fire them again. And if the ballistics tests show that Sonny's guns weren't used to kill anyone, then the worst thing that happens is that I get arrested for trespassing and you'll know that Sonny's innocent."

McCord didn't allow DeMarco to have lunch. She took him back to her office and recorded a statement from him saying how he'd obtained the slugs and after the statement was typed up, he signed it. Then she took him to an interview room and told him to sit his ass down and not move until she'd talked to a few lawyers.

She returned an hour later. She said, "Well, DeMarco, it looks like the boneheaded stunt you pulled paid off. The slug from the bullet that killed Jeff Hunter matches the bullet you fired from Sonny's rifle."

DeMarco exhaled in relief. "What about the bullet from the pistol?" he asked.

"The bullet that killed Ms. Doyle is in the custody of the Sweetwater County sheriff and I don't want the sheriff to know anything at this point because I'm afraid he'll tell Bunt senior and then Sonny's rifle will disappear. Or maybe Sonny will disappear. I'll send someone to Rock Springs to do a comparison on the pistol slug after I've dealt with Sonny."

"Yeah, okay," DeMarco said, disappointed because Shannon was his priority not Jeff Hunter.

"But you need to understand something, DeMarco. Based on what we now know, the lawyers are pretty sure they can get a warrant to seize Sonny's weapons. That's the good news. The bad news is that there's a chance, depending on the judge we draw, that any evidence resulting from the warrant might not be admissible because of what you did. And what that means is that Sonny might get away with murder. Anyway, that's the lawyers' problem, not mine. My job is to get Sonny's rifle, do another ballistic test, and go from there. In the meantime, we've all agreed that telling the sheriff that you broke into Sonny's house can wait until we've executed the search warrant, but we're going to have to tell the sheriff eventually."

"Why?" DeMarco asked, which seemed to him like a reasonable question.

"Because the FBI doesn't cover up crimes."

Before DeMarco could say that what he did wasn't much of a crime, McCord smiled and said, "DeMarco, I can't officially approve of what you did, but I have to tell you that I'm not all that unhappy about it. Now get out of here."

# 19

DeMarco practically sprinted back to Peaches' after McCord released him and stuffed himself with a pastrami sandwich and french fries. Belly full once again, he went to the Staples in Casper where he'd previously gone to make copies of Shannon's journal. He bought a flash drive, transferred the electronic file of Shannon's journal—the file that Neil had emailed him—from his laptop to the drive, and then had the kid at Staples print him out another copy.

Following that, he made the long drive back to the motel in Waverly and took a nap. He'd been up since five. After he woke up, he took a shower then called a lawyer in Washington, D.C. named Janet Evans. Evans was the lawyer who'd represented him when he was framed for killing Congressman Lyle Canton.

He told Evans that he was in Waverly, Wyoming and that he was most likely going to be arrested by a county sheriff for trespassing. After he explained why, Evans' reaction was similar to C.J. McCord's: "Jesus Christ, are you crazy, DeMarco?"

"Can you give me the name of a lawyer out here to represent me. I'm willing to plead guilty to the crime but I'm afraid they'll throw the book at me because of the people involved."

"What do you mean?"

DeMarco explained that he'd gone after the son of one of the richest, most influential members of the community, a guy wired into the county sheriff's office and politicians back in D.C. "And because of that, instead of getting probation and a fine, some local judge might decide I should go to jail for a couple of years. So I need a lawyer to make sure that doesn't happen."

"I don't know anyone in Wyoming," Evans said. "Hell, I've never even been to Wyoming. Give me an hour or two and I'll get back to you."

"Oh, and Janet, see if you can find somebody competent but who doesn't charge as much as you." Janet Evans charged about eight hundred bucks an hour.

---

DeMarco thought about continuing to read Shannon's journal while waiting to hear back from Evans, then decided to give himself a break. He turned on the television, found the Golf Channel, and started watching a rerun of a PGA tournament. He'd concluded a long time ago that watching golf was similar to transcendental meditation: he zoned out, his mind blank, thinking about absolutely nothing as he watched millionaires smack a little white ball around. He'd noticed that he didn't really learn anything from watching the pros other than that even they would sometimes miss a three-foot putt—which would actually make him feel good.

His phone rang. It was Evans. She said, "Call a lawyer named Dora Little Bear tomorrow. She has an office in Rock Springs. She's young but she's smart and has a good reputation. I called her and gave her the background on you and she agreed to represent you. One reason why is she hates Hiram Bunt. She went up against him a couple of times to stop him from drilling for gas in environmentally fragile areas, and lost both times."

DeMarco decided to go have dinner, and taking Shannon's journal with him, he walked over to Harriet's. Harriet came up to him after he was seated, order pad and pencil in hand, and said, "So you're still in town."

"Yep," DeMarco said, "but I might not be much longer."

"Does that mean you decided to give up on finding out what happened to Shannon?" He could tell from her tone of voice that she'd be happy to see him gone.

"No, I haven't given up. I think I might have found the guy who killed her."

"The guy?" Harriet said. "So who is it?"

"I'm not going to tell you. If you'd been willing to talk to me I might have, but since you wouldn't—"

Harriet shook her head. "What are you having?"

While waiting for his dinner—tonight it was venison stew and he'd never had venison stew before—he opened Shannon's journal and flipped through it until he found the place where he'd stopped reading.

*Something happened today and I feel really bad about it. When I got back to my room this afternoon I found my diamond earrings were missing. They weren't real expensive, they were only worth a couple of hundred bucks, but they were my favorite pair. I'd planned to wear them to dinner and I knew I'd put them on the ledge in front of the mirror but they weren't there. I searched my room to see if anything else was missing but nothing appeared to be. I didn't bring any other valuable jewelry with me and the only other things in the room were my cosmetics and my clothes and those were all still there. I'm glad I always keep my laptop with me.*

*I went down to the office to tell Sam what had happened. I asked him if anyone other than the maid had been in my room, like maybe he'd let someone in there to fix something. He said the only one who'd been in there was the maid and she was his daughter. He said, "Are you sure you didn't misplace the earrings? My daughter wouldn't steal from you."*

*The way he said this—the way he looked away before he spoke—I think he was lying to me. I think he knew his daughter stole my earrings. I'd seen the maid several times but I didn't know she was his daughter. She's this sullen-looking Native American girl who doesn't respond when I try to engage her in conversation. I really like Sam. He's been very helpful to me since I've been here. I feel sorry for him, knowing that his daughter's a thief. I wonder what he's going to do about it.*

DeMarco's phone rang as he was eating. The venison stew was actually pretty good. The caller was C.J. McCord.

She said, "I thought you'd like to know that I got a search warrant to get Sonny's rifle. The judge hemmed and hawed for quite a bit, but he finally signed it."

"What are you going to do when Hiram shows up at Sonny's place with a dozen armed men and tells you he won't allow you to search his son's house? The last encounter the FBI had with him didn't turn out too well for the bureau."

McCord said, "This is about the death of a federal agent not a bunch of damn cows. Bunt's not going to stop me."

DeMarco believed her. He liked C.J. McCord. He wondered what the C.J. stood for.

# 20

McCord wasn't worried about Hiram Bunt keeping her from seizing Sonny's weapons.

The standoff happened in part because the BLM was polite enough to notify Hiram that they were coming to seize his cattle, giving Hiram enough time to round up his men and his anti-government neighbors. Well, McCord had no intention of being polite or notifying anybody of anything when it came to Sonny.

She left Casper at two a.m. with five other FBI agents in a black Chevy Suburban that would seat eight. They stopped at a truck stop in Rawlins for coffee and donuts, and while there, they put on body armor and checked their weapons, a combination of automatic rifles, shotguns, and Glock pistols. At five a.m., while it was still dark outside, they drove to Sonny's place, stopped on the road in front of the house, and approached the house on foot. They didn't drive directly to the front door of the house because McCord didn't want to take the chance that Sonny or his wife might be light sleepers and hear their vehicle. One of McCord's men was holding a door knocker—a three-foot-long chunk of four-inch diameter steel pipe with handles welded on the top.

Standard operating procedure was for McCord to knock on the door, announce that she was FBI, and tell Sonny she had a warrant to search his house. McCord, however, decided it might not be wise to follow the standard procedure in this case. For one thing, Sonny might not let her into his house and she'd find herself in a situation where her men would have to storm the house of a guy who had multiple firearms inside—a guy who she was ninety-nine percent sure had already killed one federal agent. The other possibility was that while she was trying to convince Sonny to open the door, he'd call his daddy and ask for help and she'd find herself confronting a bunch of Hiram's men all armed with AR-15s. Then things would turn into a replay of the previous standoff.

So when she arrived at Sonny's front door, she knocked softly on the door—so softly the agents with her could barely hear her knuckles rapping on the wood—and then said in a low voice: "Mr. Bunt, FBI. Open the door." Now having followed the bureau's procedures, and with witnesses willing to say that she had, she said to the man holding the doorknocker: "Take it down, Hank."

Hank slammed the pipe into the door near the knob and the door flew open, making enough noise to wake the dead. McCord was the first person through the door, holding a shotgun. A shotgun had always been her weapon of choice because she was a lousy shot with a handgun.

She knew from DeMarco that Sonny kept a pistol in the nightstand next to his bed, and her biggest concern was that he'd be able to get it out before she could enter his bedroom. Yesterday, while the lawyers were imploring a judge to sign off on the search warrant, McCord got the name of the company who'd built Sonny's house, contacted the company, and had them email her the floor plans of the house. So she knew exactly where to go, and as soon as the door burst open, she sprinted through Sonny's living room—gripping her shotgun—and down a short hallway and into the master bedroom.

As she went through the bedroom door, Sonny—who'd heard the front door being bashed in— was reaching into the drawer of the nightstand for his pistol.

McCord screamed: "FBI! FBI! Put your hands up! Put your hands up! You point a weapon at me and I'll kill you." At the same time McCord was screaming, Sonny's wife was shrieking at the sight of a person in body armor, wearing a helmet with a face shield, aiming a shotgun at her husband.

Sonny stopped reaching for the weapon and raised his hands. "What the fuck is going on?" he said.

McCord reached into one of the pockets of her cargo pants, pulled out a folded multipage document, and tossed it to Sonny. "That's a warrant signed by a federal judge giving the FBI permission to search this house and seize any weapons we find. That's your copy of the warrant."

"Goddamnit, you can't do this," Sonny said.

"I am doing it," McCord said. She walked over to the nightstand on Sonny's side of the bed while another agent pointed his Glock at Sonny, opened the nightstand drawer, and removed a weapon—a .45 with a shiny chrome barrel.

Sonny said, "I'm calling my lawyer."

"That's your right," McCord said, "but we're not waiting for your lawyer to get here."

McCord had no idea how long it would take Sonny to reach a lawyer at five in the morning, or how long it would take a lawyer to get there. However long it took, she planned to be gone by then.

She turned to the men behind her and said, "Larry, find his den and empty the gun cabinet. Hank, drive the truck down here and start loading the weapons."

Sonny had gotten out of bed. He was only wearing a pair of white boxer shorts. He was a lean, well-built guy. His wife, her blonde hair tousled from sleep, was still in the bed, her hands over her mouth.

McCord searched the closets in the bedroom while Sonny was putting on a pair of jeans.

Sonny said, "I'm calling my father, you bitch. You're not taking anything from my house."

McCord said, "Call daddy if you feel like it, Sonny. Call anybody you want. I don't care."

Actually, McCord did care. Hiram Bunt lived only three miles from Sonny's place and she had no idea if any of his employees lived on his property. The last thing she wanted was Hiram driving over to Sonny's with a few of his cowboys.

McCord quickly finished searching the bedroom closet, didn't find any guns in there, then looked under the bed. To the agent who was still behind her aiming his weapon at Sonny, she said, "Murphy, keep him here. If he tries to get by you, you have my permission to beat the shit out of him. I'm going to go see how the search is going."

While she'd been speaking, Sonny had found his cell phone and made a call. As she was leaving the bedroom, she heard him say, "Dad, it's me. The fuckin' FBI—"

One of her men was carrying all the rifles and shotguns that had been in Sonny's gun cabinet to the front door. Another one was filling a canvas bag with the pistols and the ammunition taken from the drawers of the gun cabinet.

"Hurry up," McCord said.

McCord knew it would take hours to search the house, the garage, and the outbuildings thoroughly, but she didn't intend to spend hours searching. She already had what she wanted: the hunting rifle that had been used to kill Hunter. She also wanted to be gone before Hiram Bunt showed up. She wasn't afraid of Hiram—she'd spent two years in Afghanistan and gone up against guys a lot worse than him—but she knew her boss would be pissed if the situation escalated and someone got killed. She walked quickly through the house, looking into places a weapon might be stored—what she was hoping to find was a .22 caliber pistol—but didn't find another gun in the house. She really wanted to search Sonny's vehicles—a .22 was a good glove compartment gun—but for some reason the warrant didn't allow her to search Sonny's cars. Fucking judges. She looked at her watch. She'd been in the house for fifteen minutes. It was time to go.

She asked the agent who'd cleaned out the gun cabinet, "Did you inventory everything?"

"Yeah," he said. "Photographed everything in the cabinet before we took anything out too."

"Good. Give a copy of your inventory to Mr. Bunt so he'll know what we took. Oh, and thank him for his cooperation."

She rounded up her men and told them they were leaving. They piled into the Suburban, Sonny's weapons in the back, and took off. As McCord's team was driving down the driveway, she saw a pickup truck swing into the driveway. The pickup stopped when the driver saw the FBI's SUV coming toward him. His vehicle was blocking the road.

The driver got out of the pickup. It was Hiram Bunt. He was alone. McCord had to admit that the old man had balls. On his hip was a semi-automatic pistol in a holster.

McCord told the agent driving to stop and she got out of the SUV holding her shotgun, the barrel pointed toward the ground. McCord said, "Mr. Bunt, move your truck."

"Fuck you," Hiram said. Moving slowly and stiffly, the old man started to reach for the gun on his hip. McCord pointed the shotgun at his face and said, "You take out that gun and point it at me, I'll blow you to kingdom come."

Hiram stopped moving. He must have heard something in McCord's voice and realized she was serious—and different than the FBI agent he'd dealt with during the standoff. He said, "You got no right to take my boy's firearms."

"I have a warrant signed by a federal judge," McCord said. "Now move your vehicle."

"No," Bunt said.

McCord opened the SUV's passenger side front door, pushed the button to lower the window, then got in and pointed her shotgun at Bunt through the window. She said to the driver, "Go around the son of a bitch."

"You got it, boss," the driver said and drove around Hiram's pickup, tearing up the lush grass on Sonny Bunt's lawn.

# 21

Hiram stood for a moment, seething, as he watched the goddamn feds drive away. He hated the bastards. They just kept coming after him and his family. He walked up to the front door to where Sonny was standing.

"What did they tell you?" Hiram asked.

"Just that they had a warrant that allowed them to seize my guns."

"Did they give you a copy of the warrant?"

"Yeah. Those motherfuckers. Look what they did to my door."

"Show me the warrant," Hiram said.

Hiram read the warrant while standing on Sonny's front porch, but couldn't make a whole lot of sense out of it. Just government-lawyer double-talk, saying it was related to the BLM agent's murder. Then he asked the question he'd been afraid to ask ever since the agent was killed. He said, "There any reason to be worried about them taking your weapons?"

"No," Sonny said. "I don't know why in the hell they decided to raid my house."

Hiram studied his son's face, but couldn't tell if he was lying or not. Sonny was a good liar.

Sonny said, "What should I do?"

"Nothing," Hiram said. "I'm calling my lawyer."

The lawyer's office wasn't open at six in the morning—so he called the lawyer's house and woke him up.

---

Lisa was in the kitchen when Hiram returned home, having a bowl of cereal, wearing the long T-shirt she'd worn to bed. She was barefoot, her long legs visible to the top of her thighs; she wasn't wearing a bra. Her dark hair was tangled from sleeping. Goddamn, the woman turned him on. If his back wasn't so fucked up, he would have bent her over the kitchen table and taken her right there. But those days were over. He sometimes thought that he'd be better off dead than being so old and feeble.

She said, "What's going on? Why'd you go tearing out of the house this morning?"

He said, "The fuckin' FBI got a warrant to seize Sonny's weapons. They think he killed that BLM agent."

"What? I thought he was in the clear, that he had an alibi for the day that man was shot."

"Yeah, well, something's changed."

"What?"

"I don't know. I'm waiting to hear back from the lawyer. I told him to find out what's going on."

Lisa studied him for a bit as she munched her cereal, then said, "Do you think Sonny could have done it?"

Hiram shook his head and walked away.

---

Lisa couldn't tell if the head shake meant *No, I don't think he did it* or if it meant *I don't* know *if he did it.* Well, she wouldn't have been at all surprised if Sonny had killed the agent. Sonny was a snake. He'd even tried to hit on her when she first married Hiram. Cheatin' on his wife with that Mexican at the Grill was one thing; trying to screw his father's wife was in a whole different category.

All she knew was that if the FBI had enough to get a warrant, they had something. The FBI didn't go off half-cocked. And if they could put Sonny in jail for murder, that wouldn't be a bad thing—not when it came to her future. She'd already started to think ahead to what might happen when Hiram died. She'd inherit a pile of money, of course, but she wouldn't get it all. And what she really wanted was the land and Hiram's businesses, which no doubt would be passed on to Sonny. But if Sonny was serving life in prison—

She looked out the kitchen window. The sky was clear; the wind was barely blowing. Since she was up anyway, she might as well go for a ride. When she'd married Hiram she'd never ridden a horse. After ten years, though, she'd become an excellent horsewoman and loved nothing better than a morning ride.

Ten years. She couldn't believe it. And as miserable as it sometimes was living with the grumpy old bastard, it had been worth it. If she hadn't married him, God knows what she'd be doing today, most likely waiting tables or working some other minimum wage job. Her plan, from the time she'd turned twenty, had always been to marry a rich man and she doubted she could have done any better than Hiram. If she'd married a younger man, she would have had to put up with him for thirty or forty years, but Hiram . . . she wondered how much longer he'd last. His father had lived to eighty; he was now seventy-six.

Whatever the case, she really had no complaints, especially now that she no longer had to put up with having sex with him. Thank God his back would never get any better. She drove a BMW convertible, went on shopping sprees in Denver, took classes at the community college in Rock Springs, went skiing in Jackson Hole. Then there was her handsome lover. Yep, life was grand—and if Sonny were gone, it would get even grander.

# 22

DeMarco was on his laptop researching nearby golf courses. The best one appeared to be a course in Rock Springs, a place called White Mountain, only an hour away. He was anxiously waiting to hear if McCord had confiscated Sonny's weapons and to learn what the FBI planned to do next, but in the meantime, he was bored. There wasn't much in the way of entertainment in Waverly.

He was just about to dial the pro shop at White Mountain, to find out if he could rent clubs, when his phone rang. He was pleased to see it was McCord calling.

She said, "DeMarco, I decided to keep you in the loop just to keep you from doing something stupid. Our ballistics experts confirmed for a second time that Sonny's rifle was used to kill Jeff Hunter."

"So what are you going to do now?"

"What the hell do you think I'm going to do? I'm going to arrest him for murder."

"You told me that Sonny has an alibi, that he was supposedly at some gun show the day Hunter was killed."

"Well, we'll see how well his alibi holds up now. One of the first things I'm going to do is get in the face of the man who said Sonny was with him. I'll tell him that if I can prove Sonny wasn't really in Cheyenne then I'm going to arrest him for accessory to murder and for lying to the FBI."

"What will you do if he doesn't fold?"

"I've got more options than I had before. Now that we know Sonny's rifle was used to kill Hunter, I can get warrants to look at his credit card charges and cell phone records. Sonny Bunt's no genius. I wouldn't be surprised if he made a credit card charge or a call that proves he wasn't in Cheyenne. And even if I can't break his alibi, he'll go to trial and the jury will have to decide if they want to acquit a backshooter based on what one of his buddies says. Folks in Wyoming tend to have a low opinion of backshooters."

Before DeMarco could ask about it, McCord said, "Regarding the small-caliber pistol we found in Sonny's gun cabinet, it wasn't the weapon used to kill Shannon Doyle. Shannon was killed with a .22. Sonny's gun was a .25."

"Maybe he tossed the .22 after he used it," DeMarco said.

"But *why* would he kill her, DeMarco? He didn't have a motive that I'm aware of."

"Yeah, he did," DeMarco said. "She knew about the fight he'd had with Hunter and she was thinking about telling the FBI about it. But the main thing is, and like I told you the day I met you, Shannon was all over this town, talking to people, watching things, and she might have learned something directly tying Sonny to Hunter's murder. Or maybe she learned something that would break Sonny's alibi."

"DeMarco, you're grasping at straws. And there's nothing written in Shannon's journal—I've skimmed most of it—that shows she knew anything about Hunter's death other than what she wrote about the fight."

Before DeMarco could object, McCord continued. "You ought to be more concerned about the sheriff arresting you, and if I were you,

I'd get out of Wyoming. I don't think the state is going to try too hard to extradite you from D.C. to face charges for trespassing."

"I'm not going anywhere until I know who killed Shannon," DeMarco said.

# 23

McCord was looking forward to arresting Sonny Bunt—but there were some challenges.

Had Sonny been almost any other citizen, McCord would have taken a couple of agents with her, driven up to his house, knocked on the door, and slapped handcuffs on his wrists when he opened the door. With Sonny, however, she had the same concern she'd had when executing the search warrant: that Hiram Bunt might put a dozen armed men around Sonny's house to keep her from taking his son, in which case there'd be another standoff but this time people might get killed. The FBI didn't need another Ruby Ridge and for this reason, McCord had decided to take a more cautious approach when it came to bagging Sonny.

Sonny's house was on County Road 23, also known as Crooks Gap Road, a road that ran north and south. About five miles south of his house was a small wooden structure that over the years had been used as a stand for selling fresh produce and honey gleaned from local hives and, most recently, fireworks. But as they say in the real estate business, location is everything—and the location of the stand was hardly conducive to brisk sales. It had been abandoned for the past couple of years.

At six a.m., McCord pulled the big Suburban SUV she was driving behind the stand, where it would be invisible to anyone driving by on CR-23. With McCord were three other FBI agents and a technician she'd borrowed from the Cheyenne office. The FBI agents were dressed in jeans and wore dark blue windbreakers with "FBI" in yellow letters on the back. The technician was a skinny, long-haired kid in his early twenties dressed in a T-shirt, cargo shorts, and high-top, black Converse tennis shoes without socks. McCord figured he had to be exceptional at his job, otherwise, his boss in Cheyenne would have demanded that he get a haircut and dress more professionally. The kid's name was Brian.

McCord opened the rear hatch of the Suburban and Brian removed an aluminum suitcase about the size of an airplane carry-on bag. He opened the suitcase and, sitting in protective foam rubber, was an iPad, what looked like the controller for a video game with two joysticks—and a drone. The drone was a quadcopter, meaning attached to the body of the drone were four helicopter-like propellers. In the body of the drone was a camera, a powerful lithium polymer battery, and a bunch of other electronic gizmos that only Brian could understand. You could buy a drone that looked just like Brian's on Amazon for a couple of hundred bucks. This drone, however, cost *way* more than a couple hundred because of its capabilities, and was the type of drone used by the military and other federal law enforcement agencies. In other words, it was the Cadillac of surveillance drones.

It took Brian about five minutes to get the drone ready to fly and to run some tests to make sure everything was working. McCord gave Brian the GPS coordinates of Sonny's house—and the drone rose into the sky. Ten minutes later, the drone was about three hundred yards from Sonny's house at an elevation of two hundred and fifty feet. The drone, unlike the models you bought on Amazon, was so quiet you could barely hear it, and it was painted a grayish color that was essentially sky-colored camouflage. McCord had told Brian to locate the drone east of Sonny's house so that it would be even harder for anyone at the house to see it, as they'd be squinting into the morning sun.

The camera from the drone fed the scene to the iPad that Brian had propped up in the rear compartment of the SUV, so McCord and the other agents could see what the camera was seeing. And what the camera showed was not good from McCord's perspective. In Sonny's driveway was a black Dodge pickup with a king cab and there were four men armed with long rifles seated on folding lawn chairs near Sonny's front porch. This is what McCord had been worried about, and she wondered if the four men had been there all night.

She said to her team, "We're going to wait awhile and see if those guys leave or if Sonny leaves his house and goes someplace where we'll be able to make an arrest without getting into a gunfight."

If the men guarding Sonny didn't leave soon, then she'd have to figure out what to do.

There was no way she was *not* arresting Sonny Bunt today.

---

For the next two hours, McCord monitored the scene at Sonny's house via the iPad while Brian maintained the drone in position. The rest of McCord's team sat in the SUV bullshitting and drinking coffee from a couple of thermoses that McCord had brought.

At eight a.m., McCord saw a second pickup swing into Sonny's driveway and a man got out of it. McCord told Brian to zoom in on the man. It was Hiram Bunt. McCord watched as Hiram walked into Sonny's house without knocking. Five minutes later he came out with Sonny in tow and they got into Hiram's truck. The four men who'd been standing guard got into the second pickup—the Dodge with the king cab—then the two pickups left Sonny's place and proceeded south toward Waverly. They'd be driving right past the one-time fireworks stand that was blocking the view of McCord's Suburban from the road.

McCord told Brian, "Land the drone. You can come back later and pick it up."

"What if somebody finds it. That drone cost—"

"I don't care what it cost," McCord said. "Land it and pack up the rest of your shit."

A couple of minutes later, Hiram's convoy consisting of Hiram and Sonny in one pickup and Hiram's four cowboys in the other, drove past the fireworks stand. McCord waited until the two pickups were almost out of sight, then took off after them.

It was easy to follow Hiram and Sonny. The road ran almost straight and the landscape was flat. When Hiram reached the place where CR-23 intersected with I-80, Hiram merged onto I-80 and headed west—in the direction of Waverly. But Hiram didn't stop in Waverly. He kept traveling west, toward Rock Springs—and McCord thought she knew where he was headed. Hiram's lawyer's office was in Rock Springs and McCord figured that Hiram was taking his dumbass son to ask the lawyer what they should do about the weapons the FBI had seized.

She wondered if Sonny had told his daddy that his hunting rifle had been used to kill a man.

Forty minutes later, the two pickups pulled into a small parking lot in front of a two-story brick building. A sign in front of the building said it was occupied by a real estate agency, an Allstate insurance agent, an architect—and the honorable William S. Patterson, the attorney who'd represented Hiram in his never-ending fight against the federal government.

McCord parked a block away from the building, parallel parking the Suburban between two other vehicles. She watched as Hiram and his son walked into the building. The four men who'd come with Hiram got out of their pickup but didn't go inside. They stayed in the parking lot, jawboning, a couple of them smoking. Maybe Hiram had decided to leave his men in the parking lot because he thought that the FBI wouldn't dare to arrest Sonny while he was in a lawyer's office. If that's what he thought, he was wrong.

Now McCord had to make a decision. The FBI liked to outnumber its adversaries—by a lot. She'd brought three agents with her to arrest Sonny, making the odds four to one in her favor. With Hiram's four cowboys standing in front of the building, McCord would have liked it better if she'd had a dozen more agents with her, all of them armed to the teeth and dressed in body armor. But she didn't have a dozen agents, and in the time it would take to bring in reinforcements, Hiram and Sonny would most likely be gone from the lawyer's office.

She mulled the situation over for a bit then said, "Brian, I want you to go into the building and locate Patterson's office. Then I want you to find a door on the back or side of the building that me and the rest of the team can use to get inside without Bunt's men seeing us."

She'd picked Brian for this job because of the four men with her, he was the one who looked the least like an FBI agent. And she could tell that Brian was excited to be given an active role in Sonny's arrest. He may have been a geek but he wasn't a coward.

McCord watched as Brian strolled toward the entrance of the building, pretending to talk on his cell phone as he did. Bunt's men glanced over at him, then went back to bullshitting. Brian obviously didn't strike them as a man who posed a threat. McCord noticed that Bunt's men had left their rifles in their truck but all had sidearms in holsters on their belts. Nothing pissed her off more than the goddamn laws that allowed citizens to go around armed like it was fucking Tombstone in the 19th century.

A couple of minutes after Brian entered the building, he called McCord and said, "Patterson's office is on the ground floor. It's got glass doors and you can see into the reception area. The Bunts aren't in the reception area—they must be in Patterson's office—but there's a receptionist sitting at a desk. There's a door at the back of the building. It's not alarmed. If you drive around back, I can open it and let you in."

"Stand by," McCord said. Turning to one of the other agents, she said, "Larry, I want you to get out of the car and stay here and watch Hiram's men. Take off your windbreaker—"

She meant the windbreaker identifying him as an FBI agent.

"—and stick your gun under your shirt and in the back of your pants where it can't be seen. I want you to call me if any of Bunt's men enter the building."

"Got it," Larry said as he took off the windbreaker and his holster and put his Glock where McCord had told him. Then Larry left the car and strolled over to a nearby bus stop bench and sat down and pretended to study his iPhone screen.

Once Larry was in position, McCord said into her phone, "Okay, Brian. Go open the back door and wait for us."

---

"Well, Hiram, I have to tell you that things don't look good," Bill Patterson said.

Patterson had been Hiram's lawyer for the last twenty years and he'd represented him in his battles against the federal government as well as numerous other business-related disputes. And he'd represented Sonny, the time Sonny had been accused of assaulting a man in Rock Springs, the one he'd hit on the back of the head with a beer bottle. But this . . . This was first-degree murder and Hiram wasn't sure that Patterson was the right man for the job.

Patterson said, "They got the warrant to seize Sonny's weapons based on someone breaking into Sonny's house."

"What?" Hiram said. "What are you talking about?"

"I'm saying that someone broke into Sonny's house, fired his hunting rifle into a rain barrel, and then turned the slug over to the FBI so they could compare it to the bullet that killed the BLM agent. Apparently, they got a match."

Sonny shouted, "Who the hell was it? Who the hell broke into my house?"

"I don't know, but I'll find out," Patterson said.

"Well, goddamnit, they can't just break into my house and—"

"Shut up, Sonny," Hiram said.

On the one-hour drive from Sonny's house to Patterson's office, Hiram and Sonny had hardly said a word to each other. Hiram, a man who didn't normally talk all that much anyway, figured that there wasn't really anything to talk about until he'd heard what the lawyer had to say. He hadn't seen the point of asking Sonny a second time if he'd shot Jeff Hunter in the back.

Hiram said to Patterson, "So what are you going to do?"

Patterson noticed that Hiram didn't say: *Hey, there's no way my boy would have killed that man*. He appeared to have accepted the fact that his son might be a killer. Nor, he noticed, did Sonny leap up from his chair and proclaim his innocence. Sonny just sat there looking down at the floor as if he knew his world might be coming to an end.

Patterson said, "Before the case even goes to trial, I'll argue that because of the way the FBI obtained the warrant, any evidence resulting from it is inadmissible at a trial. It's a legal thing called "fruit of the poisonous tree." If that doesn't work, then I'll argue that if a person could break into Sonny's house to test-fire his rifle then somebody could just as easily have broken in, used the weapon to kill the agent, and then put the rifle back. In other words, there's a case to be made that someone is trying to frame Sonny for the crime. And because Sonny has an alibi for the time Hunter was killed, I think there's a good possibility that I can create reasonable doubt and he won't be convicted."

Hiram had never seriously questioned Sonny's alibi because he'd never seriously considered that Sonny could have killed that man. Now he had to wonder if the alibi would hold up. The man who'd alibied Sonny was almost as useless as Sonny.

---

McCord drove to the back of the building and stopped near an open door where Brian was standing. She and the other two agents got out of the car and she told Brian, "Get in the car. You're going to drive us away when we bring Sonny out." She could tell that Brian liked the idea of being the get-away driver, like the wheelman in a bank robbery. The main reason McCord wanted Brian to remain in the car was that he wasn't armed and was a technician and not a trained agent.

McCord and the other two agents walked down the hallway to Patterson's office. McCord opened the double glass doors and stepped inside. As Brian had said, there was a receptionist, a middle-aged woman, sitting behind a desk. Behind the receptionist, McCord could see a closed door with a gold plaque on it saying: *William S. Patterson. Attorney at Law.*

The receptionist jumped to her feet when the three FBI agents burst into the office. She said, "What are you—"

McCord said, "FBI. Just stay where you are." Turning to one of the two agents with her, she said, "Hank, you make sure she doesn't call anyone." Like Bunt's four cowboys standing outside the building.

McCord walked around the receptionist's desk, the other agent following her, and threw open the door to Patterson's office. Patterson, a beefy, red-faced man in his sixties, was sitting behind his desk. Hiram and Sonny Bunt were in chairs in front of his desk.

McCord said, "Steven Bunt, I'm arresting you for the murder of Jeff Hunter. Stand up and put your hands behind your back."

Patterson said, "You can't do this. Not here in my office, when I'm consulting with him as a client."

McCord said, "Yeah, I can. I have a warrant for his arrest. And if either of you tries to interfere, I'll arrest you too."

Hiram said, "You goddamn bitch. You got no right to—"

"Shut up," McCord snapped, and the agent with her yanked Sonny out of his chair, spun him around, and handcuffed him.

Hiram said, "Goddamnit, I'm not going to let you—"

He didn't complete the sentence. He stood up, his bad back making it hard for him to rise, and took a step toward the door. McCord figured he was probably going to get his men.

McCord pointed a finger at his face and said, "Sit your ass down. I'm telling you, you interfere, and you're going to be sitting in a cell next to your backshooting son."

Patterson said, "Hiram, calm down. Let me deal with this." To McCord he said, "Where are you taking him?"

"To the Natrona County Detention Center."

"Well, I'm coming with you," Patterson said, "to make sure my client is treated properly."

"No, you're not," McCord said. "But you can meet me at the jail if you want." To the agent with her, she said, "Let's go."

The agent grabbed Sonny's right arm and pulled him from the lawyer's office. So far, Sonny hadn't said a word; his face was pale and he looked as if he might vomit. McCord backed out of the office, keeping her eyes on Hiram. The old bastard had a gun on his hip and she wouldn't have been totally surprised if he pulled it. The guy was so mad he was trembling and McCord could just see him having a stroke.

McCord's team and Sonny left through the door they'd used to enter the building and Sonny was shoved into the backseat of the SUV. McCord said, "Brian, take off. Take a right. We have to pick up Larry." Larry was the agent she'd left watching to make sure Hiram's men stayed outside Patterson's building.

It didn't sit well with McCord having to take Sonny out the back door. She felt as if she was *sneaking* him away. She would have preferred to go out the front door so the good citizens of Rock Springs could see her arresting Hiram Bunt's shitbird kid, but knew it was wiser to avoid a confrontation with Bunt's men. Besides, taking him out the back door was a minor irritation compared to the satisfaction she felt for arresting the coward who'd killed Jeff Hunter.

As Brian was driving, he said, "Hey. When are we going to go back and pick up my drone?"

McCord said, "Hell, I don't know, Brian. We'll figure it out later."

Brian said, "Do you know how much that drone cost? What if someone comes along and sees it? What if a cow steps on it?"

"Shut up, Brian. You're giving me a headache. Just drive the damn car."

# 24

By the time Hiram got back to his ranch, his back hurt so badly from the one-hour drive from Rock Springs that he could barely get out of his truck. He was glad none of his ranch hands were there to see him shuffling toward the door, moving like a crippled old man.

When his back hurt this badly, about the only thing that helped was lying on a flat, hard surface. He went into his office, and with some difficulty, got down onto the floor and onto his back. He'd have to call Lisa or the housekeeper to help him get back up.

As he lay there staring up at the ceiling, he thought about his only son. Sonny had always been such a disappointment. He had no ambition, had failed out of college, and was constantly getting into some kind of scrape that Hiram had to bail him out of. And when it came to the ranch, he really had no interest in learning the business. He liked to hunt and fish, drink with his buddies, and ride around on his ATV, but that was about it. He acted more like a teenager than a grown man.

When Hiram first heard that the BLM agent had been killed, he'd wondered, but only briefly, if Sonny might have done it. He'd heard about the fight and how Hunter had kicked Sonny's ass, and he had no doubt that Sonny would have wanted to get back at Hunter for embarrassing him. He wouldn't have been at all surprised if Sonny, knowing he wasn't man enough to handle Hunter on his own, enlisted a couple of his shithead friends to help him beat the hell out of the man. But shooting him in the back? Nah, he'd thought, even Sonny wouldn't do that.

But now he knew he had.

If Hunter had been a bigger fellow maybe the fight wouldn't have shamed Sonny the way it had, but Hunter had been a little guy who had been taught how to fight. And Sonny knew the ranch hands were all snickering at him behind his back and every time he looked in a mirror in the days after the fight, he'd have been reminded of his defeat. The day he'd killed Hunter, he must have just snapped, unable to bear the humiliation any longer.

Sonny lacked *impulse control.* Those were the words a high school counselor had used when Sonny had been suspended for breaking all the windows in a car belonging to some teacher who'd embarrassed him in class. *Lack of impulse control* was a fancy way of saying that Sonny did stupid things without thinking about what he was doing or what the consequences might be. So Hiram could imagine Sonny seeing Hunter alone on the open range and working himself into a rage, and then, without giving it two seconds of thought, grabbing his hunting rifle and shooting the man. Only afterward would he have given any consideration to the potential ramifications of what he had done—and, in the back of his mind, would be the thought that Hiram would be able to save him the way he always had in the past.

But Hiram knew he wasn't going to be able to save him this time.

Maybe if his mother had lived Sonny would have turned out differently, but his mother had died when Sonny was ten. Or maybe if Sonny and his wife had had kids, or maybe if he'd married a woman with a spine, he would have changed for the better. And maybe if Hiram liked him, even a little bit, he'd be different. Maybe, maybe, maybe.

His cell phone rang. With some difficulty, he extracted it from the pocket of his jeans and saw it was Patterson calling.

He answered saying, "Yeah, what is it?"

The lawyer said, "The guy who broke into Sonny's house is someone named Joe DeMarco. I got that from a clerk I know who works for the judge who signed the warrant. You got any idea who he is?"

"Yeah, I know who he is," Hiram said.

While Hiram had been driving back from Rock Springs, he'd been seething with anger. Another man might have wept after learning that his son was a cowardly backshooter and was likely to spend the rest of his life in prison, but Hiram didn't weep. He never wept. The last time he'd cried he'd been twelve years old. His dog had been dying from kidney failure and when his father told him he had to shoot it, he started crying—and his father slapped him and told him to quit acting like a girl. From that point on, the way Hiram dealt with grief or disappointment or adversity, was to get mad.

When Sonny's mother had died of cancer, he'd been mad at God. But since there wasn't anything he could do to God, he took his anger out on his wife's doctor, suing the man for malpractice. And when it came to Sonny being a backshooting killer, the only one he could get angry at other than Sonny, was himself.

But now he had a better target for his anger: DeMarco.

He'd been annoyed when he'd learned from Jim Turner that DeMarco was in town, poking into the writer's death. His annoyance had mostly stemmed from the fact that DeMarco was an outsider and from D.C., and just about anyone from D.C. annoyed him. Then DeMarco had smarted off to him in the Grill in front of Lisa, and that had pissed him off, but not enough to do anything serious about it. But now, knowing what DeMarco had done when it came to Sonny, he could finally unleash all his pent-up fury—the fury he was feeling toward Sonny and toward himself and toward the fucking FBI.

After he finished speaking to Patterson, he called his foreman, a man named Roy Kline, and told Roy to come to the house. Roy said he was ten miles away helping a veterinarian vaccinate a herd of cows, but Hiram said he didn't care.

Thirty minutes later, Roy arrived. Roy was a lean man with a weathered face and small eyes so dark they seemed more black than brown. He was almost sixty now, but unlike Hiram, still vigorous and strong. He was a good foreman, knew the business, and knew how to keep the cowboys in line. The other thing about Roy was that he had a mean streak; he liked hurting people and was now divorced because one of the people he'd liked hurting was his ex-wife. And when Hiram wanted to send a pointed message to some drifter hanging around Waverly or some drunken gas worker causing problems in town, he would dispatch Roy to deliver the message. There had been a time when Hiram dealt with those things himself, but those days were gone.

Hiram, who was still lying on the floor, said, "Help me up." He couldn't talk to the man lying on his back, looking up at him.

Roy reached out a work-hardened hand and pulled Hiram to his feet, and Hiram moved around behind his desk and slowly lowered himself into the fancy, ergonomic chair that Lisa had bought him.

He said, "There's this bastard from Washington in town, a guy named DeMarco, staying down at Sam Clarke's motel. I want you to have a word with him."

# 25

DeMarco was sitting in the Grill, celebrating Sonny's arrest by having a martini.

McCord had called half an hour earlier, this time to say it would be at least six months before the case went to trial and there was no point in DeMarco sticking around any longer.

DeMarco had said, "But you don't think Sonny killed Shannon, do you?"

"No, but maybe I'm wrong. And now that he's in custody, I'll be able to ask him where he was the night she died. But there's no reason for you to remain in Waverly. Like I told you, you're liable to get arrested for breaking into Sonny's house, so if I were you, I'd skedaddle."

"I'll think about it," DeMarco had said, knowing he wouldn't. The fact that he'd helped put Sonny Bunt behind bars was good, but that hadn't been his primary objective. His primary objective was to determine who'd killed Shannon. And if McCord couldn't prove that Sonny had killed her, then he needed to figure out what he was going to do next, knowing he couldn't hang around Waverly, Wyoming forever.

As he was sitting there sipping his martini, mulling things over, three men walked up to his table. They all had on work-worn jeans and scuffed cowboy boots. They were also wearing gloves, which seemed odd at first. Two of the men were husky young guys in their twenties; one of them had a large belt buckle showing a cowboy riding a bucking horse. The third man was a tough-looking old bastard with a lean, sun-wrinkled face. He said, "You think we're going to allow you to break into a man's house around here and get away with it. Stand up. We're going to step outside and have a little talk."

McCord had been right: It hadn't taken long for his role in the arrest of Sonny Bunt to become known. But she'd been wrong saying that the biggest threat he faced was going to jail. He had no doubt that the three men standing near his table worked for Hiram Bunt and he knew that they hadn't come to make a citizen's arrest—and he didn't care. He'd been dying to hit someone ever since Shannon's death.

"Fuck off," he said to the old cowboy.

The man slapped the martini glass out of DeMarco's hand and reached down and grabbed his shirt to yank him up from his chair, but DeMarco came out of the chair on his own accord—and smashed his right fist into the man's jaw. The man went down—he appeared to be unconscious—but his two buddies were still in the game. One of them hit DeMarco on the side of the head, staggering him. He countered with a quick left jab, hitting the guy hard enough to break his nose, but while that was happening, the third cowboy hooked DeMarco in the ribs. When DeMarco turned to face the guy who'd hit his ribs, the man whose nose he'd broken threw a roundhouse right and hit DeMarco in the mouth, hard enough to knock him down. When he was on the floor, someone kicked him hard in the side with the pointed toe of a cowboy boot. DeMarco rolled to avoid a kick aimed at his head, but ended up beneath a table and he couldn't get to his feet. He was thinking he needed to grab the kicker's foot when he kicked again and see if he could pull the man to the ground where he could hit him. If he didn't get back up on his feet, he was liable to end up in a hospital—or maybe a morgue if one of those kicks hit his head.

A gunshot sounded. It was like a cannon going off in the enclosed space.

Bunt's men—the two still standing, one of them with blood pouring from his nose—spun around to see Jim Turner standing there, holding a pistol still aimed at the ceiling.

"What in the hell do you think you're doing?" Turner said.

"He started it," the one with the broken nose said, pointing at DeMarco who was struggling to get to his feet.

Turner looked down at the man DeMarco had knocked unconscious. "Is Roy okay?"

The young cowboy with the rodeo belt buckle knelt down next to his fallen buddy, slapped him lightly on the cheek a couple of times, and the man came to. "How you doin', Roy?"

"I'm all right," Roy said. "Lucky fuckin' punch."

DeMarco smiled, his teeth smeared red with blood.

Turner walked over to DeMarco and said, "You're coming with me. I'm placing you under arrest for trespassing and breaking and entering."

DeMarco was treated like your average hardcore criminal, processed into the Rock Springs detention center, photographed and fingerprinted. His wallet, watch, spare change, and cell phone were placed into an envelope and he was required to remove his belt and his shoelaces, apparently to prevent him from hanging himself. He was then tossed into a holding cell. His cellmates were two men who appeared to have been in a fight, who reeked of booze and stale vomit and had passed out on the floor.

An hour later he was escorted to a room where he met his lawyer, Dora Little Bear, an intense, dark-haired young lady who couldn't have been more than five feet tall. DeMarco's head hurt, his ribs were sore, he was having a little trouble breathing, and his mouth was swollen. Nonetheless, he felt pretty good, figuring he gave as good as he got. Knocking out ol' Roy with a single punch made all his aches and pains seem worthwhile.

Little Bear pointed at DeMarco's face and asked: "Did the cops do that to you?"

"No," DeMarco said. "Three of Hiram Bunt's men did."

"Huh," the lawyer said. "I would have liked it better if the law had roughed you up making a misdemeanor arrest."

"Sorry to disappoint you, but Turner never touched me," DeMarco said. "In fact, he may have kept Bunt's guys from kicking me to death."

"Let's talk about how we're going to handle the arraignment," Little Bear said. "According to what your previous lawyer told me, you broke into a man's house and—"

DeMarco said, "I didn't break in. I walked in through an unlocked back door." After telling that small lie, DeMarco proceeded to tell her the truth about everything else he did: searching Sonny's house, firing two of Sonny's guns into a rain barrel, then taking the slugs to the FBI to determine if the weapons had been used in the murders of Shannon and the BLM agent. DeMarco concluded with: "Thanks to me, Sonny Bunt is now in jail for the murder of Jeff Hunter."

"Well, you got a lucky break," Little Bear said. "The judge you'll appear before hates Hiram Bunt. Not because of the standoff, but because of some property dispute where Bunt apparently screwed him. I'd suggest you plead guilty to trespassing. I'll argue that you trespassed in the interest of seeing justice done and because of what you did, a man almost certainly guilty of murder is now behind bars. I think the judge will let you off with probation, or maybe a fine, but he won't do much more than that. I hope."

"You *hope*?"

As the town of Rock Springs didn't hold court at night, DeMarco couldn't be arraigned and, therefore, couldn't bail himself out of jail. So—and over his lawyer's objections—he spent the night in the holding cell at the detention center, sitting on the floor, his back against a wall, trying and mostly failing to sleep. The two men who'd been passed out in the cell when he'd arrived eventually regained consciousness. It turned out they were brothers who got drunk, then got into a donnybrook in a local bar when the older brother discovered that the younger one was sleeping with his woman, a gal named Trixie. Based on what DeMarco overheard, the brothers concluded—once they were sober—that Trixie wasn't exactly a prize worth fighting over and certainly wasn't worth what they were going to have to pay the bar owner for the furnishings they'd destroyed during their altercation.

In the morning, DeMarco was taken before a judge named Amos Morris, an amiable, roly-poly, red-cheeked man with wispy white hair. The first thing he said when he saw DeMarco was: "Who beat you up?" Morris just sounded curious and not particularly concerned about DeMarco's condition.

Before DeMarco could speak, Little Bear said, "Three of Hiram Bunt's men who decided to take the law into their own hands."

"But the cops didn't hit you," the judge said.

DeMarco shook his head and was about to say that Turner had probably saved him from a much more severe beating, but again his lawyer spoke first. She said, "No, the police didn't injure my client. On the other hand, the deputy involved also didn't arrest Mr. Bunt's employees for assault. It appears as if the law in Sweetwater County is willing to turn a blind eye to anything that Hiram Bunt does and the sheriff's office is more concerned about a minor case of trespassing than my client being brutally attacked."

The prosecutor, a guy wearing a string tie with an agate clasp, objected. He said, "What the deputy did or did not do with regard to

Mr. Bunt's men isn't relevant to the matter at hand, which is your client breaking into a man's house. And that's not minor at all."

The lawyers blabbed back and forth a bit, Little Bear explaining how DeMarco's initiative—*initiative* sounding a lot better than breaking and entering—resulted in the arrest of a man who had almost certainly killed a BLM agent. The prosecutor argued that no matter DeMarco's intentions or motives, it was unlawful for him to enter a home and do illegitimate ballistic tests on a man's weapons. When the lawyers finished, the judge asked DeMarco if he had anything to say. DeMarco said he was willing to plead guilty to the crime of trespassing, that being the only crime he'd committed. The judge mulled this over for about five seconds, shrugged, and said, "The court fines you one hundred dollars."

The prosecutor shrieked, "That's not right, your honor! This man should be sentenced to at least thirty days in the county lockup."

The judge responded with: "Get real, Bernie." The judge did, however, tell DeMarco that he'd better not break into anyone else's home while he was in Wyoming or the next time he would spend some time in jail.

DeMarco wrote a check to pay his fine then asked Little Bear if he could buy her breakfast as a way to partially repay her. She said she didn't have the time, that she had to meet with a client, a kid who'd almost killed an old lady when he broke into her house to steal to support his opioid addiction. She told DeMarco she'd send him her bill—and if he got into any more trouble while he was in Wyoming, to give her a call. The last thing she said to him was: "I'm really sad about what happened to Shannon Doyle. I never met her but I loved her book. I hope you find the person who killed her, but try not to break the law again."

After Little Bear left, DeMarco realized he didn't have a way to get back to Waverly as Jim Turner had driven him to Rock Springs. It took him an hour to find a taxi driver who was willing to make the forty-minute drive for a hundred dollars. Considering the fine, his lawyer's fee, and the taxi ride, breaking into Sonny Bunt's house had cost him about five hundred bucks.

It was worth it.

# 26

McCord had told DeMarco that now that she had solid evidence that Sonny had killed Jeff Hunter, she could get warrants to break Sonny's alibi and prove that he had not been in Cheyenne the day Hunter was shot. Then she thought: to hell with breaking Sonny's alibi. She was going to break the man who'd given him the alibi.

The man who'd said that Sonny had been with him at the gun show in Cheyenne the day of Hunter's murder was a short, bantamweight drunk who'd gone to high school with Sonny and had spent time on the rodeo circuit in his twenties. His name was William Warren, but as he was about five foot four with his boots on, his cowboy sobriquet was naturally *Shorty*. McCord had heard that the only reason Hiram Bunt tolerated an alcoholic working for him was because Shorty was an exceptional horse trainer. That and the fact that he was a good friend of Sonny's.

Shorty lived in a manufactured home in Waverly. The place hadn't seen a coat of paint in twenty years and the weed-filled front yard contained the carcasses of three Ford pickup trucks that had been cannibalized for parts but, for whatever reason, hadn't been hauled off to a wrecking yard. There was also a fourth Ford pickup with rusty fenders and a cracked windshield that appeared to be functional if not completely legal.

McCord had left Casper at three-thirty a.m. so she could arrive in Waverly at six. One problem with being an FBI agent in a state the size of Wyoming was you often had to drive for hours to do your job. The reason she'd risen so early was that she was hoping to catch Shorty before he left for work. She didn't want to have to go out to Bunt's ranch to pick him up as that was likely to result in another confrontation with Hiram, one which might end up with her shooting him.

She looked around before getting out of her car to see if Shorty had a pit bull roaming his yard. She'd rather shoot Hiram than a dog. She rapped hard on Shorty's door and a moment later he appeared, wearing a once-white T-shirt, stained with what looked like tomato sauce, and blue boxer shorts. His hair was sticking up, he hadn't shaved in days, and his eyes looked as if he'd spent the night drinking until he'd passed out.

He said, "What do you want?"

He recognized McCord from the time she'd questioned him after Sonny claimed Shorty was his alibi.

"I want to talk to you again about Sonny being with you in Cheyenne the day Jeff Hunter was killed."

He said, "I don't have anything more to say to you. And I'm not going to talk to you without my lawyer present."

McCord was five inches taller than Shorty and probably outweighed him by forty pounds. She shoved by him and walked into the house. She said, "Go put on some pants, you little shit. And you're going to talk to me or I'll arrest you and drag your ass to Casper and talk to you there. Which means you'll have to pay your lawyer, assuming you even have one, for the time it takes him to drive to my office."

While she was waiting for Shorty to get dressed, she looked around his hovel. It was just what she'd expected from the exterior: a pigsty. Clothes strewn about, unwashed dishes in the sink, fast food cartons and pizza boxes and beer cans on the floor and almost every other flat surface.

A moment later Shorty came back to the living room, now wearing jeans, but still barefoot. She pointed to a recliner aimed at the television and said, "Sit down." She walked over to a leather chair with a split in the upholstery and swept a jean jacket and a couple of soiled work shirts onto the floor and took a seat.

"So what do you want?" Shorty said.

"As I'm sure you must have heard by now, I've arrested Sonny Bunt because I can prove his rifle was used to kill Jeff Hunter. Well, Shorty, I'm going to give you one chance, and one chance only, to tell me the truth. And if you don't, you're going to jail."

"Going to jail for what? I didn't commit any crime."

"Yeah, you did. You lied to me. You lied when you said Sonny was with you at the gun show in Cheyenne the day Hunter was killed."

"I didn't—"

"By now I'd think that every person in America, even a dumb ass like you, must know that lying to the FBI is a crime."

Shorty started to say something but she held up a hand, silencing him. "Now I know what you're thinking. You're thinking that lying isn't that big a deal and the most you'll get is a fine or a few days in the county lockup. But you see, Shorty, lying is just going to be the first charge on your indictment. Do you know what the second one is going to be?"

"What indictment?"

"The second charge is going to be accessory to murder. You'll be charged as an accessory because you lied to help Sonny get away with killing a federal agent. So now you're not looking at a few days in jail and picking up trash on the highway. Now you're looking at *years*. Maybe you'll end up in a cell next to your buddy Sonny."

Shorty said, "I'm telling you that Sonny— "

"I suggest you stop before you tell me another lie. Because I know what else you're thinking. You're thinking that I can't prove that Sonny wasn't with you in Cheyenne that day. Well, cowboy, let me explain something to you. Now that I have evidence tying Sonny to a murder, namely that his rifle was used to kill a man, I'm getting warrants to look at his cell phone and credit card records. All it will take is a phone call Sonny made or him paying for something with a credit card to prove he's wasn't in Cheyenne."

Shorty just sat there, looking trapped.

McCord remembered this one time when she was a kid. A mouse had gotten into the house and she'd cornered it, intending to smash it with a broom, and the mouse had looked just the way Shorty did: its little black eyes darting everywhere, looking for a way out of that corner. The mouse got away that day because it had been too quick for her—but Shorty wasn't as quick as the mouse. Or as smart.

She said, "So, let's start over. Let's pretend this is the first time I'm talking to you, now that you know what'll happen if you lie to me again. Was Sonny Bunt really with you in Cheyenne the day Jeff Hunter was killed?"

Shorty's Adam's apple bobbed a couple of times as if he was trying to swallow a baseball. "No," he said.

Maybe he was as smart as the mouse.

"So why did you tell me he was?"

"Because he asked me to. He said you goddamn feds were out to get him because of his old man. He told me he didn't kill Hunter but he couldn't say where he really was that day. He said he was really with his girlfriend, you know that Mexican chick, Angela, who tends bar at the Grill. He didn't want to use her for an alibi because then his wife would find out that he was fucking around on her."

"And you believed him?"

"Yeah. Sonny can be kind of an asshole, but I didn't think he would have shot that man in the back."

McCord's parting words to Shorty were: "You skip town before you can be formally deposed, I'll track you down like a gut-shot deer leaving a trail of blood."

McCord thought that sounded pretty good—like something an old-time Wyoming lawman would say—although she'd never shot an animal in her life, much less tracked a wounded one.

---

McCord decided to stop at the café in Waverly for breakfast before driving back to Casper.

A stout woman with short white hair came over and took her order. McCord had read enough of Shannon's journal to know that the woman was Harriet and that Shannon had been close to her. Which made her wonder what that slick bastard, DeMarco, had learned from her. DeMarco was a piece of work.

"What'll you have?" Harriet asked.

McCord really wanted a stack of pancakes slathered with butter and maple syrup but restrained herself. She said, "Black coffee, bacon, and a couple of eggs over easy. No hash browns or toast." She was proud of her self-control but knew that long before noon her stomach would be rumbling.

She sipped her coffee as she waited for her breakfast to arrive, feeling good about the way things had gone with Shorty. She had no doubt now that she'd stripped Sonny of his alibi that he'd go to jail for life for first-degree murder. She also wouldn't be totally surprised if he eventually pleaded guilty to avoid a death sentence. Wyoming still had the death sentence on the books, and although no one had been executed since 1992, the state might make an exception for Sonny. But there was still the issue of whether or not he'd killed Shannon Doyle, as DeMarco thought. When she got back to Casper, she'd swing by the detention center and ask Sonny if he had an alibi for the night Doyle was killed.

Then she thought, as long as she was down in this part of the state already, she might as well go talk to Sonny's wife. She knew Elaine Bunt was a high school teacher in Rock Springs and therefore only forty minutes away. She figured that since Shannon Doyle had been shot sometime around midnight, that if Sonny was innocent he should have been lying in bed next to his wife the night Doyle was killed. And if he had been, his wife should be able to corroborate this.

There was the problem that Doyle's murder was under the jurisdiction of the Sweetwater County Sheriff and not the FBI, but she decided that she didn't care. Screw everybody's rice bowls.

McCord showed her ID to the principal of the high school and asked him to bring Elaine Bunt to her. When the principal asked if Elaine had done something wrong, she said, "Not a thing. I just need to ask her a question related to an ongoing investigation."

A few minutes later, the principal returned to his office with a worried looking Elaine Bunt following him. Elaine was a thin blonde woman with bitten-to-the-quick fingernails. She seemed so mousy and timid that McCord wondered how she was able to control classrooms filled with unruly teenagers.

McCord said, "Mrs. Bunt, why don't we step outside so we can talk privately."

They walked out together and stood on the sidewalk near the front double doors to the school. McCord had noticed when she'd arrived at the school that the front doors had thick bulletproof glass and were locked, and she had to use an intercom next to the door to request permission to enter. There was also a camera above the door so whoever opened the door could see that the person entering wasn't a kid dressed in Goth-black, carrying an AR-15. God bless America.

McCord said, "Mrs. Bunt, I need to ask—"

Elaine said, "If this is about Sonny shooting that BLM agent, I can't talk to you without Sonny's lawyer being present."

"It's not about that," McCord said. Before Elaine could speak, McCord said, "Can you tell me where Sonny was the night Shannon Doyle was killed?"

"But what does Sonny have to do with that?"

"Probably nothing, but it's just a question I have to ask. So was your husband home with you that night?"

Without hesitating, Elaine said, "No. He went to a rodeo near Fort Collins with Shorty Warren the day before she was killed, and they stayed the night in Fort Collins."

Fuckin' Shorty again.

"And you're sure he was in Fort Collins that night?"

"I'm positive. I remember when Shannon Doyle was killed because when I drove to school that morning and saw all those sheriff cars down at the motel, I knew something bad had happened. I didn't find out until later exactly what had happened, but that was definitely the morning after Sonny went to Fort Collins."

"But how do you know he really went to Fort Collins?"

"Well, I guess I don't for sure, but why would he lie to me?"

McCord saw no reason to answer that stupid question. Instead she said, "Thank you for talking to me, Mrs. Bunt. I don't need anything else."

Fuckin' Shorty.

---

McCord returned to her car and called the cell phone number Shorty had given her. When he answered, she said, "This is Special Agent McCord."

"What do you want now," Shorty whined. She could hear cows mooing in the background.

"I want to know if you were in Fort Collins with Sonny the night that writer Shannon Doyle was killed. And don't you dare lie to me."

There was a brief hesitation before Shorty said, "We didn't go to Fort Collins together. Sonny spent the night with his girlfriend, you know, the Mexican chick. Sonny told me that if his wife asked, or if she called me if she couldn't reach Sonny, I was supposed to say we went to the rodeo."

An hour and a half later, McCord was finally on her way back to Casper.

She'd gone to the Hacienda Grill and questioned the bartender, first threatening her with all the terrible things that would happen to her if *she* lied. The woman eventually admitted that she and Sonny were together at a motel in Red Desert the night Shannon Doyle was killed. The bartender, by the way, was gorgeous, and McCord couldn't imagine why such a good-looking woman would have anything to do with a snake like Sonny Bunt.

As she drove back to Casper, she remembered that this was the day that DeMarco was supposed to appear in court for trespassing. She wondered how that had gone.

# 27

When he finally got back to Waverly from Rock Springs, DeMarco took a long nap as he'd hardly slept the night before in the jail. He then took a shower and shaved in a gingerly fashion due to the bruises on his face. His ribs, almost cracked by the cowboy-booted kickers, hurt worse than anything else. He dressed in jeans, a T-shirt, and top-siders sans socks, and walked across the highway to the truck stop to buy three bottles of beer. Back at the motel, he got ice from the machine, dumped the ice into the sink in his room, and placed two of the beers in the ice. He opened the third beer, and because it was hot inside his room, he took a chair and went to sit out on the walkway in front of his room, where he was treated to the now too familiar sight of the traffic on I-80 and Harriet's place across the highway.

He'd only been sitting there a few minutes, trying to decide what he was going to do next when it came to Shannon, when his phone rang. It was McCord.

"I heard you got off with just a fine."

"Yep. Law and order prevailed once again in the great state of Wyoming."

"Well, I got some bad news for you. Sonny Bunt didn't kill Shannon. Not only was the gun you found in his house not the murder weapon, but Sonny has an alibi for the night Shannon was killed."

"Who's his alibi? The same guy who said he was in Cheyenne when Jeff Hunter was killed?"

"No. It's the bartender at the Hacienda Grill in Waverly. Sonny has been having an affair with her, and the night Shannon was killed, he told his wife that he was going to Fort Collins and would be spending the night there. He actually spent the night at a motel in Red Desert with his girlfriend and she confirmed this."

"Maybe she's lying," DeMarco said.

"She's not. The clerk at the motel confirms that Sonny paid cash for the room and cameras at the motel don't show him leaving his room until the next morning."

"Well, shit," DeMarco said.

"DeMarco, you might have to accept that Shannon was killed by some trucker like the sheriff thinks."

"She wasn't killed by a trucker," DeMarco said. "Someone who lives in this fucking place killed her."

"Just let the sheriff do his job, DeMarco," McCord said and hung up.

DeMarco looked across the road at Harriet's place. He had to get Harriet to talk to him. And that's when he remembered the last conversation he'd had with Harriet, when he'd told her that he might have found the guy who'd killed Shannon. Harriet's response had been: "The guy?"

Harriet knew it wasn't a guy.

He'd never finished reading Shannon's journal because he'd been so convinced that Sonny had killed her. He went into his room, got his copy of the journal and another beer, and went to sit back outside.

He started flipping pages—this time focusing on the entries related to the women of Waverly.

# 28

The first entry DeMarco came to concerned Harriet. He almost skipped over it as he didn't consider Harriet a likely suspect, then decided not to.

*I'm really glad Harriet's taken a liking to me. She's a tough old gal. She doesn't tolerate any sass from the truckers who go to her restaurant and isn't particularly friendly to the locals, either. But once she found out I wrote* Lighthouse, *she opened up to me. She has a hard time sleeping, and some nights she'll sit in the café at a table near a window and sip bourbon and watch the cars streaming down the highway. There's a painting by Edward Hopper of a lonely woman sitting on a bed staring out a window and that's who she reminds me of. Because I'm always up so late, I've gotten into the habit of going over to the café sometimes when I see her and we'll talk for an hour or so. She's the best source of gossip in Waverly and she likes telling what she knows.*

*I've noticed that Harriet rarely says anything about her past so last night I asked her how she ended up in Waverly. She told me that thirty years ago she and her husband owned a restaurant in Cleveland and her husband got tired of the city, and the neighborhood where the restaurant was located had started to go downhill.*

*Her husband, his name was Gene, learned that the café in Waverly was for sale. Harriet didn't know how he'd found that out, maybe from a trade magazine, but he sold the restaurant in Cleveland and bought the café in Waverly based on nothing but photographs. He'd been to Yellowstone once when he was a kid and he thought all of Wyoming looked like Yellowstone. Harriet said, "The first time I saw this town . . . Well, I could have killed him." But she said her husband, unlike herself, was an outgoing person and people liked him and the café earned them a living, if just barely. Then Gene died unexpectedly and she was pretty much stuck here. It's hard for me to imagine a woman like Harriet letting her husband push her into doing something she didn't agree with, but who knows what she was like when she was younger.*

DeMarco flipped a few pages until he came to:

*Lisa Bunt is an interesting woman. According to Harriet, there's no doubt whatsoever she married Hiram for his money and he married her because having her on his arm made him the envy of every man in the county. Harriet said Lisa was twenty-seven and Hiram was sixty-six when they wed. They met when Lisa was working at the gun show they hold at the fairgrounds near Cheyenne, dressed in a skimpy outfit, luring guys over to look at the weapons some dealer was selling. Lisa charmed the pants off him and within six months they were hitched. At the time Hiram, even though he was in his sixties, was still a vigorous, virile man, maybe with some assistance from those little blue pills. But about two years ago, right after the famous standoff, he screwed up his back riding an ATV and since then he can barely walk. But if Lisa has any regrets about being married to a man forty years her senior, you'd never guess it from talking to her. She's smart and funny, always pleasant, and acts as if life's a ball.*

The next entry was a surprise: a discussion about the motel's maid.

*I'd told Harriet last night that Sam's daughter had most likely stolen my earrings. Harriet said the girl's name is Lola and she started hanging out with the wrong crowd in high school and got hooked on drugs. "She was such a sweet kid," Harriet said. "It's a shame, what she's become. It's killing Sam."*

*I was coming out of my room to go to lunch today and found Lola Clarke with her cleaning cart standing in front of the room next to mine. She looked terrible; the drugs are definitely taking their toll on her physically. When she saw me, she said, "You gotta lot of goddamn nerve accusing me of stealing." I said, "I didn't accuse you. I told your father my earrings were missing and asked if anyone had been inside my room but you, and he said no one had." She said, "Bullshit, you're not accusing me. You better watch your fancy ass. I won't stand for you telling lies about me." I said, "Are you threatening me, Lola?" She said, "I'm just saying don't go badmouthing me or you'll regret it." I feel sorry for her. I hope she gets the help she needs. As for her threat, I'm not worried about that. Lola doesn't know I played hockey in college and whipped girls a lot tougher than her.*

The next entry DeMarco stopped to read began with: *Hoo-boy.* DeMarco smiled when he read that, "hoo-boy" being an expression Shannon had used when something struck her as scandalous or shocking.

*Hoo-boy. I saw something tonight and I'm dying to talk to Harriet about it. I'd just pulled my car into the motel parking lot and I saw a striking cloud formation to the north. It looked like the fist of God about to come down on Waverly. I decided to study it for a while; I knew taking a photo wouldn't really capture it and it was changing by the moment, and I wanted to get my head around how to describe it. So I walked around to the back of the motel, where the trailers and RVs are parked, to get a better view and I saw Jim Turner come out from amongst the trailers. I was going to say hi to him and point out the cloud formation, but he got into his cruiser and took off before I could say anything. I didn't think too much about seeing him there, figuring that he was probably on sheriff's business, checking on someone who lived in one of the trailers. After he left, I stood there for about ten minutes, studying the clouds, when I see Lisa Bunt coming from the same direction that Jim Turner had come from. When she saw me, she stopped dead in her tracks, then smiled and walked over to me, and asked what I was doing. We BS'ed for about ten minutes, literally talking about the weather, then she left. She never said what she was doing in the trailer park and I never asked, but when I first saw her, I could see she looked really uncomfortable. Or maybe guilty?*

The next page was filled with a description of the cloud formation Shannon had seen: the colors, the way it advanced toward Waverly, the pent-up energy about to be released upon the land. DeMarco was once again struck by the difference in Shannon's voice when she was writing what he guessed would be a part of her novel as opposed to the informal entries in her journal, which approximated the way she spoke.

*Harriet confirmed it. Jim Turner is having an affair with Lisa Bunt. Harriet said this is bad news for both of them. Lisa signed a prenup that says if she fooled around on him, Hiram could divorce her without giving her a cent. How Harriet knows these things is a mystery. As for Jim, he'd certainly lose his job because Hiram would make sure he did. Harriet said she suspected that Jim and Lisa meet in places other than Waverly as it was too dangerous for them to be having a tryst so close to home, but she'd seen Lisa's cute little BMW half a dozen times go around to the back of the motel and not long after that, she'd see Jim's cruiser arrive. Jim could always say he was there investigating some gas worker who'd committed a crime, but Lisa Bunt had no excuse for being there. As for the trailer they used, Harriet had no idea which one it was or who owned it. Lisa probably gets a big enough allowance from Hiram that she could afford to rent a trailer. Harriet also said that this wasn't the first time Jim had cheated on his wife. The guy was so damn good looking that women just threw themselves at him and Harriet was aware of affairs he'd had with local women, one of them married, and she imagined Jim's wife was probably aware of them too.*

*I find it hard to believe that Carly Turner would tolerate her husband cheating on her. I've spoken to her a couple of times since the dinner party at Hiram's house and have gotten to know her a bit. She comes across as a strong woman, very bright, and very independent. Yet I can't help but feel sorry for her. She told me she was at the University of Wyoming in Laramie when she met Jim, who'd just gotten out of the army and had been hired on as a city cop. She'd been planning to go for a law degree, but then gets pregnant, marries Jim, and drops out of school. The second kid, another boy, came along a couple of years later. In the meantime, Jim gets a job working for the Sweetwater County Sheriff and becomes a rising star in the department. The local scuttlebutt is that he's going to run for the sheriff's job when the incumbent retires. Anyway, I like Carly. For one thing, she's the only unabashed liberal I've met here in Wyoming, other than Gloria Brunson, and she's very outspoken about her political beliefs and doesn't care that the majority of the people in the area don't agree with her. I get the sense, however, that as much as she loves her sons and her husband, that she feels like she's wasted her life in Waverly. I also think she has a drinking problem. Every time I've seen her, she's been drinking and is always a bit drunk.*

*I'm more sure now than ever that the main character in my novel is going to be based on Carly Turner: complex, conflicted, strong yet vulnerable. Maybe I'll marry her to a younger version of Hiram Bunt, a successful rancher, an arrogant, aloof man who barely speaks to her. She'll love the land yet feel as if it's sucking the life out of her.*

A few pages later, Shannon was back to Lisa Bunt.

*Lisa Bunt invited me to go horseback riding with her and I'm so glad she did. Seeing the country from the back of a horse gave me a totally different perspective than driving around in my car. I asked Lisa if she knew someplace where I could rent a horse and she told me I could borrow one of hers any time I wanted and I'm going to take her up on the offer. During the ride she asked me if anyone in my book would be recognizable as a real person in Waverly. I told her no. I said that I was still developing the characters in my head and they would be based in part on some of the people I'd met, but that what I would be trying to do was capture the attitudes of people, their outlook on life, their feelings about living where they did and doing what they did, but none of them would be recognizable as people who actually lived in Waverly. Although she didn't say so, I think she was genuinely concerned my novel would expose her affair with Jim Turner. What I didn't tell her was that my novel was going to be centered around a couple who were married to other people and having an affair that was going to turn out very badly for both of them. If I'd told her that, she would have probably freaked out.*

*Saw Carly Turner tonight at the Hacienda Grill. She was there with a couple of women I'd never met, and when I walked in to have dinner, she waved me over. I couldn't help but notice she was drinking about twice as fast as everyone else. At first she was funny, just as she'd been at the dinner party at Hiram's, but after a while she tended to become a bit belligerent, snapping at the server, and her mood got darker the more she drank. When one of her friends pointed at the pretty Hispanic barmaid and said she'd heard that she was having an affair with Sonny Bunt—something I already knew about—Carly's reaction seemed over the top. She said, "These goddamn bitches who go after other women's husbands oughta be shot." I couldn't help but wonder if Carly knew about Lisa's affair with her husband. Or maybe she was reflecting on past affairs that he'd had with other women. Harriet had told me that he's had more than one. Whatever the case, there's a lot of anger in Carly that she probably suppresses when she's not drinking. Seeing that she was in no condition to drive I offered to drive her home, but she just laughed and said, "You think anyone's going to give a deputy sheriff's wife a DUI?"*

The next section he came to was about Harriet, which DeMarco again almost skipped over because he couldn't imagine that Harriet would have anything to do with Shannon's death. But he decided to read it anyway.

*I was at Harriet's last night and something odd happened. I told her I wanted to find a book with photos of the area, maybe one which identified the plants and discussed the geographic formations. I said I could find things on the Internet but sometimes it's easier to flip through an old-fashioned book. Harriet said her husband had bought a book like that when they first moved out here and it was upstairs in her apartment, and she asked me to go upstairs with her and try to find it. I'd never been in her apartment before. It's a loft with a sleeping area at one end and a sitting area with a TV at the other end. There's a fairly large bathroom with a huge, claw-footed bathtub, but no kitchen. Her kitchen is the restaurant. There were two bookcases in the place, one in the sleeping area and one in the sitting room. She told me to check the books in the sitting room and she'd look in the other bookcase.*

*I didn't find a book showing photos of Wyoming, but on an end table near a recliner I saw a photo in a silver frame partially hidden by a lamp. I picked it up. It was a photo of Harriet and her husband taken years ago when they were both very young. Harriet's hair was dark and wavy and framed her face. She looked so pretty. Her husband was a thin guy, several inches taller than her, and he had curly dark hair and a crooked smile. He wasn't handsome but still very appealing. They were standing in front of a restaurant but the name of the restaurant was only partially visible. All I could read was "gretti's" but I couldn't see the letters in front of the "g."*

*Anyway, Harriet found the book she was looking for and came back into the sitting room and when she saw me holding the photo she said, "What are you doing with that?" She practically shrieked at me and I could see she was upset. Maybe she was afraid I'd drop the photo or just angry that I'd picked it up in the first place. I said something like "Oh, look how pretty you were. And your husband, he looks like he'd be a lot of fun. Where was this taken?"*

*I could tell she was still upset but she said, "Cleveland, thirty, forty years ago." I pointed at the restaurant in the background of the photo and asked, "Is this the restaurant you used to own in Cleveland?" She said, "No, that's just where the picture was taken, somewhere on the street. I can't remember where or who took it." The thing is, I got the distinct impression she was lying, but about what, I have no idea. After that she pretty much shooed me out. I hope I haven't damaged our relationship by being so nosey.*

*Carly Turner needs to get some help. I was walking back to my room after picking up a few things at the convenience store and she was waiting in the parking lot in her car. As soon as she saw me, she got out of her car and yelled at me, "Are you having an affair with my husband?" She was obviously drunk. I asked her what on earth she was talking about and she said she saw me talking to Jim the other day, standing outside my room. And I had been talking to him. I'd just come out of my room to go for another horseback ride and I saw him in the parking lot, by his car, talking to someone on his phone. When he saw me, he walked over and said hello. He told me that Sam Clarke had called him to the motel because a couple on the second floor had gotten into a screaming match and Sam had called Jim to settle them down before they killed each other. So he and I just chatted for a bit, and he went on his way—and I told Carly this. She said, "I don't believe you." For a moment I thought she was going to attack me, in which case I would have been forced to kick her ass, but she didn't. She said "You stay away from him," and got into her car and roared off, almost getting t-boned by a semi as she pulled onto the highway. The thing that occurred to me after she left was: How did Carly know Jim had talked to me? Had she been following him?*

DeMarco almost missed a short paragraph that said:

*I don't know why, but sometimes I just can't seem to stop myself. I called John Bradley and asked him about the photo I saw in Harriet's apartment. I couldn't believe what he told me.*

He came to the last entry in Shannon's journal.

*I talked to Harriet tonight, to tell her I'd probably be leaving soon, then, like a dummy, I had to go and show off and tell her what I'd learned. When I did, I thought she was going to faint. I told her repeatedly how I admired what she'd done but I could see that it had been a mistake to say anything. I scared her to death.*

*It's time to leave. Carly Turner thinks I'm screwing her husband, Lisa Bunt thinks I'm going to write a book about her affair with Handsome Jim, and then I almost go and give the person who's helped me the most a heart attack. It's definitely time to get back to California and write the book. I've gotten everything I need here. I can see the land and I can see the characters in the novel. It's time to go home and do the work.*

DeMarco flipped the last page over and sat back to think. He had three female suspects and one male, the male being Jim Turner. Either Jim Turner or Lisa Bunt might have killed Shannon because they were worried about her exposing their affair, in which case Turner would lose his job and Lisa would lose whatever chance she had of inheriting Hiram Bunt's fortune. Then there was the drug-addicted maid. She could have killed Shannon to steal her laptop and sell it to pay for drugs. That seemed unlikely though, that the girl would murder for whatever price she could get for a pawned laptop. But then addicts aren't known for being rational. The final possibility was Turner's alcoholic wife. Carly Turner could have killed Shannon in a drunken rage because she believed Shannon was trying to steal her husband from her.

Whatever the case, he had no proof that any of these people had killed Shannon. He also had no way to eliminate suspects. He could question them to see if they'd tell him where they were the night Shannon died, but the murderer would lie to him and the others most likely wouldn't answer his questions. Nor could he think of any way to force law enforcement to get a warrant to do ballistics tests on any weapons they might have. For one thing, a member of law enforcement was one of his suspects and DeMarco wasn't about to break into the homes of three people to see what firearms they had. And after what had happened to Sonny Bunt, if the murderer hadn't already disposed of the murder weapon, he or she certainly would have done so by now.

He needed to get Harriet to talk to him. Shannon had confided in her and Harriet knew more about the people in this snake pit than anyone. She might know if Shannon, in the last few days of her life, had done something or learned something that could have pushed one of them over the edge. He didn't know what it was that Shannon had learned about Harriet—obviously something to do with her past—but whatever it was, Shannon had said that she admired Harriet for what she'd done. Being admired wasn't a motive for murder. Yeah, it was time to force the ol' gal to talk to him.

# 29

DeMarco had dinner at Harriet's, again taking his time eating so that he was the only customer left when it was time for the café to close. When Harriet presented him with his bill, he said, "Harriet, you have to talk to me about Shannon's murder."

"No, I don't. And it's time for you to get going."

"Yeah, you do. If you cared about her, and I know you did, you have to help me catch the person who killed her."

Before Harriet could respond, DeMarco said, "Shannon kept a journal, like a diary, while she was here in Waverly."

When he said this, Harriet's reaction surprised him. She blurted: "Oh, my God! What did she say about me?"

"She said how much she liked you, and how she enjoyed talking to you, and how grateful she was for the help you gave her. "

"That's all she said?"

"Yeah, pretty much, but I'm not here to talk about you. I know from reading her journal that there are four people who might have killed her. Two of those people are Jim Turner and Lisa Bunt because they were afraid that Shannon might reveal that they were having an affair. Then there's Sam's daughter, Lola. She stole Shannon's earrings and, because she's a junkie, she might have killed Shannon to steal her laptop and whatever cash Shannon had in her purse. Lastly, there's Carly Turner. She's got a drinking problem and she thought Shannon was having an affair with her husband. She even confronted Shannon, accusing her of the affair."

"I didn't know that," Harriet said.

"That was almost the last entry in Shannon's journal, Carly Turner showing up at the motel and accusing her of sleeping with Deputy Jim. Anyway, I think you saw something the night Shannon was killed. Right before Sonny Bunt was arrested, I told you that they might have caught the guy who killed her and you acted surprised when I said it was a guy. Like you knew it *wasn't* a guy. So talk to me, Harriet. Tell me what you know. You owe it to Shannon."

Harriet closed her eyes briefly, then finally, reluctantly, sat down at DeMarco's table. The woman looked bone-weary and ancient, and DeMarco felt momentarily sorry for the way he was pressuring her.

"I don't know who killed Shannon," she said. "The night it happened, I was sitting here in the café in the dark because I couldn't sleep and I saw someone knock on her door. I saw the door open and the person who knocked walked into her room, then just a minute later she walked back out. I thought Shannon must have invited her in but I didn't know why she left so soon. I thought that maybe Shannon gave her something she came to collect. I didn't know until the next morning that Shannon had been killed."

"So who was she?"

"I don't know." When she saw the look of disbelief on DeMarco's face, she said, "Hey! Look across the highway at the motel. You can't make out a person's face from this distance, or at least I can't, not with my eyesight. But it looked like a woman to me, one with dark hair. The thing is, in case you haven't noticed, is that Lisa Bunt, Carly Turner, and Lola Clarke are all about the same height and build, and they all have dark hair. But I don't know if it was any of those three who came to see Shannon that night because, like I already said, I couldn't see her face. So I can't help you, DeMarco. I don't know who visited Shannon that night."

"You could have told the sheriff that it was a woman."

Harriet said, "What good would that have done? Do you seriously think that Jim Turner was going to investigate either Lisa or his wife?"

---

DeMarco left a few minutes later, satisfied that Harriet had finally told him the truth, although there was something off about why she didn't tell Jim Turner what she'd seen. DeMarco wondered if the reason could be that she hadn't wanted to get involved because of whatever Shannon had learned about her past.

Whatever the case, he could only think of two things he could do to expose Shannon's killer. One of those was to let it be known that Harriet had seen the murderer. If he did that, the killer might go after Harriet—and that was unacceptable. He couldn't use an old woman for bait.

But the person he could use for bait was himself.

# 30

A couple of years ago, an enormously wealthy couple in Boston was killed in a plane crash. Their fifteen-year-old daughter miraculously survived the crash and became the beneficiary of a five-billion-dollar trust fund. The girl was also the goddaughter of John Mahoney and DeMarco had been sent to Boston to check on her and stumbled into a case of murder and embezzlement. It turned out that the lawyer managing the family trust fund had been stealing from it, had sabotaged the girl's parents' plane, and then fled to Montenegro to keep from being arrested. She'd picked Montenegro because the country had no extradition treaty with the United States.

To bring the woman to justice, DeMarco employed the help of an ex-Boston cop named Tommy Hewlett. And because the lawyer couldn't be legally extradited from Montenegro, DeMarco, with Tommy's help, *illegally* extradited her. That is, they kidnapped her and shipped her murderous, thieving ass back to Boston where she was arrested and convicted. Tommy Hewlett was currently employed by a security company in Boston; he was competent and experienced and carried a gun. DeMarco figured that Tommy might be useful insofar as keeping him from getting killed.

DeMarco called Tommy, told him what was going on, and generally what he had in mind. Tommy said, "Things are never simple with you, are they, DeMarco?" Nonetheless, Tommy said he'd tell his boss he needed some time off and would be in Rock Springs tomorrow.

The next afternoon DeMarco was waiting for Tommy at a restaurant on the outskirts of Rock Springs that had parking spaces long enough for RVs. The restaurant was also conveniently located near a gun shop where DeMarco had purchased a bulletproof vest. That is, the vest was bulletproof provided he wasn't shot with a .50 caliber bullet. Considering what he was about to do, and knowing how Shannon had died, the vest seemed a prudent investment.

About the time Tommy had predicted he'd arrive, DeMarco saw a white Jeep Grand Cherokee pulling an Airstream travel trailer roll into the parking lot. There'd been no accommodations available for Tommy in Waverly so he'd rented the light Airstream in Salt Lake, along with a vehicle with enough power to tow it.

Tommy walked into the restaurant dressed in a T-shirt, jeans, and work boots, attire which DeMarco had suggested so he'd fit in better with the folks in Waverly. Waverly wasn't a place where you saw men in suits and ties. Tommy was almost sixty, a lean six-footer with gray hair, blue eyes buried in wrinkles, and an aquiline nose. The first time DeMarco met him, DeMarco thought he looked like an old-time Western gunfighter; the fact was that in twenty years on the Boston PD, Tommy had never fired his weapon in the line of duty. DeMarco was just assuming he knew how to use a gun.

Tommy sat down at DeMarco's table in the café and ordered a piece of apple pie and a glass of milk. He said, "So. We got a plan here?"

"First, we need to discuss your fee. Naturally, I'll pay for your flight and the rental fees for the Jeep and the trailer, but I don't know your daily rate."

"For you, my daily rate is zero. We both know I owe you."

DeMarco was relieved to hear this. This adventure was putting a major dent into his savings account between flights, lodging, lawyers, and accessories like the bulletproof vest, which had cost him four hundred bucks. As for Tommy owing him, that was true. Tommy owed him big time.

DeMarco met Tommy under odd circumstances, those circumstances being that Tommy had been trying to blackmail John Mahoney. After Tommy retired from the BPD, he'd taken a job on Mahoney's security detail, functioning as Mahoney's driver for a few years, and while performing that job learned about one of Mahoney's affairs. Mahoney, a man who'd had many affairs, wouldn't have been particularly damaged if the affair had been revealed, but the woman involved would have been.

DeMarco had been sent to pry Tommy off Mahoney's back and learned that Tommy had fallen on hard times. After he left Mahoney's service, he went to work for a Boston security company as an investigator, but then his wife contracted cancer and her medical expenses wiped out his savings—after which he tried to drink himself to death and was fired from his job. At the time DeMarco met him, Tommy was about to lose his house and blackmailing Mahoney had been an act of desperation and completely out of character for the man. DeMarco, however, took pity on him and gave Tommy a second lease on life by getting the security company to rehire him so he could help DeMarco in Montenegro. He also got a banker, one who wanted some political suck with Mahoney, to give Tommy some breathing space when it came to the loan he had to repay to keep his house.

So yeah, Tommy owed him.

As for DeMarco's plan, it was pretty simple: Tomorrow he was going to poke a stick into a hornet's nest and see which hornet tried to sting him. Tommy's job was to swat the hornet if it came too close.

# 31

Bright and early the next day, DeMarco strolled into Jim Turner's office and plopped down into the chair in front of the deputy's desk.

"What do you want?" Turner said. "And why the hell are you still here in Waverly?"

"To answer your second question first, I'm still here because you haven't arrested Shannon Doyle's killer. As for what I want, I don't want anything. I'm just here to tell you what I'm planning to do."

"And what's that?" Turner said. His tone and relaxed body language made it clear that he wasn't concerned about anything DeMarco might do.

"Jim, as I'm sure you know, I got a copy of a journal that Shannon Doyle had been keeping while she was here in Waverly. In this journal, she wrote down all her observations and opinions and the gossip she collected on the fine folk of Waverly."

"No, I didn't know that."

"Come on, Jim. Of course you knew about the journal. That night when I was smacked on the head at my motel, a copy of the journal was stolen. Now I can't prove this, but I think there's a very good possibility that you're the guy who hit me."

DeMarco had originally thought that Sonny Bunt might have attacked him to steal Shannon's journal—but he now knew that Sonny hadn't killed Shannon. And he figured that if Sonny had wanted to see the journal and stop DeMarco's investigation, Sonny probably would have shot him in the back the way he had Hunter. It now seemed more likely that Turner or one of his three female suspects had attacked him. He knew it wasn't Lisa Bunt, as she'd still been in the restaurant when he'd left that night. So too had Lola Clarke; she'd been having dinner with her dad. Which left Carly or Jim Turner. He'd seen Turner in the restaurant but hadn't noticed if he was still in the bar when he left. And of the two Turners, a large, healthy male struck him as a more likely suspect than a small female.

Turner came out of his chair and pointed a finger at DeMarco's face. "Hey! Are you accusing me—"

"Jim, I'm going way beyond accusing you of mugging me. That journal made it clear that you've been having an affair with Lisa Bunt, and what that means is that both you and Lisa had a motive for wanting Shannon dead. If your affair became known, you'd lose your job, Hiram would divorce Lisa, and she'd have wasted the last ten years being married to the old goat."

"That's a goddamn lie!" Turner said.

DeMarco didn't know what part of what he'd said was a lie, but it didn't matter. He said, "What I'm going to do is get the FBI or the Wyoming State Police to take over the investigation of Shannon's murder. This has happened before when local police forces are proven to be corrupt or poorly managed. They bring in the feds and they set up some kind of task force or commission to oversee things. Well, that's what's needed here, my man. You can't have the guy in charge of Shannon's investigation screwing one of the main suspects."

Turner looked as if he was about ready to come out from behind his desk and start whaling on DeMarco. Considering the guy's size that probably wouldn't turn out well for DeMarco—but DeMarco kept going. "Now I know what you're thinking. You're thinking that I don't have the clout to make this happen. Well, what I'm going to do is take a copy of Shannon's journal to the biggest newspaper in this state and let them read it. And maybe the feds or the state cops won't come in and take over, but sure as shit you'll lose your job, any chance you have of being elected sheriff will evaporate, and, like I said, your girlfriend will walk away from ten years of marriage with nothing more than the clothes on her back."

"Goddamnit, you can't do that," Turner said. "I'm not going to let you do that."

"Oh, yeah? What are you going to do to stop me?" DeMarco said. He was sure that as soon as he left, Turner would be calling Lisa Bunt.

---

Turner said, "We need to meet. Right now."

Lisa said, "Well, I can't just—"

"This is serious. It's that fucking DeMarco. We need to talk."

"All right. Calm down."

"I'll wait for you in the trailer. How long do you think it will take you to get there?"

"I don't know," she said. "Give me an hour."

---

Fortunately, Lisa had been alone when Jim called, brushing down her horse after her morning ride. If he had called while she was having breakfast with Hiram, the situation could have gotten a little tricky.

She didn't know what was going on, but it was something bad. Jim had sounded almost hysterical.

She'd always known it was a huge mistake to become involved with Jim. But she just couldn't help herself. For one thing, the man was absolutely gorgeous. The other thing was, and this had actually surprised her, he was incredible in bed. It had been her experience that a lot of good looking men weren't particularly good lovers; they were just too caught up in themselves. Jim, however, wasn't that way at all and maybe that was because the man had been with so many women. He'd told her that he lost his virginity when he was thirteen and she could believe it.

It was just one of those things that happened. Sleeping with Hiram had been disgusting and then the old bastard hurts his back so he wasn't even capable of sex. When she'd started the affair with Turner, she hadn't been laid in two years and she hadn't been laid *right* in ten years. She had needs, for Christ's sake. She was only thirty-seven. But she'd also known that the affair would ruin her if Hiram ever found out. A man as proud as Hiram wouldn't tolerate being a cuckold and God knows what she'd do to make a living if he divorced her. She did *not* want to go back to the life she'd been living before she met him.

She thought for a moment about some excuse to give Hiram for why she had to leave immediately and came up with one. She called out to one of the hands who was mucking out a stall and told him to finish wiping down her horse and went back to the house. She found Hiram in his den but he was just sitting behind his desk, staring off into space. Normally, this time of day, he'd be poring over the financial news to see what was happening with gas prices or the price of cattle or a dozen other things. Or he'd be giving his foreman orders on what he wanted done around the ranch that day. But the thing with Sonny had really gotten to him and he hadn't been able to focus on business or anything else for several days.

He wouldn't admit it to her, but Hiram knew Sonny had killed the BLM agent and was likely to spend the rest of his life in jail. And the fact that Sonny had shot the man in the back would have been particularly hurtful to a man as proud as Hiram Bunt. Had Sonny walked up to Hunter and looked him in the eye before he shot him, Hiram wouldn't have been pleased, but at least he wouldn't have felt ashamed. And even though he knew it was probably hopeless, he'd hired another lawyer to defend Sonny, a man from Denver who'd defended a couple of high-profile murderers. It pissed Lisa off that he was spending his money—which, with any luck, would soon be *her* money—by wasting it on a high-priced lawyer.

She said, "Honey, I have to go to see Dr. Parker."

"What?" he said.

*Oh, God, was he going deaf too?* "I said, I have to go to Dr. Parker's office. You know that physical I had last week?"

"Yeah. What about it?"

"One of the lab tests came back with a weird result and the doctor's office just called and told me they need me to retake the test." She actually had had a physical last week. She was in perfect health.

"What's wrong?" he asked, sounding genuinely concerned.

"Some number having to do with kidney function was high. The nurse said the number was so high that she thinks they most likely screwed up the test. Anyway, I have to drive to Rock Springs and pee in a cup. I'll probably have lunch there and then come right back. I'm sure everything will be fine."

---

Jim was sitting in the RV at the fold-down dining room table behind the driver's seat. All the ratty curtains in the vehicle were pulled closed.

The RV was a class C motorhome with bald tires and over two hundred thousand miles on the odometer. Lisa had bought it from a gas worker who had needed a quick infusion of cash. It had a small propane stove that didn't work and a sink barely big enough for a frying pan. With a couple of exceptions, however, the age and condition of the RV were irrelevant. The exceptions were a queen-sized bed in the back that Lisa had installed to replace the motorhome's original bed, a miniscule shower that actually worked, and a small refrigerator that would hold a couple bottles of wine.

Jim stood up when she walked into the motorhome. He was so tall his head almost touched the ceiling. His face was grim.

"What's going on?" she said, taking a seat at the table.

"That guy, DeMarco," Jim said. "He said he's going to give Shannon's journal to a newspaper and claim that I shouldn't be investigating her death because I'm involved with you. He thinks if he does that the FBI or the State Police will take over the investigation."

"Goddamn him," Lisa said.

She'd flipped through the journal after Jim had stolen DeMarco's copy. She'd actually been flattered by some of the things Shannon had written about her, Shannon saying how much she liked her and enjoyed her company. She hadn't been pleased to see Shannon discuss her affair with Jim or to learn that old bat Harriet Robbins also knew about it, but she hadn't been too concerned. With the writer dead, there wouldn't be a novel coming out to expose her adultery and she seriously doubted any respectable paper would publish the journal in its current form. A newspaper wouldn't want to face the possibility of a libel suit for passing on a lot of what amounted to nothing more than titillating, unsubstantiated gossip. But DeMarco was putting a new twist on the journal. He was going to say that Shannon's knowledge of her affair with Jim was a motive for murder and also a reason why Jim shouldn't be leading the investigation. She wasn't worried, however, about the FBI or the State police. She was one hundred percent confident they wouldn't connect her to the writer's death. But what would happen is that Hiram would divorce her and, because of the damn prenup she'd signed, there wouldn't be any alimony to compensate for all those years of being married to him.

"What are you going to do?" she asked.

"I don't think there's anything I can do," Jim said. "Destroying DeMarco's copy of the journal won't do any good. He'll just print out another one. He obviously has access to an electronic copy."

"I wasn't thinking about destroying the journal. I was thinking about destroying *him*. He's the only one pushing this thing. If he's gone—"

*Jesus, he'd always known there was a cold streak in her*. Her marrying Hiram was proof of that. But murder—

"Hell, Lisa, I'm not going to kill the man."

"He's going to ruin us! You'll lose your job, your wife will probably divorce you and take what little money you have, and without a doubt, Hiram will divorce me."

Turner shook his head.

"Honey, Hiram will be gone in a few years. In fact, he might be gone even sooner than I'd hoped. This thing with Sonny is killing him. And when he's gone, and with Sonny in jail, I'll be the wealthiest woman in Sweetwater County, and you and I can get married and you won't have to worry about what divorcing your wife will cost you. And if you want to be the sheriff, I'll help you get elected. But if DeMarco goes to a newspaper with that damn journal—"

"I'm not going to kill him," Turner said.

As if he hadn't spoken, she said, "And you need to act quickly, and I mean like right away. You gotta stop him before he tells anyone else what he knows."

When Jim just sat there, his head hanging, looking down at the tabletop, she stood up and started to unbutton her blouse. "Maybe this would be a good time to remind you of what you'll be missing if you don't deal with DeMarco."

# 32

DeMarco had noticed that Sam Clarke's daughter usually started cleaning the motel's rooms around nine in the morning, moving at a glacial pace, slowly pushing her cleaning cart from room to room, spending about twenty minutes in each one. He'd also noticed that sometimes she'd forget to provide clean towels or toilet paper or to empty the wastebaskets. The only reason she'd be nominated for employee of the month was because she was Sam Clarke's only employee.

DeMarco took his room chair outside and placed it on the walkway to wait for Lola. He was wearing an extra-large, button-up sport shirt to conceal the bulletproof vest. The vest was hot and uncomfortable and he wondered how cops could stand to wear them all day.

At nine-thirty, a dusty blue Toyota with a dented left front fender pulled into the parking lot with Lola Clarke behind the wheel. She didn't immediately exit the vehicle; she sat for about five minutes smoking, making DeMarco wonder *what* she was smoking. Finally, she left her car and walked reluctantly over to the locked closet at the east end of the motel and removed her cleaning cart.

DeMarco waited until she finished cleaning the first room before approaching her. As he was walking toward her, he looked around the parking lot and spotted Tommy Hewlett sitting in his rented Jeep drinking coffee. Good.

Lola was about to enter the next room and DeMarco called out to her. "Hey, Lola, hold on a minute."

She said, "Yeah, what is it? You need something?"

"Nope, don't need a thing. Just wanted to let you know something. You know that writer who was killed here?"

"Yeah," Lola said. DeMarco noticed she had the pinpoint pupils often seen in heroin users and was wearing a long-sleeved shirt on a warm June day.

DeMarco said, "The writer was a friend of mine. Maybe your dad told you that."

Lola didn't respond.

DeMarco said, "Well, she left a journal in which she talked about all the fine people she met here in Waverly, one of those fine people being you. She wrote you stole her diamond earrings."

"That's bullshit," Lola said. "And I'm gonna tell my dad you're giving me a hard time and he's going to kick you out of your room. And good luck finding another place to stay."

DeMarco almost said *I've been kicked out of a lot of better places than this—* but decided this wasn't the time for humor.

"Lola, I'm going to get the FBI to investigate Shannon Doyle's death because I don't think that the sheriff is doing his job. And when the FBI starts poking around they're going to check pawn shops to see if someone hocked the earrings or Shannon's laptop."

"I don't give a shit what you or the FBI does," Lola said. "Now if you don't stop bothering me, I'm gonna go get my dad."

"Lola, I don't care about the earrings you stole from Shannon, but if the cops find out you pawned them, they'll arrest you, and those earrings were expensive enough to make stealing them a felony. And if they find out you pawned the laptop, well, then you're going to jail for murder. I've heard addicts have it really hard when they have to go cold turkey inside a jail cell."

"Hey, I didn't murder anyone, and you get the fuck away from me." Lola walked into the room she'd been planning to clean next and slammed the door behind her.

DeMarco suspected he might not have fresh towels this evening.

---

Inside the room, Lola sat down on the unmade bed, trying to decide what to do. As she sat there, she unconsciously began to scratch her left arm, near the scabs over the needle marks. She could hardly think, she needed a fix so bad.

She pulled out her cell phone. When he answered, she said, "Donny, I'm in trouble."

"Oh, yeah? How's that?" Donny said, his voice conveying how little he gave a shit.

Donny was a fat, long-haired creep who lived in Rock Springs. He supplied her with dope and when she didn't have enough cash sometimes he'd make her give him a blow job. Other times, he'd sell her to some gas worker or a trucker if he could find a guy who wanted her. He was always telling her that if she'd fix herself up a little, wear some makeup and a short skirt, they could both make more money and life would be easier for her. Yeah, Donny was a peach of a guy and, God help her, the only one she could think of to call about DeMarco.

"There's this guy here at the motel," Lola said. "He's investigating that writer's murder. You remember, I told you about the writer."

"Yeah, but so what?" Donny said.

"I want you to make him stop hassling me. He says he's going to tell the cops I stole the bitch's earrings and they'll check with the pawnshops, and when they find out I hocked them they'll arrest me."

"Well, I guess you shouldn't have stolen those earrings."

"Hey, you listen to me. If you don't help me and I get arrested, I'm going to tell the cops all about you."

Donny was silent for a moment. His voice no longer carefree when he said, "You don't want to threaten me, girl."

"I'm not threatening you," Lola said, even though she was. She said, "But you know if the cops catch me, they won't give me anything to help me unless I tell them whatever they want to hear. Plus, you don't want me arrested. I know you don't make a lot of money off me, but you make some, and I won't be able to earn for you if I'm in jail."

Another long silence. "What this guy's name."

"DeMarco. He's in room nine here at the motel."

# 33

The last person on DeMarco's list was Carly Turner, the deputy's wife. He wasn't sure exactly how to approach Carly. He could simply drive over to her house and knock on the door, but the problem with that bright idea was that Jim Turner might arrest him. He wasn't sure exactly what Turner would charge him with. Harassment? Trespassing? Certainly, someone in law enforcement would be able to come up with a suitable charge and DeMarco imagined a local judge would tend to be unsympathetic toward a man who was bothering a cop's spouse.

On the other hand, if Turner did arrest him then he'd have to think about the possibility of DeMarco telling the judge and everyone else in the courtroom the reason why he was hassling Carly Turner, the reason being the contents of Shannon's journal. That is, DeMarco would be able to say that the journal indicated a number of folks in Waverly had motives for killing Shannon, one of those people being the wife of the deputy and another being the deputy's lover. Yeah, it seemed pretty unlikely that Turner would want to take the chance of DeMarco shooting off his mouth in a courtroom.

Jim and Carly Turner lived in a modest, single-story home with an attached two-car garage. There was a fair-sized lawn, and in a carport on one side of the house was a riding lawn mower and two ten-speed bikes. Over the double garage doors was a basketball hoop, reminding DeMarco that Carly Turner was the mother of a couple of teenage boys.

DeMarco couldn't help but feel sorry for Carly Turner. According to Shannon's journal, she'd never had the opportunity to live up to her full potential, her college ambitions having been cut short by her marriage to Turner. Now she was a woman who had become addicted to booze and had a husband who cheated on her. And if the contents of Shannon's journal were made public—that her husband was screwing Hiram Bunt's wife—it would not only hurt her but also her sons. On the other hand, if she was the one who'd killed Shannon, he didn't care how the truth affected her children. That was on Carly, not him.

It was eleven a.m. on a weekday and DeMarco figured Carly's boys would be at school and her husband would be off doing whatever a sheriff's deputy normally did. She answered the door wearing shorts, a white tank top, and flip-flops. She had unruly dark hair and bright blue eyes and although not as striking as Lisa Bunt, she was an attractive woman. DeMarco had never met her but he realized he had seen her before at the Grill having drinks with a couple of other women.

"Can I help you?" she said to DeMarco.

"My name's Joe DeMarco. I'm—"

"Oh, you're DeMarco. My husband's told me about you. Said you're the one who broke into Sonny's house and got him arrested. Jim was pretty upset about what you did, but I can tell you that it didn't bother me a bit. Sonny's an asshole."

"Mrs. Turner, I'm going to cut right to the chase here. Shannon Doyle left a journal, documenting observations she made while visiting here. From her journal I've concluded that several people had a motive for killing her." He paused then said, "You're one of those people."

"What! Are you serious?"

"Right before Shannon was killed you accused her of having an affair with your husband. Shannon wrote that you threatened her."

Carly didn't speak for a moment, then shook her head. "That was pretty stupid of me. I saw her talking to Jim one day when I'd had too much to drink, and I said a few things I shouldn't have." She hesitated. "My husband's a good-looking man and women are always throwing themselves at him and sometimes I get a little jealous, especially if I'm drinking. But it was just the booze talking and I never would have killed her. And I can tell you right now, my husband is going to be pretty upset that you came to our house and accused me of murder. You don't really want to piss off the law in this town and my husband is the law."

"I'm not accusing you of murder. I said you were one of the people who had a motive. And I can take you off my list pretty easily if you'll answer a couple of questions."

"Who else is on your list?"

"It doesn't matter. Do you own a small-caliber pistol?"

"Half the women in Wyoming own small-caliber pistols. They keep them in their cars or their purses for self-protection."

"Yeah, but do *you* own one?"

"You said you had a couple of questions. What's the other one?"

"Where were you the night Shannon was killed?"

"Right here. I'm almost always right here, except for maybe once a week when I get together with a couple of the other moms."

"Can anyone vouch for you being here?

"Yeah. My boys and my husband. Now I'm going to do you a favor, Mr. DeMarco. I'm not going to tell Jim you were here today because I'm afraid he'll forget that he's a cop and beat the living hell out of you. Now I wouldn't really mind that, seeing as how you've insulted me, but he might lose his job. So go away and don't come back or I will tell Jim you're hassling me."

Because she couldn't stop herself, Carly went to the kitchen and pulled from the refrigerator a half-full bottle of white wine and filled up a jelly jar glass. Normally she didn't drink until at least four p.m. At four, she'd have a couple of glasses of wine while making dinner before the school bus dropped the boys off. Then after dinner she'd sip wine until she went to bed, making sure Jim and her sons didn't see how often she refilled her glass. She never got drunk when her sons were home; she just maintained a pleasant glow. The times she really drank were when she went out with her girlfriends, which, as she'd told DeMarco, she did once or twice a week. Jim had told her she was drinking too much and even though she knew he was right, she'd pretty much told him to go fuck himself. He was the reason she drank.

She wondered how long after they got married that he started cheating on her. She guessed it hadn't been that long, as the first three years they were married she'd been pregnant about half the time and Jim would have had his pick of a lot of women who didn't have a belly the size of a microwave. Whatever the case, she knew he'd slept with other women in the fifteen years they'd been married. There'd been too many nights when he'd come home with the scent of some bitch on him. And what had she done about it? Not a damn thing.

She had two sons. How would she support them as a single mother? She'd never worked outside the home, never finished college, and she didn't have any marketable skills. She imagined Jim would pay child support if she divorced him—he loved his boys—but that was never certain. Then there was the fact that she knew Jim didn't really want a divorce. He loved his sons and in his own way, he loved her too. And that was the root of the problem: love. She loved the son of a bitch, she didn't want to give him up, and she'd do anything to keep from losing him.

And now, as if her life couldn't get any worse, she had DeMarco accusing her of murder. There was no way the sheriff's office would investigate her or even think she was a viable suspect, but what if it wasn't the sheriff's office who did the investigating? It was the FBI who'd arrested Sonny Bunt.

She was pretty sure she hadn't killed Shannon Doyle. She'd *wanted* to kill the bitch, no doubt about that, but she didn't think she had. The problem was, she wasn't positive. That night . . . Well, it was a blur. All she had were fragments of memory, and mostly of things she didn't want to remember.

She gulped down the wine in the glass and went into the garage. She opened the passenger side door of her car, sat in the passenger seat, opened the glove box, and pulled out the little .22 auto that Jim had given her for a Christmas present ten years ago. He'd actually put it in her Christmas stocking.

She pulled the magazine from the gun and shucked the shells out into her lap. The magazine held seven bullets; there were only two bullets in it. She reached back into the glove compartment and pulled out the small box of ammunition. There were only three bullets rattling around in it; the box held thirty.

The last time she'd used the gun—or at least the last time she *remembered* using it—was about three months ago. The boys had needed new tennis shoes and they'd gone shopping in Rock Springs. On the way back they passed this spot where there was a high sandy bank and where the locals would go for target practice. As they were passing it, the boys begged her to stop and let them shoot her gun. They knew how to use the gun, of course. In a house filled with firearms, Jim had given them gun safety training when they were about eleven. So she stopped the car and they fired about twenty or so shots at a bunch of tin cans and afterward she forgot to clean the gun and reload the magazine.

And she was almost positive that was the last time she'd used the gun—but, goddamnit, she wasn't sure.

She took the gun and the box of bullets into the house and got the gun cleaning kit. She poured another glass of wine and started to swab the barrel when she thought: *What in the hell are you doing?* If they got her gun and did ballistic tests on it they'd be able to prove it was the murder weapon whether it was clean or not.

That is, they'd be able to prove it *if* it was the murder weapon.

She finished the wine in the glass, then got a quart-size baggie from a drawer and dropped the gun and the bullets in it. She grabbed the baggie, her car keys, and her purse and went back to the garage, where she got a shovel and tossed it into the trunk of her car.

She'd bury the damn thing someplace out on the prairie, someplace where she could recover it after that damn DeMarco was gone. That is, she'd recover it if she could remember where she buried it.

# 34

DeMarco had noticed that Carly Turner hadn't denied owning a gun. In fact, she'd pretty much confirmed that she did. As for her being with her husband and her boys the night Shannon was killed, he couldn't figure out a way to prove if she was lying. Oh, well, he'd accomplished what he'd intended: He'd made sure all his possible suspects knew that he was pursuing them and didn't intend to stop.

As he drove back to his motel, he checked in his rearview mirror. Tommy was behind him.

DeMarco and Tommy had lunch at Harriet's, although Tommy sat at the counter while DeMarco ate at one of the tables. When one of the other customers asked Tommy what he was doing in Waverly, Tommy pointed across the street at the trailer park and said, "Waiting for parts for my Airstream. The generator's on the fritz."

Following lunch, DeMarco returned to his motel room while Tommy parked in the lot where he could see DeMarco's room. After ten minutes DeMarco called Tommy and said, "There's no point you hanging around all afternoon. I don't think anyone's going to try anything in broad daylight."

"That BLM agent was shot in broad daylight," Tommy said.

"Well, if somebody shoots me with a rifle from half a mile away, there won't be anything you can do about it anyway. Go sightseeing or something. I'll meet you down at the Grill for dinner at seven."

"The Grill?

"The Hacienda Grill. It's the only other place to eat in this town."

"Okay, but keep the damn vest on."

Tommy drove off and DeMarco stood in his room for a moment, trying to decide his next move. There wasn't much to do until one of his suspects took some sort of action, assuming any of them actually would. It was hot in the room and the air conditioner wasn't working, even though it had been working the night before. He wondered if Lola could have something to do with that. There was a slight breeze outside, so he took the chair from the room and again placed it on the walkway. The walkway had become his balcony, his porch, his front yard.

As he sat there, he wondered why he hadn't heard from Mahoney. He'd been in Wyoming over a week. Certainly, Mahoney would have returned from China and Vietnam by now.

He used his phone to google Mahoney. Mahoney made the news almost every day by doing or saying something outrageous or picking a fight with one of his brethren across the aisle.

Google informed him that Mahoney was indeed back in the country, but he wasn't in Washington. He was in Boston. Yesterday some nut had decided to shoot up a Boston shopping mall for reasons no one yet understood and fourteen people had died. Mahoney had gone back to his district to console the survivors and rant about the Republicans' failure to do anything substantive when it came to gun control. DeMarco was sorry about the reason his boss was too preoccupied to call him and ask what he was doing about the leaker—but he was grateful, nonetheless.

DeMarco looked up from his phone just as a BMW convertible drove through the parking lot, the BMW having come from the area behind the motel where the trailers were parked. He could see Lisa

Bunt at the wheel—and at that moment she saw him sitting in front of his room, his chair propped up against the wall. She slammed on the brakes, put the BMW in reverse, and burned rubber steering to a spot in the parking lot near DeMarco. She flung open the door, and without bothering to close it or shut off the BMW's engine, she strode toward him, looking mad enough to kill.

DeMarco's first thought was that he'd been wrong about someone not willing to kill him in broad daylight. He was glad he was wearing the vest. His second thought was that he'd been right about Turner calling Lisa after he'd met with Turner in his office. The good news was that Lisa wasn't carrying a purse or holding a gun in her hand, so DeMarco didn't move. He just sat there, trying to look nonchalant.

Lisa stopped about two feet from him and pointed a finger at his face. She said, "Listen to me, you jackass! I didn't have a thing to do with Shannon being murdered. And if you say anything to a reporter about me, I swear to God, I'll kill you."

DeMarco said, speaking calmly, "If you didn't have anything to do with her death then you have nothing to worry about. Where were you the night she was killed?"

"Fuck you!" Lisa screamed and returned to her car. She drove out of the parking lot, her tires squealing on the asphalt, and turned onto the highway without stopping first.

DeMarco was surprised that Lisa had confronted him. He'd figured that if anyone would lose control, it would be Carly Turner. He could see Carly having a few drinks, working herself into a rage, and threatening him the way she'd threatened Shannon. He'd thought that Lisa was different, that she was a woman who wouldn't allow passion to affect her judgment; there'd certainly been no passion involved in her marrying Hiram Bunt. On the other hand, she was having an affair with Jim Turner, so maybe she wasn't as cold and rational as he'd thought.

DeMarco and Tommy had dinner at the Hacienda Grill, again sitting apart. DeMarco ordered a pre-dinner martini and a ribeye steak. He was feeling good because he'd spent the day riling people up, which might eventually result in something positive. Tommy didn't order any alcohol with his dinner, but not because he was on duty. Tommy had sworn off booze some time ago.

About nine, as it was growing dark outside, they left the restaurant, DeMarco departing first and Tommy immediately after him.

DeMarco pulled into the motel parking lot, and into a vacant parking space twenty feet from his room. The only parking spot Tommy could find was at the far end of the parking lot, a good fifty yards from DeMarco's room, but he could see DeMarco's door from his position. The plan was for Tommy to stick around for a while and see if any of DeMarco's suspects came to pay him a visit. When DeMarco turned out the lights in his room, to indicate he was going to bed, Tommy would go back to his trailer. DeMarco would call Tommy if he had any late night guests and Tommy knew DeMarco was smart enough not to open his door to anyone who came a-knockin'.

DeMarco had almost reached the door to his room when two men got out of a van that was parked close to DeMarco's room and started walking rapidly toward DeMarco. Tommy hadn't been able to see the men when they were sitting in the van, but now he could see that one of them was holding something in his right hand. A pistol with a long barrel? Whatever it was, Tommy flung open his car door, pulling his gun from its holster as he did, and started jogging in DeMarco's direction—but he could tell the men were going to reach DeMarco before he could.

DeMarco had his back to the two men as he was inserting the key card in the door to his room. The men were now only a few feet from him. One of them was a tall, fat man with greasy black hair hanging down to his shoulders. He must have weighed almost three hundred pounds. He was wearing a floral-patterned Hawaiian shirt, baggy shorts that reached below his knees, and flip-flops. The other guy was shorter than the fat man but had the build of a weightlifter; he was wearing a white wife-beater T-shirt to show off his muscles. Both men were holding pieces of pipe that were about eighteen inches long.

Before DeMarco could open his door, the fat man called out, "Hey! We want to talk to you."

DeMarco turned to face whoever had spoken—and saw it was two men holding pipes. He thought: *Aw, shit.* Fortunately, he could also see Tommy coming up rapidly behind them.

DeMarco said, "What about?"

Neither of the two men answered. Instead, they rushed DeMarco and that's when Tommy also saw they were holding pipes. Tommy thought for a second about shooting one of them in the back but didn't; he didn't want to kill anyone. The weightlifter, being faster than the fat man, reached DeMarco first and swung his pipe at DeMarco's head. DeMarco ducked and the pipe hit the cheap door behind him hard enough to crack the wood. DeMarco immediately charged the weightlifter before he could swing again, wrapping his arms around the man's thick torso, but by then the fat guy was close enough to swing at DeMarco. His pipe was in position, high above his head, ready to deliver a blow that could possibly be fatal—and Tommy fired a shot into the air.

Both men jerked their heads toward Tommy and DeMarco released his grip on the weightlifter and shoved him away. Tommy said, "Drop those fucking pipes or I'm going to shoot you."

Tommy was aiming at the two men, holding his pistol in a two-handed grip and moving it from one man to the other. Tommy's face was grim and it must have been apparent to DeMarco's attackers that he wasn't bluffing. The weightlifter looked over at the fat man for guidance. The fat man was looking at Tommy. The fat man finally dropped his pipe on the ground, where it clanged off the concrete walkway, and the weightlifter followed suit.

Tommy said, "Lay down on the ground."

"Fuck you," the fat man said. "You're not a cop. We're leaving and you can't stop us. This was just a . . . a misunderstanding."

Tommy didn't hesitate. He pulled the trigger and the bullet hit the motel's siding, about a foot from the fat man's head. "Son of a bitch," the fat man shrieked.

Tommy said, "The next shot's going to be in your kneecap. Now lay the fuck down."

The two men knelt—the fat man grunting as he did—and lay face down on the walkway in front of DeMarco's room. Tommy said to DeMarco, "Call the cops. If these two pieces of shit move, I'll shoot them."

Before DeMarco could do anything, a voice called out, "What the hell's going on?" DeMarco turned his head to see Sam Clarke limping toward him as rapidly as he could. Sam said, "I heard a gunshot." Then Sam saw Tommy pointing a gun at the two men on the ground.

Sam started to back away when DeMarco said, "Call the sheriff, Sam. These two assholes just tried to kill me."

The fat man said, "We weren't going to kill you. We were just going to tune you up a bit."

"Shut up," DeMarco said.

Sam returned to his office to call the sheriff. DeMarco kicked the fat man in the side and said, "Who sent you?"

"Fuck you," the fat man said.

For the next ten minutes, no one said anything. The fat man and the weightlifter remained on the ground, the fat man wheezing, while DeMarco and Tommy stood over them, the pistol in Tommy's hand pointed at the fat man's thick left thigh. Sam Clarke had returned from his office after calling 911, but was observing from several feet away. Sam didn't know what was going on, but he had no intention of getting close enough to get hit if Tommy should fire. A siren could be heard coming down the highway, and a moment later Jim Turner's cruiser pulled into the parking lot, the light bar on the roof flashing blue and red.

Turner killed the siren but left the roof rack lights spinning and got out of his car. DeMarco noticed that Turner was in civilian clothes, not his uniform. He might have been at home when the call came in about the shooting at the motel and he may have decided to respond himself because he didn't live that far away.

When Turner saw Tommy was holding a gun, he immediately pulled his service weapon, pointed it at Tommy, and yelled, "Drop that gun!"

Tommy said, "Yes, sir" and put his pistol on the ground.

"What's going on here?" Turner said. Turner had been so preoccupied with Tommy that he hadn't noticed DeMarco, but now he did. Turner said, "What the hell? DeMarco, what's this all about?"

"These two assholes tried to bash in my head in with those pipes," DeMarco said, pointing to the two pipes laying on the walkway near the fat man and his companion.

"Why?"

DeMarco said, "You shouldn't be investigating this."

"What are you talking about?" Turner said.

"You know what I'm talking about. For all I know, you or your girlfriend sent these guys."

"You better shut your mouth," Turner said.

Turner glared at DeMarco for a moment, then kicked Tommy's gun into the parking lot, under a car so Tommy couldn't reach it. While still aiming his pistol in the general direction of the men near DeMarco's room, he took out his phone and made a quick call. Call completed, he asked the men lying on the ground: "What are your names? And why did you attack Mr. DeMarco?"

The fat man said, "We're not saying anything without a lawyer."

A second Sweetwater County sheriff's cruiser pulled into the parking lot a moment later. DeMarco noticed there was a wire mesh screen separating the front and back seats in the cruiser. A deputy got out of the cruiser and Turner pointed at the men on the ground. He said, "Ray, take these two down to the jail in Rock Springs. They're being arrested for aggravated assault. Read them their rights and let them get a lawyer if they want one. I'm going to take statements from these two," Turner said, jerking a thumb toward DeMarco and Tommy. "I'll be down in the morning to talk to the prisoners."

Ray handcuffed the fat man and the weightlifter, escorted them to his cruiser, and took off. Turner walked over to DeMarco and Tommy. "Now tell me what happened."

DeMarco said, "I had dinner at the Grill and when I got back to my room, those guys were waiting for me. They rushed me and one of them swung a pipe at my head." DeMarco pointed to his room door. "Take a look at the door and you'll get an idea of how hard the guy swung."

"Why did they attack you?"

"I don't know. I asked them and the fat guy with the long hair told me to go fuck myself."

Turner turned to Tommy and said, "Who are you?"

Tommy said, "My name's Tommy Hewlett."

"Show me some ID."

Tommy pulled out his wallet and handed Turner his driver's license. Turner studied it for a second and said, "Boston?"

"Yeah," Tommy said, but didn't elaborate.

"What are you doing here in Waverly?"

"I'm on vacation, just driving around seeing the country. I'm pulling a trailer—it's parked over there in the lot—and the generator failed. I'm just waiting for parts so I can fix it."

"So how did you get involved in this?"

Tommy said, "I'd just driven into the parking lot and saw those two guys attack this guy." Tommy pointed at DeMarco. "So I pulled my gun and fired a shot into the air to stop them. I didn't know what was going on, but I could see they were trying to kill him, or if not kill him, seriously injure him. After that, we just held them until you arrived."

DeMarco noticed that Turner didn't ask why Tommy would be carrying a gun. In Wyoming, a man packing a weapon wasn't considered abnormal.

"And that's it?" Turner said.

"Yeah," Tommy said.

To DeMarco, Turner said, "And you don't know why they attacked you?"

DeMarco didn't answer Turner's question. Again, he said, "You shouldn't be investigating this. You have a conflict of interest."

Turner just shook his handsome head. "I'm going into Rock Springs tomorrow morning to question those guys. After that, and depending on what they tell me, I may call you down to the sheriff's office in Rock Springs to provide formal statements."

Before Turner left, he put the pipes used by DeMarco's assailants in an evidence bag and took a photo of the crack in DeMarco's door.

---

After Turner left, DeMarco said to Tommy, "This fuckin' place. I was hoping someone other than Turner would respond to the 911 call. It's like I told him, for all I know Lisa Bunt hired those guys to kill me."

Tommy hesitated for a moment, then said, "You know, DeMarco, you might want to give law enforcement around here a little more credit than you're giving them."

"I don't know what you mean."

"What I mean is, Turner has a boss and maybe you should go talk to him. You've threatened Turner with getting the FBI involved and talking to the media, but the straightforward thing to do is talk to Turner's boss and tell him what you know."

"Turner's boss is the sheriff of this redneck county. He's Hiram Bunt's buddy. What do you think he'll do if I tell him that Hiram's wife might have killed Shannon, and then maybe hired those two thugs to kill me to keep me from revealing her affair with Turner?"

Tommy said, "I don't know what he'll do. But you shouldn't assume that everyone out here is corrupt. The sheriff may know Bunt and may take campaign contributions from him, but that doesn't mean he'll be willing to overlook the fact that one of his deputies is the wrong guy to investigate a murder. Go talk to the man and see what he says."

# 35

Jim Turner took a seat at a table in an interview room at the Rock Springs detention center. On the other side of the table was the fat man he'd arrested the night before and the fat man's lawyer. The fat man's name was Donald Mullen, "Donny" to his pals. Before speaking to Donny, Turner had taken a look at his record and talked to a cop in the Rock Springs Police Department. He learned that Donny owned a bar that catered to a shady clientele and ran a small string of prostitutes, but his major source of income was from distributing heroin, meth, and marijuana. The Rock Springs cops, however, hadn't been able to pin an actual crime on him because Donny was apparently brighter than he looked.

Turner said, "Donny, as I'm sure you've already figured out, you and your boyfriend are going to jail for aggravated assault."

"He's not my boyfriend," Donny said, clearly offended that Turner might think he was gay.

"Whatever," Turner said. "I got two eyewitnesses, the weapons you used, and a photo of a door that shows you guys swung a pipe hard enough to kill a man. So maybe they'll charge you with attempted murder and not simple assault."

Donny's lawyer, a bored public defender, said, "So if you got all that, why are we here, Deputy?"

"Because I want to know why your client assaulted Mr. DeMarco."

Turner *had* to know the reason. Specifically, he had to know if Lisa had hired the guy, although he couldn't imagine how she would know a man like Donny Mullen. But because he was afraid of what Donny might say, he'd decided to interview him alone and hadn't turned on the tape recorder in the interview room.

"And what does my client get if he cooperates?" the lawyer asked.

"I'm not sure," Turner said. "But I imagine if Donny here is willing to testify against his boyfriend—"

"Goddamnit, he's not my boyfriend."

"—and also testify that someone hired him or conspired with him to attack Mr. DeMarco, then he could get a lighter sentence."

The lawyer turned to Donny and said, "Go ahead and tell him, Donny. You're pretty much screwed here, so it can't hurt."

"Yeah, all right. There's this girl, this Indian girl. She's, uh, sort of a friend and she told me DeMarco was hassling her. She wanted me to get him to back off."

"What's this girl's name?"

"Lola Clarke."

Turner had to stop himself from saying *Thank God.*

Turner said, "I don't understand. What's this girl's connection to DeMarco and what was he hassling her about?"

Donny said, "It had to do with some dead writer, something about how Lola stole the writer's fancy earrings, and DeMarco was going to tell the cops and Lola was afraid she'd get arrested."

"I see," Turner said. "And you, being the nice guy you are, just decided to help this poor Indian girl out."

"Yeah," Donny said.

Turner knew Donny wasn't the sort to help anyone unless it was in his own self-interest. He knew Lola Clarke had a drug problem and suspected she bought her drugs from Donny and was most likely one of Donny's whores. And maybe Donny decided to help her when it came to DeMarco because he was afraid of what she might tell the Rock Springs cops about his various criminal endeavors.

It was a crying shame the girl had sunk so low. But Lola Clarke conspiring with Donny was infinitely better than Lisa having done so. Then it occurred to him that maybe Lola had done more than steal the Doyle woman's earrings. Maybe Lola had been so desperate for money that she'd killed Doyle to steal her laptop. Then another thought occurred to him: *Even if Lola hadn't killed Doyle, it would be better if she went to jail for murder than Lisa Bunt.*

Turner said, "Okay, Donny. I'm going to tell the prosecutor to cut you some slack if you testify that Lola conspired with you to attack Mr. DeMarco, and if you testify against your buddy. I don't know what kind of deal you'll get, but less time in jail is less time in jail. And if you can come up with a better reason for why Lola wanted Mr. DeMarco harmed, that might go a long way."

"What better reason?" Donny said.

"The dead writer," Turner said. "Could Lola have had something to do with that?"

"Nah, no way," Donny said.

"Well, think about it," Turner said. He'd planted a seed; now he'd allow some time for it to grow.

Turner left the interview room and made a call. "Ray, would you mind swinging by Sam Clarke's motel in Waverly and arresting Lola Clarke for conspiracy to commit murder. Bring her to the jail here in Rock Springs so I can talk to her."

Turner left the detention center, and since he'd skipped breakfast, drove over to a Starbucks to get coffee and a breakfast sandwich. As he was munching on the sandwich, he glanced at his watch. This time of the morning Lisa was normally out riding, but in case she was with her husband, he texted her. *We may not have a problem when it comes to DeMarco. Something happened last night related to Lola Clarke. So don't do anything you'll regret.*

She immediately texted back. *What happened last night?*

*I'll tell you the next time I see you.*

His last encounter with Lisa hadn't ended well. After they'd made love . . . No, "made love" wasn't right. She went after him in bed like she'd been living in a convent the last ten years. Sex with her was always good, but yesterday it had been incredible; the lady had a lot of experience and no inhibitions. But as they lay there afterward, Jim just enjoying the sight of that marvelous body, she started in on him again about how he had to do something about DeMarco. She'd apparently thought that he'd be more malleable after she'd screwed his brains loose. But again he'd told her that he had no intention of killing anyone, and that they'd just have to hope for the best. To this she'd responded. "Hope for the best, my ass. I didn't get to where I am today by hoping for anything. And I'm telling you, if you don't have the balls to protect me, I'm going to deal with this on my own."

But maybe now, with this thing with Lola, no one would have to do anything.

Knowing it would be at least an hour before Lola Clarke arrived in Rock Springs, he decided to drop in on the sheriff and tell his boss what he'd learned from Donny Mullen. As he was parking his cruiser in the lot in front of the sheriff's building, he saw DeMarco walk out of the building. What the hell? A minute later, while still sitting in his car, he gets a call from the sheriff's secretary saying the sheriff wants to see him immediately.

# 36

DeMarco's phone alarm went off at five. He slapped the offending device to make it stop ringing and reluctantly got out of bed. He used the bathroom, brushed his teeth, and splashed some water on his face to force himself fully awake. He hated getting up so early but he wanted to talk to Congressman Wilbur Burns back in D.C. before Burns went off to do whatever it was he did on a normal workday. Not that any workday in our nation's capital seemed normal these days.

Burns came on the line saying, "I heard about what you did in Wyoming, breaking into Sonny Bunt's house. I guess I shouldn't have been surprised that a guy who would work for that bastard, Mahoney, would—"

"Congressman, doesn't it bother you that Sonny killed a BLM agent?"

"Of course, it bothers me. And if he really killed the man and is convicted, then jail's where he belongs. But what you did . . . Hell, why are you calling me?"

"I'm calling to ask you to get me a meeting with your pal, the Sweetwater County Sheriff. If he doesn't meet with me, I'm going to give him a major media headache."

"What are you talking about?"

DeMarco began by saying, "Congressman, you've got a real mess out here in Waverly."

DeMarco went on to tell Burns about Shannon's journal, what he'd learned from it, and how it was possible that one of three women had murdered her: Lola Clarke, Lisa Bunt, or Carly Turner. "The problem is that the man investigating Shannon's murder is sleeping with two of those women and will probably do anything to protect them."

"So what do you want from the sheriff?" Burns asked.

"I want him to assign a different person to investigate Shannon's death. Jim Turner can't continue to be involved because he's got a conflict of interest, and for that matter may be complicit in the crime. In other words, I'm willing to give the sheriff a chance to do the right thing, and if he doesn't, then I'm going to the press."

Sheriff Clay Webber—short gray hair, thick white mustache, skeptical blue eyes—was dressed casually in a dark blue polo shirt and jeans. His badge was clipped to his belt, but he wasn't wearing a weapon, which surprised DeMarco. His office contained a large mahogany-colored desk and a couple of plain wooden visitors' chairs; on one corner of the desk was a photo of a pleasant-looking middle-aged brunette and two pretty younger women who appeared to be in their twenties. The walls didn't have any plaques or certificates or anything else to glorify Webber's long career. His desk had a computer monitor on it, a phone, and a simple in/out basket. There was a single manila file folder in the basket. DeMarco got the impression that Webber was a no-frills, all business, organized guy.

Webber studied DeMarco for a few long seconds when DeMarco entered his office, then pointed him to one of the visitors' chairs.

"All right, DeMarco," he said, "say your piece. Wilbur Burns told me what you told him, but I want to hear it directly from you."

DeMarco dropped a copy of Shannon's journal on the sheriff's desk. Before arriving at the sheriff's office he had two copies made, one for the sheriff and one for Tommy who wanted to read the journal. DeMarco said, "That's a copy of a journal Shannon Doyle kept while she was in Wyoming researching her book. So you can read it yourself and see if you come to the same conclusions I did."

"How'd you get a copy of her journal?"

DeMarco hesitated, then said, "A friend of mine hacked into Shannon's iCloud account."

Webber shook his head. "You're a real piece of work. That stunt you pulled with Sonny Bunt's rifle and now this."

"That may be," DeMarco said, "but let me tell you what the journal says."

For the second time that day, DeMarco told how Shannon was aware that Jim Turner and Lisa Bunt were having an affair, how their affair would ruin them both, and so maybe one of them had killed Shannon. He told how Lola Clarke had stolen Shannon's earrings and may have murdered Shannon to steal her laptop and purse because she was an addict. Lastly, he discussed how Carly Turner was under the mistaken impression that Shannon had been sleeping with her husband, had threatened Shannon, and Carly may have killed Shannon in a drunken rage. He decided not to tell the sheriff that Harriet had seen the killer. For one thing, Harriet couldn't identify the person. Maybe later he'd tell Webber what Harriet had told him, but for now he'd let the investigation proceed without involving her.

The sheriff didn't say anything for a moment, then said, "And you're planning to run to the media and tell them all this stuff?"

"That's what I was planning but a friend of mine convinced me that I should give you a chance to do the right thing and investigate Turner and these three suspects on your own. My worry is that I know you're close to Hiram Bunt."

"What makes you think I'm close to Hiram?"

"Because I've heard he supports you politically and because you took his side in the standoff against the feds."

"I didn't take his side. I just didn't jump into the middle of his fight with the government. That was a federal problem, not mine, but I didn't approve of what he did."

DeMarco figured that the sheriff might be telling the truth: he didn't approve of Hiram defying the federal government, but on the other hand, why should he take the feds' side in an issue that might cost him votes?

"Okay," DeMarco said, keeping his tone neutral.

"How 'bout these two men who attacked you last night?" the sheriff said.

"You know about that?"

"Of course, I know. I know about every crime committed in this county."

DeMarco said, "I don't know how they fit into this yet. I'd never met those guys so one possibility is that one of the suspects, like Lisa Bunt or Carly Turner, could have hired them. The problem is that the guy investigating the attack on me is Turner."

Webber stroked his mustache as he studied DeMarco, "Okay, DeMarco. Because of these complaints you're making, I'm going to remove Jim Turner from the investigation and assign another guy to take the lead. I don't know if you're telling me the truth or not but—"

"Read the journal," DeMarco said,

"I'll read it, but regardless of what it says, I'm not going to have some cloud hanging over the investigation of that woman's death. What I want from you is your word that you won't go running to the press until I've had a chance to do my job."

DeMarco nodded. "You have my word."

# 37

Webber sat for about ten minutes mulling everything over. He wasn't totally surprised that Jim Turner might be screwing Lisa Bunt, but he was *somewhat* surprised. He'd always known that Jim ran around on his wife, but in the past, his infidelities had never led to any problems with him doing his job. Jim was one of those guys who'd always been lucky that none of his past affairs had come back to bite him because a woman made a formal complaint or the woman's husband decided to go after him with a shotgun. The other thing about Jim was that he was the most viable candidate to replace him when he retired next year. He was popular with folks—the ladies, of course, loved him—and other than his sexual escapades, he'd been a good law enforcement officer, and would probably make a good administrator.

But if his fling with Lisa Bunt became public knowledge—and there was a good possibility it would if he assigned another man to the case—then Jim's political ambitions would be finished. And God knows what Hiram Bunt might do. If a man as prideful and ornery as Hiram didn't shoot Jim outright, he might make a big stink about the whole thing with the governor and the governor might demand that Webber fire Jim. And if Jim really had interfered in the investigation of the writer's death in such a way that he'd intentionally steered the investigation away from viable suspects, then he'd fire the man on his own, and not because of any grief Hiram might give him. He wouldn't tolerate an officer on his force who helped a murderer get away.

He punched a button on his desk phone and said, "Irene, tell Pat Morse I need to see him right away. Then track down Jim Turner. I'll want to see Jim after I'm done with Pat."

Pat Morse was the best investigator he had and didn't harbor any political ambitions to be sheriff. He would have initially assigned Pat to the Doyle case if Jim hadn't lived in Waverly.

---

Jim watched Pat Morse walk out of the sheriff's office. He'd been waiting twenty minutes to see his boss and the longer he'd sat there, the more apprehensive he became.

He said, "Hey, Pat, how you doin'?"

Pat gave him an odd look, then said, "Fine, Jim, just fine. I'll talk to you later."

*Talk to me later?* What did that mean?

Jim entered the sheriff's office, saying, "Gonna be a hot one out there today."

The sheriff looked at him for a long beat then pointed to a chair and said, "Jim, sit down. We need to have a serious talk."

---

Jim left the sheriff's office less than ten minutes later. He thought for a second that he might throw up right there in the sheriff's waiting room.

The sheriff had told him that Pat Morse was taking over the Shannon Doyle murder investigation because Jim had been accused of having an affair with Lisa Bunt. But the affair wasn't the reason he was being removed from the case. The reason was that the sheriff had been given information indicating that Lisa might be a suspect when it came to the writer's murder and that Jim, therefore, had a conflict of interest.

The information given to the sheriff had obviously come from DeMarco, and he wondered if Doyle's journal was what Pat Morse had been carrying when he left the sheriff's office. Morse had been carrying a brown accordion file folder like the type DeMarco had used to hold his copy of the journal. Folks joked about people coming back from the grave to haunt them, but the damn Doyle woman was literally doing that with her fucking journal.

He hadn't denied that he was having an affair with Lisa—he'd just dig his hole deeper by lying to Webber—but he had said, "Clay, Lisa didn't have anything to do with that woman's death. I'm certain of that. But last night a couple of guys attacked DeMarco because Lola Clarke sicced them on him. I just got through interviewing one of the men involved, and I think there's a chance that Lola might have killed the Doyle woman."

"Yeah, well, I'm sure Pat will look into that," the sheriff had said, clearly no longer interested in Jim's opinion when it came to Lola Clarke or anything else connected to Doyle's murder. "Now, as much as I hate to do it, Jim, I'm suspending you until Pat completes his investigation."

And that was that.

His next thought was: *What the hell am I going to tell Carly when I don't go to work tomorrow?* He supposed he could say he'd decided to take some time off to paint the house like she'd been bugging him to do—but he wondered how long he'd be able to get away with that. But he was going to have to tell Lisa what was going on. There was no doubt Pat would be interviewing her and Pat was going to ask if she had an alibi for the night Doyle was killed. He might even get a search warrant to obtain any weapons Lisa might have. Pat Morse was a good guy, and he'd been a friend for years, and he'd probably try to investigate Lisa in such a way that it wouldn't get back to Hiram that she'd been screwing him—but that wasn't certain. And when Hiram found out, there was no doubt that Lisa's marriage would be over.

Jim wasn't ready to go home to face his wife. Before leaving the sheriff's building, he changed into civilian clothes, then headed to a bar on the east side of Rock Springs, a scruffy place with a scruffy clientele. It was only eleven a.m. but the bar would be open for the neighborhood alkies it catered to.

The bartender, a good-looking young gal with a lot of tattoos, smiled at him in a way that indicated she approved of his looks. He didn't return the smile. The last thing he needed right now was another woman.

He sat for a bit, sipping a beer, trying to figure out what Pat Morse might do. He'd certainly interview Lola Clarke, and if Pat was as smart as he thought he was, he'd toss Lola into a cell and let her sit for twenty-four hours until she'd be dying for a fix and willing to tell him anything. If Lola had actually killed Doyle, Pat would get it out of her, and that would be best for everyone. Pat's investigation would then end quickly and he might not see any reason to question Lisa. But the truth was, and as much as he hoped Lola had killed Doyle because she needed money to support her habit, he had a hard time imagining Lola being able to pull off a cold-blooded murder.

Lisa was a different story. Lisa was a beautiful woman but at her core, hard as steel. As repulsive as it might have been for her, she'd married Hiram Bunt to give herself a chance for a better life. That in itself was pretty cold-blooded. And if she thought Doyle might destroy her life and her future, he had no doubt Lisa could muster up the courage to do something about it. The big thing was going to be Lisa's alibi. Lisa thought she had an alibi but she really didn't, and he knew Pat Morse wasn't going to buy it unless Lisa had some way to prove where she'd been at the exact hour Doyle had been killed.

He finished the first beer, asked for another, and while he was waiting for the bartender to bring it, he texted Lisa. "*Call me as soon as you can. It's important.*"

Ten minutes later, Lisa called and he stepped outside the ratty bar into the sunlight to talk to her.

"What's going on?" she asked.

"I've just been suspended. That bastard DeMarco went to the sheriff, gave him a copy of Doyle's journal, and accused me of having a conflict of interest since I've been sleeping with you. Now the sheriff has assigned another investigator to the case."

"I thought you said everything was going to be okay?"

"Well, it still might be," Jim said, and told her about Lola Clarke.

When he finished, Lisa didn't say anything for a moment, then she shrieked, "That son of a bitch! I told you, you had to do something about DeMarco. I told you!"

"Well, it's too late now."

"What's going to happen next?" Lisa asked.

"I'm assuming Pat Morse, he's the investigator who's been assigned, is going to question you. He's going to ask if you have a .22 caliber pistol. If you do—"

"I don't."

"If you do, he's going to ask you to give it to him voluntarily to do a ballistic test." He assumed she really didn't have a .22. Not now anyway. If she'd shot the Doyle woman certainly that gun would be someplace where it would never be found. "And if you don't give him any weapons you have voluntarily, he might get a search warrant."

"Hiram would never let him search our house."

Jim ignored that comment; he knew Hiram wasn't going to keep Clay Webber from executing a lawful search. "The other thing he's going to do is ask if you have an alibi for the night Doyle was killed."

Lisa said, "You know I do, but what should I say? That I was fucking you the night Shannon was killed?"

"Lisa, what you do is tell the man the truth. And you ask him, you beg him, to keep what you tell him to himself. But there's something you need to understand. You don't really have a solid alibi."

"What are you talking about? I was with you in a motel room in Rock Springs the night she was killed."

"The thing is, Lisa, I left about eleven that night. Doyle was killed after midnight as best anyone can tell. So unless you can prove you stayed in the room after I left, Pat's going to say that you could have driven to Waverly and killed Doyle and then returned to the motel."

"I'll just tell him you were with me all night."

"That's not going to work. I got home around midnight and if Pat questions my wife, she's going to say I was there. So there's no way I can lie and say I was with you. This whole mess is bad enough without us lying and making it worse. So tell the truth. Say that I left at eleven and you spent the rest of the night in the room. And unless you really killed Doyle, Pat won't be able to prove otherwise."

"I didn't kill her, goddamnit. How could you say such a thing?"

"Good," Jim said. "So tell the truth. Now I have to go home and figure out what I'm going to tell Carly. I can't—"

"Shut up a minute," Lisa said. "I need to think." A moment later, she said, "What do you think will happen if Pat Morse can't find Shannon's killer? Like what if Lola has an alibi or Pat can't prove she or anyone else did it?"

"Well, if he can't prove anything, then that will be the end of it and her death will go down as an unsolved homicide."

Lisa said, "No, that won't be the end of it. That fucking DeMarco is going to destroy my life no matter what Pat Morse learns."

---

Lisa knew she was right. If Morse couldn't find Shannon's killer, DeMarco wouldn't let it go. The man was obsessed. He'd go to the media and get them all stirred up and maybe eventually the politicians in Cheyenne would decide to get the state police or the FBI involved. That's what DeMarco had told Jim he was going to do. In fact, it puzzled her that DeMarco had even bothered to talk to Clay Webber. And once the media got involved, there was no doubt her affair with Jim would come out. The goddamn media jackals loved nothing better than a sex element in a story.

But what could she do? She could see that Jim didn't have the guts to deal with DeMarco. And she couldn't go to her husband and say: *Honey, I'd like you to kill that nasty man from Washington because he's going to expose the fact that I've been fucking around on you.*

---

Jim got home about two hours before he normally did, and Carly couldn't help but smell the beer on his breath. Jesus, it was bad enough she drank as much as she did; now it seemed as if her husband had a drinking problem, too.

She said, "What are you doing home so early?"

"I decided to take some time off. Told the sheriff I needed a couple of weeks, that it was time for me to get some work done around this place like you've been saying. You know, paint the house, get the air conditioner running right again before it gets really hot."

She studied his face for a moment, then said, "Jim, what the hell is going on?"

He started to say something, then he dropped into a chair and started crying.

"What's wrong?" Carly said. "You're scaring me."

Jim shook his head, blew his nose, and said, "I've been having an affair with Lisa Bunt."

She was too stunned to speak.

"That guy, DeMarco, convinced the sheriff that I had to be taken off the Doyle case because there's a possibility that Lisa might have murdered Doyle and that I've been covering up for her. So I've been suspended and another investigator has been assigned."

Carly was only half listening to what her husband was saying. She was thinking: *My God, I was wrong. He hadn't been sleeping with Shannon.*

# 38

She would wonder later if she did it because of the mirror.

She had one of those magnifying mirrors that she used sometimes to put on her makeup, and as she was applying her lipstick, she noticed she was getting a small network of wrinkles at the corners of her mouth. Her eyes, too. She'd always had a few crow's feet—she preferred to call them *smile lines*—but it seemed as if there were more of them, these harsh furrows in her skin.

She turned off the light on the fucking magnifying mirror and looked into the regular one over the sink. She was still a beautiful woman—there was no doubt about that—and the big four-oh was still three years away. But thirty-seven wasn't twenty-seven, the age she'd been when she'd snagged Hiram. What the hell would she do if he divorced her? There was no way she could go back to living the way she was before she met him.

She'd left home when she was seventeen because her mom was a violent, abusive drunk and her stepdad kept trying to fuck her. She moved in with a guy she knew who was a few years older than her, a loser who couldn't keep a job, then had to drop out of school so she could make enough money to eat and pay the rent. The best paying job she could find was dancing topless in a bar, a job her asshole boyfriend at the time encouraged her to take. The job was demeaning, but she kept it longer than she kept the boyfriend.

She finally quit dancing—*dancing* sounding better than *stripping*—and got a job at a Hooters in Denver. With her body, she was the perfect Hooters girl and made a lot in tips, but was still always living paycheck-to-paycheck and was never able to afford decent clothes or a nice place to live. Luckily, while she was still working at the restaurant, she got a part-time job with an agency that provided models for trade shows and conventions. She'd be the girl in the short-shorts and the lowcut halter top luring men over to look at the boats or the trucks or the snowmobiles. Which turned out to be the best job she ever had because that's how she met Hiram, at the gun show in Cheyenne.

Marriage to Hiram had its downsides, but it opened up a whole new world to her. She started shopping at Neiman Marcus instead of J.C. Penny. She drove a late-model BMW and not some beater that she was never sure would start. Then there were the horses. She *loved* horses. She'd never ridden one until she met Hiram, and now couldn't imagine not owning a horse. She grew mentally as well. She got her GED, then started taking business classes at a community college in Rock Springs so she would be able to manage Hiram's businesses when he was gone. She was surprised to learn that managing a business was something that actually appealed to her, and she knew she'd be good at it.

Yes, she had a good life—a *wonderful* life—and there was no way she was going back to the life she'd had before. Even if she'd wanted to do it—which she didn't—she was getting too old for pole dancing or modeling at trade shows or prancing around as a waitress in a place like Hooters. She knew she'd be able to find a job of some kind because she'd have to, but whatever it was, it most likely wouldn't pay for shit, and she'd find herself once again living in a small, crummy apartment in some crummy neighborhood. Most important, she knew that the likelihood of finding another man as rich as Hiram to marry would be slim, and the odds would diminish with each passing year.

No! She wasn't going to lose what she had. She wasn't going back to what she'd been. And with Sonny in jail, she was in a perfect position to get *everything* Hiram had—his millions, his land, his businesses—and she wasn't going to allow that fucking DeMarco to take all that away from her.

The problem was, she could only think of one way to stop him. And she needed to do it quickly. Hiram didn't yet know about her affair with Jim, but every minute DeMarco was around, and the longer Pat Morse kept talking to people about Doyle's death, the higher the likelihood that Hiram would learn of her unfaithfulness—and then cast her back down into the pit that she'd clawed her way out of.

---

The prevalent theory when it came to Shannon Doyle's death was that some trucker, who was most likely an addict, had killed Doyle in her motel room and then stolen what valuables she had. If DeMarco were to die and the evidence pointed to a trucker, that would tend to fit what Jim and all the sheriff's men were already thinking. Jim would, of course, suspect her—but he wouldn't pursue her. But there was no way that DeMarco would open his door if she were to knock on it in the middle of the night. Not to mention that the motel was a really dumb place to kill someone. Someone could drive into the parking lot at any time. Or one of the gas workers who stayed there could come stumbling back from a bar. Yeah, whoever had killed Doyle was probably either high or stupid, and just got lucky.

So killing him at the motel wouldn't do. But how about the truck stop? That was close to the first murder and a trucker would again be a likely suspect.

She grabbed her car keys and thirty minutes later she decided that yeah, the truck stop would do. DeMarco was on his own. No one in town was helping him and it was just a matter getting him alone where she wanted him.

# 39

DeMarco took a seat in Tommy's rented trailer. DeMarco really wanted a beer after his meeting with the sheriff, but Tommy was an alcoholic, in his third year of sobriety, so he and Tommy just sat there in the small trailer drinking Cokes.

"How'd the meeting with the sheriff go?" Tommy asked.

"I think you were right about him. He's assigning another investigator to the case. We'll see what happens."

"And how much longer do you plan to hang around here bugging people?" Tommy asked.

DeMarco shrugged. "At least a couple more days to see what the sheriff comes up with. But if you need to go back to Boston—"

"Nah, I'm okay spending a couple more days here."

DeMarco's phone rang. He looked at the caller ID, hoping it wouldn't be Mahoney. It wasn't; it was from a number with a Wyoming area code. He thought about letting the call go to his voicemail in case it was one of those annoying robocalls, then decided to answer it in case it was someone in the sheriff's office, like the new investigator the sheriff had assigned.

He answered the phone saying, "Hello, this Joe."

The caller said, "Mr. DeMarco, my name's Marla. My husband's a truck driver." The woman had a twang in her voice, an accent DeMarco associated with places like Texas or Oklahoma.

"Okay, but why are you calling me?" DeMarco asked.

"I ride with my husband and we stayed overnight in Waverly when that writer was killed. I know who did it."

"You do? Then why didn't you tell the sheriff?"

"Because my husband wouldn't let me. He didn't want me getting called to testify at some trial, which might mean having to hang around Wyoming for a couple of weeks or more."

"So who did it?"

"A trucker who was staying there the same night we were. I don't have a name but I know the rig he drives and I have a plate number."

"So give me the plate number."

"Well, I was thinking that might be worth something to you. Like maybe five hundred dollars. I could use the money."

"You need to call the sheriff. Maybe he'll give you a reward for the information."

"I told you, my husband don't want me talking to the sheriff. But I heard you were real interested in that woman's death."

"Who'd you hear that from?"

"I can't talk anymore right now. My husband will be back soon and he wouldn't like me talking to you. We're staying overnight here in town, over at the truck stop, and pulling out in the morning. My husband drives a red Kenworth with a shiny chrome bumper and fancy chrome wheels. You come see me tonight, but not until after midnight, say one a.m. My husband's a drunk and as soon as we stop for the day, he starts drinking and he'll be passed out by then. Now I gotta go. Earl's coming. So one o'clock if you want to hear what I have to say. And don't forget to bring the money."

The woman hung up.

"Who was that?" Tommy asked.

"Supposedly the wife of a truck driver who knows who killed Shannon. She said it was another trucker whose name she doesn't know, but says she has a license plate number. And oh, by the way, she wants five hundred bucks to tell what she knows. She claims her husband won't let her tell the sheriff, plus she doesn't think the sheriff will offer her a reward."

"Well, if she's telling the truth, a trucker would fit the sheriff's theory for who murdered Shannon."

"Yeah, but how would she know the sheriff's theory? And how did she get my name and number?"

Tommy shrugged. "I'm guessing a lot of people in this town know by now that you're looking into Shannon's death. And if she's really the wife of a truck driver, she could have gotten your name from someone who eats at Harriet's. As to how she got your number, maybe she found out you were staying at the motel and got it from Sam."

"Yeah, maybe. The other possibility is that she's the person who killed Shannon and tonight she's planning on taking a crack at me. People around here think I'm the one driving the investigation and—"

"Which you are."

"—and that if I'm gone, everything will be okay."

"So what are you going to do?" Before DeMarco could answer, Tommy said, "What you should do is call the new investigator the sheriff's assigned to the case."

DeMarco thought that over for a moment and said . . .

# 40

There were six big rigs at the truck stop, all parked in a row, next to each other. The area in front of the truck stop, where the convenience store and the gas pumps were located, was well lit but the parking area wasn't lighted at all. A pale half-moon provided the only illumination. The eighteen-wheelers loomed in the darkness; they had high cabs and were about eighty feet long with the trailers they were pulling. It took DeMarco a couple of minutes to find the red Kenworth, parked between two other big rigs. There was no one standing near the cab of the Kenworth, but he looked down the row on the driver's side of the truck. About halfway down, he could see a woman standing there. She was about five foot six, slender, dressed in a dark T-shirt and jeans, but he couldn't see her face; it was too dark and she was looking down at the ground and her features were obscured by a long-billed baseball hat. As Harriet had said, all his suspects were about the same height and had about the same build. The woman could be Lola Clarke, Carly Turner, or Lisa Bunt—or it could be the mysterious Marla.

DeMarco didn't see Tommy and wondered where he was.

She was thinking: Come on, come on. Why are you standing there?

She wanted him a bit closer to be sure she wouldn't miss. Ten feet was the perfect distance.

When he was within range, she'd do it quick. No talking. No hesitation. One shot and run like hell. She hadn't taken her car because the BMW was too recognizable. She'd taken one of the ranch's older pickup trucks, one that looked like a thousand other pickups in Wyoming, and smeared mud on the license plates. The pickup was parked by the truck stop's dumpsters and she could reach it in less than thirty seconds and be gone. And if somebody saw her, all they'd see was a woman dressed in dark clothing running. No way would anyone be able to make out her features the way the area was illuminated. And if anyone did suspect her, she'd have an airtight alibi. She'd slipped out of bed with Hiram sleeping next to her, dead to the world, because he had to take sleeping pills to sleep because of his back. If anyone were to ask where she was the night DeMarco was killed, Hiram would swear that she was with him and no one would ever doubt Hiram.

So she'd thought it through completely, but everything depended on speed. One quick shot and it would be over with before anyone just happened to walk by and see her.

But the bastard wasn't moving. He was just standing there.

COME ON!

---

The plan had been for DeMarco to walk to the front of the red Kenworth while Tommy circled around to the trailer end of the truck so he could come up behind the woman while she was talking to DeMarco. What Tommy hadn't realized was that because the parking area was unlit, he couldn't tell which truck was a red Kenworth from the trailer end. So he glanced down each row looking for a woman standing there, hoping DeMarco wouldn't approach her until he was in place. He was too slow. By the time he saw the woman standing between two trucks, DeMarco was already walking toward her.

Tommy thought: *Goddamnit, DeMarco, you're going to get yourself killed.*

---

DeMarco walked toward the woman. Just as he began walking, he saw Tommy behind her, at the rear of the trailer the Kenworth was pulling. The woman was about twenty feet away from him. Tommy was forty feet away, now coming up quietly behind her.

DeMarco stopped about ten feet from the woman. He still couldn't see her face because of the ballcap. He said, "Marla?"

She lifted her head. It was Lisa Bunt—and without any hesitation whatsoever, she raised the gun she was holding in her right hand and shot DeMarco in the chest.

The bullet slammed into the vest DeMarco was wearing, the impact knocking him backward, and he stumbled and landed on the ground, on his back looking up at her.

Seeing he wasn't dead, Lisa said, "Shit." She took a step toward him, planning to shoot him a second time, but before she could Tommy fired a shot into the air and screamed, "Stop or I'll shoot you."

Lisa spun toward Tommy, and again without hesitating, fired at him. DeMarco heard the bullet zing off the side of one of the trucks. When Lisa had turned to shoot at Tommy, DeMarco had scrambled to his feet and rushed her from behind. He couldn't stop her from firing the first shot at Tommy but before she could fire a second time, he slammed into her like a linebacker tackling a quarterback and drove her to the ground. He clamped his right hand on her right wrist, and with his left hand wrenched the gun from her.

DeMarco stood up. By that time, Tommy was standing over Lisa, breathing hard, his weapon pointed down at her. DeMarco said, "Are you okay?"

"Yeah," Tommy said. "And you're damn lucky she didn't shoot you in the head."

Lisa was lying there face down on the ground. Finally, after several seconds, she started to push herself to her feet, but Tommy said, "Don't get up. Stay on the ground. Just sit there."

Lisa looked up at Tommy then over to DeMarco. The ballcap had fallen off her head when DeMarco had tackled her and her long, dark hair had tumbled down to her shoulders. Her eyes were filled with tears.

She said to DeMarco, "You son of a bitch. You've destroyed my life. Why in the hell did you have to come out here and stir everything up?"

DeMarco didn't answer her question but if he had answered, the answer would have been: *Because* someone *had to.*

---

Tommy called 911, and less than ten minutes later, a deputy DeMarco had never seen before arrived. He listened to what DeMarco and Tommy had to say about Lisa Bunt shooting DeMarco and taking a shot at Tommy. DeMarco also unbuttoned his shirt and showed the deputy the slug embedded in the vest he was wearing under his shirt. The deputy asked Lisa, who was still sitting on the ground, "Are they telling the truth?" Lisa didn't answer. The deputy confiscated Tommy's weapon as well as Lisa's, put handcuffs on Lisa, and placed her in the back seat of his cruiser. He also took DeMarco's bulletproof vest, taking care not to dislodge the slug.

DeMarco asked, "What kind of gun did she shoot me with? Was it a .22?"

"It was a .38 revolver," the deputy said. "Why are you asking?"

"Just curious," DeMarco said. Actually, he'd been wondering if Lisa had used the same caliber weapon that had been used to kill Shannon.

The deputy told DeMarco and Tommy to stay where they were, and walked back to his cruiser and made a phone call. By now three truckers were watching the proceedings. They'd been sleeping inside the cabs of their trucks and had been awakened either by the gunshots, or by the sound of the deputy's siren when he arrived. One of the truck drivers was wearing nothing but boxer shorts and cowboy boots and was drinking a beer.

Fifteen minutes later Pat Morse showed up. Morse was close to fifty, a blocky guy with a crew cut who looked as if he might have wrestled in high school and had stayed in wrestling-shape afterward.

DeMarco told Morse what had happened: how he got a call from a woman who claimed to have witnessed Shannon Doyle's murder.

"And you decided to come talk to her yourself instead of calling the sheriff's office," Morse said.

"Yeah," DeMarco said, seeing no reason to elaborate.

"I guess it was a good thing you just happened to be wearing a vest."

"Yeah," DeMarco said again.

Turning to Tommy, Morse said, "And you, you just happened to be here with a gun?"

Before Tommy could respond, DeMarco said, "Tommy's a friend of mine, an ex-Boston cop, and I asked him to come out here and act as my bodyguard in the event something like this happened. Fortunately, Lisa didn't know about him."

"Jesus," Morse said. "What if she'd shot you in the head?"

# 41

The next morning, Pat Morse decided to start with Lola Clarke. She'd been sitting in a cell for over twenty-four hours. The first thing she said when led into the interview room was, "I'm sick. You gotta help me."

Pat had to admit that the woman looked like death warmed over: pasty, sallow complexion, red-rimmed eyes, scratching her left arm as if it was covered with ants. He said, "You're having withdrawal symptoms, Lola. We'll get a doctor over here in a bit to see if there's anything that can be done to help you. But first I need to ask you some questions."

"I can't think right now."

"The questions are easy," Morse said. "But, Lola, I'm required by law to tell you that you're allowed to have a lawyer here for this interview. If you want one, it's going to take a couple of hours to line one up, and, well, I can't get you that doctor you need until after we've talked."

"Just ask your damn questions," Lola said. "I think I'm gonna throw up."

"That's a good decision," Morse said. "Now you have to sign this form here that basically says I've read you your rights and you don't want a lawyer right now."

Lola scrawled her name on the form and Morse said, "Okay. Now, did you tell Donny Mullen to kill Mr. DeMarco? Before you answer, you should know that Donny's already agreed to testify against you to get a reduced sentence."

"He's an asshole and he's lying. I didn't tell him to kill the guy. I didn't even tell him to hurt him. All I told him was I needed him to get DeMarco off my back. I thought he'd, like, you know, just intimidate him."

"Good," Morse said. "I'm glad you're being honest with me, Lola. But there's something else I need to know. Where were you the night Shannon Doyle was killed?"

"Hell, I don't know. I can't tell you where I was yesterday. I'm so sick I can't think."

"Come on, Lola. That writer getting shot at your dad's motel was a big deal. Certainly, you'd remember that day. When you got to work there would have been cops all over the place."

"I'm tellin' you, I can't re—Wait a minute, I know where I was." She laughed. "I was in jail, right here in Rock Springs. The Rock Springs cops arrested me and a couple of other girls for what they called *loitering* and I spent the night in jail. The next morning, they kicked us all loose. They'd only picked us up to hassle us. After they let me go, I went home and changed and went to work."

Morse looked at her for a moment, then said, "I'll be back in a minute."

"Can I have a cigarette?"

"Sorry, but you can't smoke in this building." Then he stopped and moved a trash can sitting in a corner closer to her. "If you get sick, use that."

He left the room and called a Rock Springs vice cop he knew. Sure enough, Lola was telling the truth. In response to complaints from a couple of businesses, the Rock Springs cops had made a sweep the night Shannon Doyle was killed and rounded up some of the girls working the usual corners. One of the girls was Lola Clarke. They'd picked her up around ten p.m., at least two hours before Doyle was killed, and had held her until seven the next morning.

---

Lisa Bunt seemed almost catatonic, looking down at the table in the interview room. When Pat Morse asked if she wanted him to call her husband or arrange for a lawyer, she didn't respond.

He said, "Mrs. Bunt, is there anything about what happened last night that you'd like to tell me. For example, did you really call Mr. DeMarco and pretend to have information regarding Shannon Doyle's murder? And did you really shoot DeMarco like he said, without him doing anything to provoke you? I mean, did DeMarco threaten you or make you fear for your life, and was that why you shot him?"

Lisa didn't respond.

"Okay, well there's something else I have to ask. Did you kill the writer?"

Lisa finally looked at him. She was a bright lady and had to know that attempted murder would probably get her half a dozen years in jail, and maybe less if she pleaded guilty and saved the county the expense of a trial. But murder, particularly premeditated murder, was a whole different ball game.

"I didn't kill her."

"Lisa, you should know I'm going to get a search warrant to look for the weapon that killed Ms. Doyle. It would be in your best interest to tell me the truth."

"Get a warrant. I didn't kill her."

"Can you tell me where you were the night she died?"

Lisa made a sound that might have been a laugh. "Yeah. I was fucking Jim Turner down at the Best Western, right here in Rock Springs."

Pat had never seen Jim Turner looking so bad. He hadn't shaved since the last time Pat had seen him, and it didn't look as if he'd slept much either. Pat had thought briefly about going to Jim's house to question him, but decided it would be better to interview him at the sheriff's office in Rock Springs. He was pretty sure Jim wouldn't want his wife hearing the questions he planned to ask. Goddamn, but he felt bad for Carly Turner.

Pat said, "Jim, Lisa Bunt says you were with her at a motel in Rock Springs the night Shannon Doyle was killed. Is that true?"

Jim said, "Yeah."

"So you're willing to testify, under oath, that at the time the Doyle woman was murdered, that you and she were both in that motel room?"

Jim looked away, sighed, then said, "I was with her that night from about eight until eleven. I left at eleven. But I know Lisa was planning to stay in the room until the next day because she'd told Hiram that she was spending the night in Denver with a girlfriend."

"In other words, you don't know where she was at the time the writer was killed."

"She wouldn't have killed that woman, Pat. I mean, I know she was worried about Doyle revealing that we were having an affair, but she wasn't *super* worried. She said Doyle liked her and doubted that she'd do anything to hurt her. DeMarco was the one who worried her, stumbling around like a bull in a china shop. She was afraid he'd tell Hiram or leak what he knew to the press."

"You know she tried to kill DeMarco last night."

"Yeah, I heard."

Of course, he'd heard. The story of Hiram Bunt's wife being arrested for shooting a man would have gone through Waverly like a flash flood.

Pat said, "What time did you get back to your house the night Doyle was killed?"

"About midnight."

"And your boys and your wife will confirm this?"

"No. My sons were in Denver. One of our friends took them to see the Rockies play. They stayed in Denver overnight."

"And your wife?"

Jim hesitated and Pat said, "Jim, don't lie to me."

Jim said, "When I got home, Carly wasn't there. She'd been out drinking with her girlfriends. She got home about one o'clock, maybe a little later."

"Aw, shit," Pat said.

---

"Carly, I'm sorry to have to ask you these questions but I don't have a choice."

Pat had told Jim he'd be driving to his house to question Carly and suggested that Jim make himself scarce when he got there. He said he wasn't going to allow Jim to be in the room when he talked to Carly.

He was now sitting at the table in Carly's kitchen. He noticed a bunch of photos of her sons, two handsome, happy-looking boys, taped to the refrigerator door. He also noticed that like her husband, Carly didn't look good; her blue eyes tinged with red, as if she might have had a few too many the night before. Which he could understand if Jim had told her the reason he'd been suspended.

Pat said, "I need to know where you and your husband were the night Shannon Doyle was murdered. Your husband told me he was in Rock Springs until about eleven p.m. and he got back home about midnight."

There was no reason to tell Carly what Jim was doing in Rock Springs if he didn't have to. Plus, he figured that Carly probably already knew. Wives usually knew when their husbands were cheating on them.

"But Jim said when he got home, you weren't here. He said you didn't get home until about one. Is that true?"

"Yeah. I mean, I don't know what time Jim got home but when I got back at one, one thirty, he was here."

"Is there anyone who was with you between, oh let's say, eleven p.m. and one thirty a.m. when you returned home."

"No, I was by myself. Since Jim and the boys were both gone, I went down to the Grill. I got there about seven and started drinking. At some point, I don't know the exact time, I went out to my car and passed out. When I woke up it was about one and I drove home."

Pat could tell she was lying.

"Carly, you know I'm going to ask folks at the Grill to confirm you were there. You need to tell me the truth."

She eventually did. She said she went to a dive called the Desert Bar, not the Hacienda Grill—and Pat could understand why she'd initially lied. The truth was embarrassing.

But the truth also didn't disprove that she'd killed Shannon Doyle.

Pat thought: No one has an alibi. Not Lisa Bunt, not Jim Turner, and not Carly Turner. And they all had a motive for killing Doyle.

Lisa could have driven to Waverly and killed Doyle then driven back to the motel in Rock Springs. Jim Turner could have killed the woman after he left the motel and before going home. And Carly Turner, who thought Jim was having an affair with the writer, could have left the bar, drunk as a skunk, and killed her before going home. So one of them was lying. Or maybe all of them were lying. Or maybe none of them were lying.

There was one thing, however, that distinguished Lisa Bunt from the Turners. Lisa had proven that she was capable of killing someone when she took a shot at DeMarco. And if she had killed Doyle, even if he couldn't prove it, at least she'd spend some time in jail and by the time she got out, her looks would have faded and Hiram would have divorced her. She'd end up completely broke, with a felony conviction on her record, and would have a tough time finding a decent paying job. Her life would be pretty much ruined so justice would be at least partially served.

Pat left the Turners' home and as he did, he saw Jim sitting in a lawn chair out on the patio, drinking a beer, staring off into space. Which made him think that if one of the Turners had killed Doyle, justice would be served in another way. He was about ninety percent sure Jim Turner was going to lose his job with the sheriff's office and it wouldn't be easy for him to find another that paid as well. Yeah, Jim and Carly were both going to suffer and he couldn't help but feel sorry for their two boys.

The only thing Pat could do at this point was a lot of time-consuming, strenuous, good old-fashioned police work—the kind of work Jim Turner should have done. He was going to have to do everything he could to see if Lisa Bunt had left the motel in Rock Springs before Doyle was killed. He'd question everyone he could find, look at all the surveillance cameras in the area. He'd get search warrants to search the Turners' home and Hiram Bunt's ranch to see if he could find the murder weapon or Doyle's laptop. The likelihood of finding anything was practically zero. All the people involved were too damn smart to leave evidence lying around where he could find it. Not to mention, how was he going to search the thousands of acres that made up the Bunt ranch? Which then made him wonder how Hiram Bunt would react when presented with a search warrant. Well, he'd cross that bridge when he came to it.

The other thing he should do was talk to DeMarco and tell him everything he was doing before the bastard came up with another hair-brained scheme on his own. DeMarco had already proven he wouldn't stand idly by if he didn't think law enforcement was doing its job.

Hiram Bunt lay on the floor in his den because of the pain in his back. Since Sonny and Lisa had been arrested, it had gotten even worse. He wouldn't be able to get up without someone helping him, and with Lisa in jail, the only one left in the house to help was the housekeeper. It occurred to him that with both his wife and his son in jail, and the way his back had practically turned him into a cripple, there wasn't much reason to get up off the floor.

His son was going to spend the next thirty years in jail if he was lucky. If he wasn't lucky, the judge would give him the death sentence or he'd spend the rest of his life in prison without the possibility of parole. As for Lisa, his lawyer said she was probably going to spend at least half a dozen years in prison.

Goddamnit, Lisa, why did you do it?

He'd known in his heart that she'd been screwing someone. All those late nights when she didn't get home til eleven or twelve, all those trips she supposedly made to Denver to see old girlfriends or to go shopping where she'd have to spend the night. The truth was, he'd been willing to overlook her infidelity because if he didn't overlook it, for the sake of his pride, he'd have been forced to divorce her—and the last thing he wanted was a divorce. He loved her and he really couldn't blame her. She was a beautiful, young woman and he was a broken-down old man who could hardly move.

He never would have guessed that she'd been getting it on with Jim Turner, however. He could understand her being attracted to Turner but he would have thought that Turner would have been afraid to fuck his wife, knowing he would destroy Turner's career if he ever found out. He supposed that Turner couldn't help himself any more than he could when it came to Lisa.

But why did she try to kill DeMarco? There'd been no reason to do that. If DeMarco had claimed she was having an affair with Turner, all Lisa would have had to do was deny it—and Hiram would have pretended to believe her. Now he couldn't pretend anything. All he could do was wonder how he was going to spend the rest of his miserable life.

The housekeeper came into the room and said, "Mr. Bunt, you want me to help you up? You been lying there for almost two hours."

"Go away, God damn you. I'll call you when I want you."

# 42

Pat Morse called DeMarco and asked him to meet him over at the municipal building in what used to be Jim Turner's office. DeMarco decided to bring Tommy with him.

Morse told them how he'd questioned everybody, that Lola Clarke had a solid alibi for the night Shannon was killed but that he couldn't pin down where Jim Turner, Carly Turner, and Lisa Bunt were that night.

He concluded by saying, "I've got a lot of work to do, Mr. DeMarco, to see if I can prove any of these people killed your friend. I don't know how long it's going to take but I can guarantee you I'm going to keep digging until I either have a case against someone or decide I never will. You can do what you want, but I'd suggest you go back to D.C."

As DeMarco and Tommy were leaving the building, Tommy said, "He seems like a good cop and I think he's right. There isn't anything you can do that he can't do better. He knows the area, he's got the force of the law behind him and putting criminals in jail is what he does for a living."

DeMarco hated to leave before Shannon's killer was found, even though he knew Tommy was correct. And he'd gotten what he wanted: a competent, unbiased cop to investigate her murder.

He said, "I'm going to go play golf and think things over, but you can head back to Boston. I don't think anyone else is going to try to kill me at this point."

Tommy said, "I wouldn't be too sure about that, the way you tend to piss people off. But it's too late for me to leave today. I'll take off tomorrow morning."

"If you're not leaving until tomorrow, you want to go play with me? There's a nice course in Rock Springs called White Mountain. We can rent clubs."

"Nah, I've only golfed a couple of times in my life and I thought it was a stupid game. I'm thinking I'll go for a ride and see if I can spot some of these wild horses you were telling me about."

---

White Mountain Golf Course is a picturesque, twenty-seven-hole course with mountains visible in the distance, striking rock formations, and a couple of small ponds that DeMarco assumed were man-made. It was cheaper than comparable courses he'd played, which he appreciated considering the current state of his finances. He bought a cigar—he liked to smoke a cigar occasionally while he golfed—and three beers which he put in the cooler attached to the cart. Now fully equipped for strenuous athletics, he drove to the first tee box.

His first drive ended up in a bunker on the right side of the fairway, which he attributed to playing with rented clubs. He took a mulligan, drove again, and ended up in the same bunker. Things didn't go much better after that.

As he played he tried to decide if he should take Tommy's advice and head on home. As Tommy had said, Morse was much more likely to track down Shannon's killer than he was. On the other hand, Morse would play by the rules, something that DeMarco didn't think was necessarily advantageous. But when he tried to come up with something he could do that Morse couldn't do—or wouldn't do—he drew a blank. Yeah, it was time to head on home. Not to mention that at some point, Mahoney was going to wonder where he was.

On the fifth hole, DeMarco sunk a twenty-foot putt, the second miracle putt he'd made. He was thinking that he liked the putter he'd rented better than his own and was wondering if he could buy it. His phone rang. He looked at the screen. Aw, shit. It was Mahoney.

"Hello, boss," he said.

"Where the hell are you?"

DeMarco said, "Didn't Mavis tell you? My mother broke her hip and I'm in New York. I'm trying to get her set up with someone who can come in and take care of her until she's able to get around on her own."

Right after he said this, he remembered that he'd never told Mavis his fictitious reason for leaving D.C. because before he could tell the lie, she'd told him that Mahoney was in China. That was the problem with lying: keeping all the lies straight.

"No, she never told me," Mahoney said. And being Mahoney, he also didn't make a sympathetic comment about DeMarco's mother's hip. "But you being in New York is good. There's this freshman congresswoman from the Bronx and she's becoming a major thorn in my side. She's constantly shooting her mouth off on TV and twittering a bunch of nonsense."

DeMarco knew the congresswoman Mahoney was talking about. She was a young Hispanic woman and DeMarco liked her passion. He also knew what had raised Mahoney's hackles. Last night, MSNBC had shown a clip of Mahoney in Boston, comforting the survivors of the mall shooting and saying how it was time for action. But immediately following the clip, the newscaster interviewed the congresswoman, who let loose with both barrels, calling Mahoney a hypocrite who'd never really done anything when it came to passing meaningful gun legislation. The kicker was her saying that there were five firearm manufacturers in Massachusetts and she claimed that someone close to Mahoney had told her that Mahoney was taking under-the-table contributions from all of them. DeMarco had no idea who'd told the congresswoman this, but he knew she was right. He knew because he was the one who collected the money from the gun makers.

Mahoney said, "I need you to do some research on this woman. She's completely out of control."

By "doing some research" Mahoney meant that DeMarco was to find something damaging that Mahoney could use to hold over her head. DeMarco also knew that he probably wouldn't be able to find any dirt on her because if there had been any, the Republicans would have already found it. She was more of a pain in the ass to the Republicans than she was to Mahoney. At least normally she was.

Then, just because he felt like screwing with Mahoney for disturbing his golf game—and for giving him an assignment he didn't want—he said, "What about the leaker? You know, the one who talked to Anderson Cooper about you supporting the merger? Don't you want me to keep going on that?"

He knew Mahoney had no interest in the leaker whatsoever—which Mahoney confirmed.

"Forget about that for now. Go look into this congresswoman."

"Yeah, I thought that's what you'd say," DeMarco said. "I hope you covered your tracks well."

"What in the hell are you talking about?" Mahoney said.

"I figured out that the person who leaked the story was you, which is why you haven't been bugging me about it. I'm guessing that someone you know bought stock in both companies before the story broke, you made a killing when the stock prices jumped, and then you had this person sell the stock before it could drop again after it came out you weren't backing the merger. Like I said, I hope you covered your tracks." DeMarco had no doubt that Mahoney had. Mahoney could have written a book on how politicians could avoid being convicted for insider trading.

Mahoney didn't say anything for a moment, then said, "DeMarco, do you like having a job where you barely have to work?"

"Yes, sir," DeMarco said.

"Well, keep that in mind before you start lipping off to me. Now start digging into the freshman like I told you."

Mahoney hung up.

DeMarco smiled and moved onto the next tee box. As for the freshman, he'd wait a week then call Mahoney and tell him that he'd given it his best shot but struck out. And, by the way, his poor mother's broken hip was much better and he was ready to come back to Washington.

---

When DeMarco finished playing, he tore the scorecard into about sixteen pieces and drove back to Waverly. He took a shower then walked over to Tommy's trailer to see if he was there and wanted to go to dinner—what he'd decided would be his last dinner in the lovely town of Waverly. He was going to let Pat Morse do his job.

He knocked on the trailer door and Tommy answered.

DeMarco said, "Want to go get dinner? My treat."

"Yeah, but come in for a minute. I want to tell you about something."

DeMarco stepped into the trailer and took a seat. Tommy said, "I spent the afternoon reading Shannon's journal. I figured I was probably the only one who hadn't read it. Anyway, did you follow up on this thing with Harriet and whatever Shannon learned from John Bradley?"

"No. I didn't know who John Bradley was and I didn't see any reason to find out. The old lady loved Shannon."

"Yeah, maybe, but it seemed like a loose end to me. John Bradley, or at least I think it's the John Bradley Shannon was referring to, is a writer. He lives in Cleveland and writes true crime books, and he and Shannon have the same publisher. He wrote a book last year about some serial killer in Milwaukee. Why don't we call him?"

"How would we get his phone number?"

"I already got it. I called a pal still working for the Boston PD and he called a cop in Cleveland."

DeMarco shrugged. "Okay. Let's give him a call."

DeMarco made the call. Bradley didn't answer. DeMarco left a voicemail saying, "My name's Joe DeMarco. I work for Congress and I'm investigating Shannon Doyle's murder because she was a close friend of mine. I found a journal Shannon kept and she mentioned that she called a man named John Bradley and apparently asked about an old photograph. If you're the John Bradley she called, I'd like to know what you discussed." DeMarco left his phone number and disconnected the call.

"Let's go eat," he said to Tommy. "I'm starving."

# 43

When they walked into the Hacienda Grill, DeMarco felt as if everyone in the place was staring at him. He doubted there was a person in Waverly who didn't know that Lisa Bunt had tried to kill him, and most of them probably thought DeMarco deserved it. Yeah, it was definitely time to get out of this fucking town.

During dinner, Tommy told DeMarco about the last case he'd worked on for the security firm that employed him in Boston.

"Customers at a hotel in Brookline were being videoed having sex with hookers and people they weren't married to and then blackmailed. I have no idea how many people were blackmailed, though, because I suspect a lot of them preferred to pay rather than have their wives or their bosses learn what they'd been doing. But eventually, when a couple of people did come forward, the hotel manager was worried that word would get out that his guests were being videoed in their rooms, which would definitely hurt his bottom line, and he asked us to investigate.

"I thought at first that maybe it was the hookers or their pimps who'd set up the cameras. Or maybe some employee at the hotel, like the concierge who's a first-class creep. It turned out it was the fifteen-year-old son of the hotel manager. He planted cameras in a dozen rooms and would get into the hotel's registration system to find out who'd rented the rooms. And he was not only blackmailing people, he was selling videos of naked people to his buddies. He used hotel customers' credit cards to buy the cameras and a few other toys for himself. He even blackmailed one of the call girls, this gorgeous gal in her twenties who charged about a grand a night, into having sex with him. This little bastard was a one-man crime wave but because he's a juvenile he got off with probation. I can hardly wait to see what he does when he gets older."

DeMarco was laughing when John Bradley called him back.

Bradley said, "I got your message and I was intrigued."

DeMarco said, "Mr. Bradley, I'm not in a place where I can talk right now. Can I call you back in ten minutes?"

DeMarco paid the bill and he and Tommy went out and sat in DeMarco's car. DeMarco put his phone in speaker mode and dialed Bradley's number. He said, "Like I said in the voicemail I left, you were mentioned in a journal Shannon kept while she was in Wyoming researching her next book. She wrote that she talked to you about a photograph."

"That's right. She said she found an old photo of a man and woman standing in front of a restaurant in Cleveland. She said she could only see part of the restaurant's name in the photo. The part she could see was gretti's. That's spelled g, r, e, double t, i, apostrophe s. But she couldn't tell what was written before the g."

"Yeah, I know that," DeMarco said. "That's what Shannon said in her journal. But why did she call you?"

"She called me because I'm sixty-nine years old and have lived in Cleveland my whole life. I'd never met her but we have the same publisher and she was such a big deal that I was happy to talk to her."

"Would you mind telling me what you told her?"

"Tell me again why you're interested in this."

"I'm interested because I'm trying to find out who killed her and whatever she learned from you could be relevant."

Bradley hesitated. "Okay. I told her there wasn't any restaurant in Cleveland with a name ending in gretti's but the first thing that popped into my head was a restaurant named Sangretti's in Chicago. That's probably the first thing that anyone who writes true crime books would have thought of."

"What's the significance of—"

"I'm getting there. I told Shannon to give me a day to do some research and I found a photo of Sangretti's in Chicago online and I texted it to her. She called me back and said that was the restaurant in the photo that this man and woman were standing in front of."

"I didn't know that," DeMarco said. "In her journal, she said she'd heard back from you but never said what you told her. And her phone was taken when she was killed so I don't know what was in it. But what's the significance of this restaurant in Chicago?"

Bradley said, "In 1990, a hot-headed punk named Tony Russo shot a man in Sangretti's. Tony was the son of John Russo, a major mafia figure in Chicago. The FBI knew about the killing because Sangretti's was John Russo's hangout and they'd wired his favorite table there. But the FBI wasn't monitoring the wire full time. They'd had the bug installed for months and it wasn't producing anything, so some agent would listen to the recordings in the morning when he got to the office. The next day, the day after Tony shoots a guy, an agent hears three gunshots and people screaming. The FBI goes barreling down to the restaurant and naturally, there's no body. A tech finds a couple drops of blood on the floor but the owner of the restaurant claims the blood belonged to a customer who'd cut himself with a steak knife. The owner of the restaurant was a man named Gino Sangretti. His wife was Helena Sangretti.

"Well, the FBI's not buying Gino's story and they squeeze the shit out of him. They knew that John Russo owned a piece of Sangretti's and they suspected he'd been laundering money through it, which of course he was. The FBI tells Gino that he's going to do time for a dozen financial crimes, like money laundering and wire fraud and tax evasion, and if they can prove someone was killed in his restaurant—and keep in mind they have a recording of the shooting—they're going to put Gino away for being an accomplice.

"Gino eventually caves. But he didn't see the killing. He was in the back cooking. Helena Sangretti was the one who saw it. She tells the FBI that Tony got into a screaming match with some guy he was eating with, went completely nuts, and shot the guy. John Russo, who was also there at the time, gets the names of all the customers and tells them he's going to kill them if they talk. Then Russo's guys haul off the body and Gino and Helena mop up all the blood.

"At Tony's trial, Helena Sangretti testifies, Tony is sentenced to twenty years for murder, and John Russo swears he's going to kill Helena and her husband. The FBI knows Russo isn't kidding about killing them so they disappear them into the witness protection program. Then, just to add a little more drama to the whole thing, Tony gets killed in prison and there's no doubt that if John Russo could ever find Gino and Helena, he'd have them both whacked."

"This happened thirty years ago," DeMarco said. "Is John Russo still alive?"

"Yeah, he's my age, about seventy. His kid was twenty-five when they sentenced to him to prison and Russo was forty at the time."

"And this is what you told Shannon?"

"Yeah. DeMarco do you know who the people in the photo are? I'm willing to bet you the advance on my next book that it's Gino and Helena Sangretti."

"No," DeMarco said. "I've never seen the photo." That was true, he hadn't seen it, but he knew who the woman in the photo was.

"Man, I would really love to see this journal," Bradley said. "Can you send me a copy? I'm starting to think this could be my next book."

"I can't do that. The journal is part of Shannon's estate and the property of her younger sister. Maybe her sister will allow you to see it, but I can't give it to you without her permission. Look, Mr. Bradley, I really appreciate you talking to me, but I have to go."

"Hey, wait a minute," Bradley said, but DeMarco hung up.

---

Tommy said, "You know what this means?"

DeMarco said, "I know what it *could* mean. Shannon said in her journal that she almost gave Harriet a heart attack after she told her something."

"She obviously told her what she'd learned from Bradley," Tommy said.

"Yeah, but do you think that old lady was so scared that she would have killed Shannon?"

"I don't know. According to Bradley, if Russo found out Harriet—or Helena—was still alive, he wouldn't care how much time had passed. He'd send someone out here to kill her and Harriet knew that. And there's another thing. Maybe Harriet's a lot cagier than you think. She might have intentionally told you about seeing a woman kill Shannon just to throw you off the trail."

"I can't see it," DeMarco said.

"DeMarco, Harriet knew that if Shannon ever told anyone who she really was, she could end up dead. The *best* thing that would happen to her is she tells the marshals handling her in witness protection what Shannon learned, and they relocate her. Having to start life over at her age would be traumatic, and she might have been willing to do anything to keep that from happening. Including murder."

DeMarco shook his head. He couldn't believe that Harriet had killed Shannon.

Tommy said, "DeMarco, you need to tell Pat Morse what you know about Harriet."

"I want to talk to Harriet first."

# 44

"Hey, Clara Jane. I think you ought to read this."

McCord looked up from her computer monitor to see an agent named Potter standing in front of her desk, holding a piece of paper in his grubby hand.

Potter was the office prankster. He was also an asshole. He'd gone out of his way to find out what "C. J." stood for and it couldn't have been easy because she'd done everything possible to hide her real name. She'd even had her name legally changed from Clara Jane McCord to C. J. McCord when she was eighteen. Her mother had named her Clara as that had been her grandmother's name and C. J. *hated* the name. Clara was a name you gave a cow and she'd called herself C. J. since junior high. She figured that Potter, the devious bastard, had sweet-talked some gal in HR into looking at her original FBI application, which required her to list any previous names or aliases.

She said, "Potter, the next time we have hand-to-hand training I'm going to insist that I get paired up with you. And then I'm going to pound the snot out of you."

Potter elected to ignore the threat, which was genuine. "Weren't you working on something connected with that big-name writer who got killed?"

"Yeah, although the case belongs to the Sweetwater County sheriff."

"Well, take a look at this," Potter said and handed her the piece of paper he was holding

---

Pat Morse was sitting in his temporary office in the Waverly municipal building, creating a timeline of where all his possible suspects had been the night Shannon Doyle died.

He'd talked to Jim Turner, Carly Turner, and Lisa Bunt several times to get the facts straight and they were all cooperative, knowing that being uncooperative could put them at the top of his list. He'd talked to several other people as well to confirm, as best he could, what his primary suspects had told him. He'd also looked at surveillance camera video footage, the cameras belonging to gas companies who stored expensive equipment along I-80.

Two cameras showed Jim Turner's cruiser, one outside Rock Springs and one near Table Rock. The times Jim was videoed were consistent with his story that he'd left the Best Western in Rock Springs at eleven and would have reached Waverly about midnight. The problem was that no camera showed exactly where he was after midnight, which meant that he could have stopped at Shannon's motel and killed her before driving home.

The video footage seemed to prove that Lisa Bunt hadn't killed Shannon because Lisa would have taken the same route that Jim took to drive from Rock Springs to Waverly. But none of the cameras showed a BMW convertible zipping down I-80 around midnight. In fact, the cameras should have caught Lisa twice, once driving to Waverly to kill Doyle and then a second time when she drove back to the motel in Rock Springs. Morse knew she was in Rock Springs the morning after Doyle's death because a clerk at the motel saw her leave about ten a.m. The problem was that there was a possibility that Lisa could have driven on backroads to get from Rock Springs to Waverly, but it seemed unlikely that she would have known about the cameras along the highway and taken them into account when she planned the murder. On the other hand, Lisa was a bright woman so maybe she did think about cameras on the highway.

As for Carly Turner, she didn't pass near any surveillance camera in Waverly. The bartender at the Desert Bar confirmed she was there from seven until nine, left the bar for an hour or so, then came back and drank until midnight when he cut her off. The problem was that from midnight until one thirty when Carly returned home, even *she* didn't know where she'd been. She woke up at one, having passed out in her car, but she couldn't remember anything after she'd left the bar. She'd had a blackout, not unexpected for an alcoholic.

Pat had put off doing a search of the Turners' house and Hiram Bunt's ranch for the murder weapon, knowing in advance that he'd most likely be wasting his time, but he guessed that was the next step he'd have to take. He sat back in his chair and closed his eyes for a moment, and when he opened them he saw FBI Agent C. J. McCord standing in the doorway to his office.

Morse stood up, smiled, and said, "What can I do for you, Agent?"

Morse had met McCord before and thought she was a fine-looking woman. His ex-wife had been a full-figured gal like her. He knew she wasn't married but he wondered if she was seeing anyone.

"Nothing," McCord said. "I'm here to do something for you. I drove all the way from Casper because this was something I wanted to do in person."

# 45

The café had just opened. The day shift cook, Billy, was in the kitchen cooking bacon on the grill. Harriet was putting money into the cash register. When she saw DeMarco come through the door, she closed her eyes as if she was saying a prayer, the prayer most likely asking God to make DeMarco disappear.

DeMarco walked up to her and said, "Harriet, we need to talk."

"I can't talk right now. We'll be getting customers in a couple of minutes."

"The customers are going to have to wait. I talked to John Bradley last night."

"Damn you," Harriet hissed. "Why can't you leave me alone?"

"Let's go up to your apartment," DeMarco said.

He thought Harriet would refuse but she let out a sigh, one of resignation, and called out to the cook, "Billy, I'll be back in just a minute."

DeMarco followed her to the back of the café where there was a staircase leading up to the second floor. The stairs were steep and DeMarco could see she was having a hard time ascending them. Bad knees, bad hips, and too much weight. Inside her apartment, Harriet collapsed into a recliner in the living area Shannon had described and pointed DeMarco to a couch. DeMarco looked for a photograph in a silver frame on an end table but didn't see one. Harriet had most likely hidden it, or maybe she destroyed it, after Shannon had seen it.

"So what do you want?" Harriet said.

"Like I said, I talked to John Bradley. I know who you are."

"How many other people know?"

DeMarco decided not to mention Tommy. He said, "The only one who really knows is me. All Bradley knows is that Shannon found a photo showing a man and a woman standing in front of a restaurant called Sangretti's. He suspects that the people in the photo are Gino and Helena Sangretti, but he doesn't know your current name or that you own this café or anything else about you. I suppose Bradley could come to Waverly to look for you but I'm guessing that you look quite a bit different than you did thirty years ago."

Harriet made a sound that might have been a laugh. "I look fifty pounds different than I did thirty years ago."

DeMarco said, "What I need to know is if you killed Shannon because you were afraid that she'd expose you."

"No!" Harriet said. "I would never have killed her."

DeMarco studied her face. He believed her. Maybe she was the consummate actress but he didn't think so.

"And did you tell me the truth about seeing a woman knock on Shannon's door the night she was killed?"

"Yes. I wasn't lying about that and I wasn't lying when I said I couldn't tell who the woman was."

DeMarco rose. "All right, Harriet."

"So what are you going to do?" Harriet asked.

"About you? Nothing. Well, I may have a word with John Bradley and tell him that bad things are going to happen to him if he decides to come out here and poke around."

Bradley had no idea how much—or how little—clout DeMarco had. What he might do was tell Bradley that he was going to have his taxes audited by nitpickers at the IRS. If Bradley collected Social

Security—at his age that was likely—he'd tell him that his payments might suddenly be interrupted and hopelessly snarled in red tape. His biggest threat would be Bradley getting a visit from U.S. marshals telling him about the trouble he'd be in if he exposed a federal witness they were protecting. Yeah, he was going to squeeze John Bradley's nuts a bit when he returned to Washington to make him stay away from Harriet.

DeMarco returned to his room and started to pack. A knock on the door interrupted him. He started to open the door, which didn't have a peephole, then stopped. It occurred to him that maybe there was someone in addition to Lisa Bunt who wouldn't mind shooting him.

He called out: "Who is it?"

"Deputy Pat Morse."

DeMarco opened the door.

Morse said, "I know who killed Shannon Doyle."

"You do?"

"Yeah. Why don't we go over to Harriet's and have a cup of coffee and talk. "

DeMarco thought about that and said, "If you wouldn't mind, let's go to my friend Tommy's trailer. I know he'd like to hear the story too."

DeMarco was afraid if he walked into Harriet's with the deputy she'd have a stroke.

Tommy was outside the trailer, looking everything over to make sure it was okay to make the trip back to Salt Lake. DeMarco said, "Tommy, let's go inside. Deputy Morse has something to tell us."

The three men stepped into the small trailer and found seats.

Morse took off his hat, wiped his brow, and placed the hat on the table. He said, "After I was assigned to the case, I tried to build a timeline showing where everyone was that night. I looked at surveillance camera videos. I interviewed Lisa Bunt, Carly, and Jim Turner multiple times as well as half a dozen other people who were able to corroborate, in one way or another, what they all told me." Morse paused and said, "Here's what happened the night Shannon Doyle died."

# 46

*Carly got the boys out the door at three. One of their friends was taking them to see a Rockies game in Denver and they'd be staying the night. She got dinner ready to go, took a shower, and put on some makeup. Also a short skirt and a low-cut top that she knew were flattering. She may have been the mother of two teenagers but her figure could still turn a head or two.*

*She was looking forward to tonight; with the boys gone it would give her and Jim a chance for some "quality time," which to her meant ending up naked and sweaty and tangled in the sheets. It seemed as if it had been forever since they'd had sex and the last time they did, Jim had acted as if he was just going through the motions. Maybe tonight would be different: a nice dinner, an empty house, a bottle of wine—*

*Jim got home at five, took a shower—which was a bit unusual as he didn't normally shower until right before bed. That should have set off the alarm bells, but didn't. Dinner was pot roast, his favorite, accompanied by small potatoes and a fancy salad with cranberries and artichoke hearts. She'd made an apple pie for dessert. It was sitting on the kitchen counter and the smell of it filled the house.*

*During dinner he hardly said a word, other than mumbling how good everything tasted. He mostly only talked when she asked questions. She noticed him glance at his watch a couple of times, as if he had someplace he had to be. At six—on the dot—his phone rang. He looked at the caller ID, frowned and said, "Hello, boss." A pause, followed by, "Tonight?" Another pause, "Yeah, I get it. I'll be there as soon as I can."*

*"What is it?" Carly said.*

*"Sorry, babe. Clay's decided to bring down a meth cooker tonight. The guy's got a big operation outside Superior, lots of firepower, four or five guys helping him. Clay wants all hands on deck for this one. I have to change and take off."*

*He left the table, with her glaring at his back, thinking,* Sorry babe, my ass. *He was meeting someone.*

*Ten minutes later, he was in his uniform, all the cop crap on his belt. While he'd been getting dressed, she drank an entire glass of wine and poured another one. As he headed toward the door, he said, "Don't wait up. This might take a while."*

*She didn't say a word; she just kept sipping the wine. Normally, she would have said something like, "You watch your ass and make sure you don't get shot." Not tonight. The last thing she was worried about was him getting shot. She sat for about a minute after he was gone, swallowed the remaining wine in a single gulp, then slammed the wine glass on the table. Goddamn it, she wasn't going to put up with this shit any longer. She got up, swept her purse and keys off the table near the door, and went barreling out of the house.*

*She figured he was heading toward the highway. She was going sixty before she reached the corner—it was a good thing she didn't hit one of the neighbors' kids—and spotted his car a couple blocks later, heading toward I-80 as she'd thought. She slowed down and stayed behind him.*

*She was puzzled, when a moment later, the light rack on the county cruiser's roof lit up. Was he in such a hurry to get laid that he'd decided to use lights and a siren to get to wherever he was going? But then, just half a mile farther down the road, he pulls off the highway and turns into Sam*

*Clarke's motel. Certainly, he wouldn't be so brazen as to meet someone there, not after making such a dramatic entrance.*

---

*Jim's phone rang. It was Sam Clarke. All the local businessmen had his number. Sam said, "Jim, those two on the second floor are going at it again. It sounds like they're killing each other."*

*He thought about calling another deputy to take the call but figured he might as well deal with it himself. He had plenty of time. Then there was the possibility that those drunken nuts would actually hurt each other if another deputy took too long to get to the motel. He didn't want to have to explain why he hadn't responded himself if someone died or was seriously injured.*

*He pulled into the motel parking lot, left the blue and red lights on the cruiser spinning, and headed for the second floor. This was the third time he'd dealt with this particular pair, a gas worker and his girlfriend who'd get a load on and then start screaming and throwing things at each other. He went up the stairs, taking the steps two at a time. He could hear the couple yelling all the way down the walkway. He hammered on the door, shouting, "Sheriff. Open up, goddamnit."*

*A man opened the door, a little guy, eyes red as cherries, hair springing out from his head as if he'd been electrocuted, his breath a Budweiser fog. Before he could say anything, Jim grabbed him by his filthy T-shirt and yanked him out of the room.*

*He slammed him up against the wall and said, "I don't have time to mess with you tonight. But I've told Sam that if you two start up again after I leave, he's to call the deputy on duty and he's going to take your ass to jail, whether your girlfriend presses charges or not. I've also told Sam, that if you're arrested, he's to evict your dumb ass and good luck finding another place to stay."*

*"Hey. She started it. She said—"*

*Jim slammed him against the wall again and said, "Did you hear what I just said?'*

*"Yeah, I heard you."*

*Jim returned to his car, and while standing outside it, made a call to Bob Parker, who was patrolling tonight, and told him to swing by the motel in half an hour and see if everything was okay.*

*He'd just hung up when Shannon Doyle came out of her room. It was six-thirty and he was supposed to be in Rock Springs in an hour.*

*Lisa left the ranch at three p.m. She'd told Hiram she was meeting Cherry in Denver. Cherry was her best friend and a girl she used to work with at Hooters. She'd said that they were going to a Lady Gaga concert, and because it would be so late when the concert ended, she'd spend the night at Cherry's place. She'd gone to concerts with Cherry several times before—or so Hiram thought. She'd reminded him twice about the concert during the preceding week, and had even asked him if he wanted to go with her, knowing he wouldn't. But instead of making the four-hour drive to Denver, she drove to Rock Springs, arriving a little after four, and checked into the Best Western. She spent the next hour studying for a business class she was taking at the college and at exactly six p.m., she called Jim.*

*When he answered his phone saying, "Yes, boss," she laughed. "Ooh, I like it when you call me boss." He ignored her and said, "Tonight?" like the call was a big surprise. She responded saying, "If you're late, I'm going to start without you. Picture that, big boy." Call completed so Jim would have some excuse to give his wife, Lisa walked over to a nearby store and bought a bottle of expensive wine, most of which she'd drink herself. Jim wouldn't arrive until seven-thirty, giving her plenty of time to take a shower, splash on some perfume, and put on the outfit she'd bought online from Victoria's Secret.*

---

*Shannon said, "Hey, how you doin'?" when she saw Jim Turner standing near his cruiser. She walked over to him.*

*He said, "The couple upstairs was going at it again and I had to have a talk with them."*

*Shannon rolled her eyes. "They need to find something they can do together other than drink and fight. And if I were you, I'd be more worried about him than her. She outweighs him by a hundred pounds." Jim laughed.*

*Shannon said, "I was just going to get Sam, but maybe you can help me. I can't get the window shut." She pointed at one of the two sliding windows next to the larger picture window at the front of her room. "I open it because the air conditioner doesn't work but I don't like to leave it open when I'm gone. But the damn thing jams in the rail and you need really strong fingers to push it back."*

*Jim glanced at his watch. Shannon noticed and said, "But, hey, if you need to be somewhere."*

*"No, it's okay. I've got time. But let me get my cruiser out of the way." He hopped into his car, which had been sitting in the middle of the parking lot, and pulled it into a parking space near the end of the lot.*

*Then followed Shannon into her room.*

---

*When Jim turned right into the motel's parking lot, Carly made a left turn and pulled into the lot in front of the truck stop convenience store. She backed into a parking space so she could see across the highway and watched Jim go up to the second floor, where he bounced some scrawny little guy off the wall a couple of times, and then returned to his cruiser. It looked as if she'd been wrong about him meeting someone at the motel—and could feel the relief washing over her.*

*But then Shannon Doyle walks out of her room, dressed in a pair of skintight jeans, and walks up to Jim, who's standing near his cruiser. They talk for a second or two, and Carly sees her husband laugh, then get into his car. Carly thought he was leaving the motel, but instead he parks in a spot a short distance from Shannon's room. While he's parking the car, Shannon stands in the doorway to her room.*

*Then Jim walks up to Shannon, follows her into her room, and closes the door.*

*Carly shrieked, "You bastard!" and slammed her fist on the steering wheel.*

*And goddamn Shannon Doyle to hell. The first time she'd seen Shannon talking to Jim and later accused her of having an affair with him, she'd almost believed Shannon when Shannon denied it. She should have known better.*

*Shannon Doyle had everything. She was beautiful. She was famous. She was rich. She had the greatest job in the world—but it wasn't enough for her. She had to have Jim, too.*

*Carly was so mad the veins in her temples were throbbing. She opened the door to the glove compartment and pulled out the little .22 that Jim had given her.*

*Then she thought:* What are you doing? You can't kill them. You have two sons.

*Her next thought was: Okay, I'll give them ten minutes to get their clothes off and then go pound on the door and embarrass the shit out of him and his fucking girlfriend.*

*Yeah, she could see the scene play out in her mind. She hammers on the door. After a moment Shannon answers, maybe a towel wrapped around her so she could claim she'd been in the shower. But Carly shoves past her, knocking her out of the way, and there's Jim lying in the bed.*

*Then what? She screams at Jim for being a lying, cheating, son of a bitch. Maybe she slaps Shannon across the face for being a man-stealing bitch. But what happens after that? She leaves in tears, totally humiliated, and Jim comes home and swears he's sorry, swears he loves her, swears he'll never cheat on her again? But of course he would.*

*Well, she wasn't going to be his fucking doormat forever.*

*And there was a way for her to get back at him.*

*She peeled out of the truck stop parking lot and headed for the Desert Bar. Normally, she drank at the Grill but the Grill wasn't the place to find what she wanted. The Desert Bar was a dive, not somewhere a respectable married woman would go, and that's what she wanted: a dive. At this time of the evening it would be filled with horny drunks who worked for the gas companies and she was going to pick up the best-looking one she could find and fuck him.*

*If her husband didn't want her, she'd find a man who did.*

---

*Five minutes after entering Shannon's room, Jim left. The damn window had been harder than hell to shut. He checked his watch. He had plenty of time, mainly because he drove a vehicle equipped with a siren and the speed limit didn't apply to him.*

---

*After Jim shut the window—God, he was a dreamboat—Shannon left her room. She put her laptop case in the trunk of her car—she never left her laptop in the room after Lola Clarke stole her earrings—and headed toward the Grill for dinner.*

---

*Carly Turner walked into the Desert Bar, and picked a spot near the center of the long bar. She was glad she was wearing the short skirt that she'd put on for Jim. She normally drank wine but tonight she wanted something stronger and ordered a Jack Daniel's on the rocks. Before she could finish it, a guy walked up and said hi.*

---

*At seven-thirty, right on time, Jim arrived at the Best Western in Rock Springs. He called Lisa and asked what room she was in. She said, "108." Jim knocked on the door and Lisa called out, "It's open, sugar." He walked into the room and she was lying on the bed in a transparent nightie which was more erotic than if she'd been nude. He took off his hat and sailed it toward the chair in the corner of the room.*

---

*By nine o'clock Carly Turner had had four, maybe five, drinks but she'd only paid for one. This lanky guy with curly dark hair spilling over his forehead had bought all the rest. She'd told him her name was Julie and that she was a teacher in Rock Springs. She thought his name was Dave, but wasn't sure. He took his time, asking her a lot of questions about herself, maybe thinking he had to romance her a little. Finally, he worked up the nerve to ask if she'd like to go back to his RV, which was within walking distance of the bar and where they could enjoy a quiet drink alone. She slammed down the last drink he'd bought her and said, "Hell, yes."*

---

*Sex with Dave or Dan or whoever the hell he was, was awful. The whole time he'd been on top of her, all she could think about was Jim and Shannon doing the same thing in Shannon's room. After he finished, she started crying. He kept asking her what was wrong as she got dressed—he seemed like a decent guy—but she just yelled at him to shut up and leave her the hell alone.*

*She stumbled out of his RV and walked back to the bar—and started drinking. She didn't want to go home. She sat alone at the end of the bar, thinking about that bitch, Doyle, and her husband, and whenever a man would approach her she'd snarl at him to get the fuck away from her.*

---

*Shannon had dinner at the Hacienda Grill, then hung around for a while afterward BS-ing with some of the cowboys drinking in the bar. She got back to her room around ten. She booted up the laptop and fiddled for about an hour with a scene involving a herd of wild horses she'd seen that morning, but she couldn't get it right. She just couldn't capture in words not only the beauty of the animals but how they were a metaphor for the spirit of the Wyoming plains.*

*She looked across the highway and saw a single light on in the café and Harriet sitting alone at a table. She decided to go talk to her—and then made the mistake of telling Harriet what she'd learned from John Bradley. At eleven she was back in her room working. She made an entry in her journal then went back to trying to describe the horses, but again the words refused to come.*

*At eleven, Jim told Lisa he had to leave. "What the hell?" she said. "Slam, bam, thank you ma'am?" She'd been expecting him to spend the night.*

*It had hardly been slam, bam. They'd been in bed for the last three and a half hours. And he actually had been planning to spend the night, but the look on Carly's face when he left the house told him that it would be better if he got back home. So now he had not one, but two women pissed at him.*

*As soon as he was back in his cruiser, he called a deputy and asked how the meth lab raid had gone. The sheriff actually had planned a raid for tonight but it hadn't been that big a deal, had only involved about six deputies, and had gone down without a hitch. Jim just wanted a few details he could relay to Carly, like the one he got about one of the deputies getting bitten by the asshole's Rottweiler.*

*He figured he should be home a little after midnight. He might even try to make love to Carly if she was still awake, although he doubted he'd have the strength to do so.*

*A few minutes before midnight, Shannon walked down to the ice machine. She had a can of Coke in her room and felt she needed the caffeine to keep working, but the Coke was warm. She looked over at the café. It was dark; Harriet must have gone to bed. Along the way to the ice machine, she passed a bearded, bear of a man named Phil Parker. He worked for an outfit called Black Hills Energy and had just gotten off his shift. They nodded to each other.*

*Phil knew who Shannon was—he'd even read her book—but he didn't have the nerve to approach her and tell her how much he'd enjoyed it.*

*At midnight, the bartender at the Desert Bar told Carly he was cutting her off. When she yelled that she wanted another drink and he damn well better pour her one, he said, "Mrs. Turner, you really don't want me to have to call your husband." God, she hated this fucking town where everyone knew everyone else. But she wasn't worried about the bartender telling Jim she'd left with Doug, Dan, whoever he was. She didn't give a shit if her husband found out or not.*

*She staggered back to her car. She'd really had too much to drink; she could barely walk. She climbed into the driver's seat, then immediately flung open the door and vomited. Then she made the mistake of putting her head back and closing her eyes—and passed out.*

*She woke up a while later, not knowing how long she'd been unconscious. She glanced at her watch. It was a little after one. She started the car and headed toward the highway—and then noticed the little .22 sitting on the passenger seat. What was it doing there? Had she taken it out of the glove compartment because she'd been thinking about shooting Shannon again? She reached over and tossed the gun back into the glove compartment. She hoped she could make it home before she passed out again.*

*Jim walked into the house about twelve-thirty, surprised to see Carly's car gone and the front door unlocked. He wondered if something had happened to the boys. He called her cell phone but it immediately went to voicemail, meaning she most likely had the phone turned off or the battery was dead. Where the hell could she be? He took off his uniform, took a quick shower to wash away Lisa's scent, but didn't go to bed. He called her cell phone a couple more times, and again she didn't answer. Finally, at one thirty, she walked into the house, glassy-eyed, reeking of booze.*

*He said, "Where have you been?" She answered, "Fuck you," stumbled into the bedroom, and collapsed face down on the bed.*

---

*At four thirty a.m., Henry Clemson left his ground-floor room at Sam Clarke's motel. He normally started work at six but there was a problem with a leaky relief valve on one of the wellheads, and he had to go in early to see if he could get it working right. As he passed Shannon Doyle's room he noticed the door was open and he glanced inside.*

*Shannon Doyle was on her back, on the floor. There was a spot of blood the size of a silver dollar on her blouse, directly over her heart.*

# 47

"So which one of them did it?" DeMarco said. He was frustrated. Morse's timeline of what had happened that night didn't clarify anything.

"None of them did it," Morse said. "They all told me the truth."

"Well, shit," DeMarco said. "Then why did you tell me you know who killed Shannon?"

Morse said, "One of the first things Jim Turner did at the beginning of the investigation was get the names of all the truckers who passed through Waverly that day, and people in the sheriff's office followed up to see if any of them had records."

"Yeah, I already knew that," DeMarco said. "Turner told me. But Turner also told me they hadn't found anyone who was a likely suspect."

"That's true. But the other thing Jim did was send the ballistic test photos of the slug used to kill Ms. Doyle to the FBI in Cheyenne, and asked them to check their database to see if the gun had been used in another homicide. Well, Jim never heard back from the FBI, but this morning Agent McCord, who works out of the Casper field office, dropped in on me."

"So?" DeMarco said.

Morse said, "A year ago, a woman in a house close to a highway rest stop outside of Fallon, Nevada was shot to death and robbed. The rest stop is a place where long-haul drivers will spend the night. The cops in Fallon never found out who killed the woman but the weapon used was a .22.

"Four months ago, an old man who lives in a trailer park in Kearney, Nebraska was shot. He opened his door, someone shot him, took his wallet and his watch, and split. The old man didn't die but all he could tell the cops was that a kid wearing a hoodie had shot him and he couldn't describe the kid. The cops in Kearney took the slug they dug out of the old man's chest, noticed it was a .22, and placed it in an evidence envelope, but that's all they did with it. They didn't bother to notify the FBI. Next, Shannon Doyle was killed."

"Shit," DeMarco muttered. He could already see where this was going. "So who—"

But Morse wasn't through. He said, "Two days ago, a woman, a tourist from Germany, staying in a motel outside of Salt Lake was shot and killed. Like Ms. Doyle, she had a ground floor room in a motel near a truck stop and she opened the door to whoever shot her. But the Utah cops got the shooter. It was one of those fluke things where a state cop just happened to be passing by when the shooting occurred. Someone heard the shot, called 911, and the trooper sees someone running from the scene and gets her."

"Her?" DeMarco said.

"Yeah. She used a piece of shit .22 revolver to kill the tourist."

Morse said, "At that point, it all comes together, although I don't know who connected the dots—it could have been a computer, for all I know—but someone finally realizes that Salt Lake City, Fallon, Nevada, and Kearney, Nebraska are located on I-80. Like Waverly. Then someone remembers the Doyle case, mainly because Doyle was a celebrity, and they find the ballistic test results that Jim submitted, which were still waiting to be entered into their database. Eventually, the FBI concludes that the same weapon was used in all four crimes. Right now they're looking to see if any other people were shot in towns along the highway."

Morse took out his phone and showed DeMarco and Tommy a photo. It was of a girl, maybe sixteen years old, with a thin, acne-scarred face, dull brown eyes, and long dark hair. Morse shook his head and said, "The media will probably end up calling her the I-80 Killer."

Morse said, "That girl's father is an independent trucker and his route is I-80 from Sacramento, California to South Bend, Indiana. She travels with him, doesn't go to school or anything. They sleep in the truck and take showers at truck stops. The father was one of the truckers who passed through Waverly when Ms. Doyle was killed. The cops in Utah who nabbed the girl are about ninety percent sure her father's molesting her, although she hasn't admitted it yet. Mentally, she's slow and all fucked up, pardon my language. When she was asked why she killed these people she said it was to steal things so her father wouldn't get sick."

"Sick?" DeMarco said.

"The guy's an opioid addict. After he was threatened with being indicted as an accessory to murder, he admitted his daughter would sometimes steal things and he'd pawn what she stole, but he said he had no idea she'd used his gun to shoot anyone. So far he hasn't admitted to pawning Ms. Doyle's laptop but I'm guessing he eventually will."

Pat Morse paused and said, "So Mr. DeMarco, now you know who killed your friend."

Before DeMarco could say anything, Morse said, "And now what I'm hoping is that you'll get the hell out of Waverly. You came in here like a wrecking ball and destroyed a lot of lives and I'd like to see you in my rearview mirror."

"Hey, wait a minute!" Tommy said. "If it wasn't for Joe, the guy who killed the BLM agent would never have been caught."

"That's probably true, but if it wasn't for Joe stirring the pot, Lisa Bunt wouldn't have felt the need to kill him. Her life is destroyed. And because of what's going on with Lisa and Sonny, the stress is really getting to Hiram. Last night they had to send an ambulance to his place because he was having chest pains."

"Fuck Hiram and his chest pains," Tommy said

"And Jim Turner is most likely going to lose his job. That'll be up to the sheriff but if he does lose it, I don't know what he'll do to support Carly and his boys."

DeMarco didn't bother to say that the other life that was almost ruined was Harriet's. And maybe it still would be depending on what John Bradley did.

DeMarco said, "I'll be leaving this afternoon. Thanks for—"

"Good," Morse said. He put on his hat and left the trailer.

# 48

Driving west on I-80, toward Salt Lake City to catch a plane back to D.C., DeMarco took in—and hopefully for the last time—the rolling, sagebrush landscape. There was an unforgiving, harshness to this place that he found disheartening and he couldn't even imagine what it would be like in the winter, with the wind whipping the snow across the plains.

He rounded a curve and glanced to his right and on a low hill near a striking red rock formation he saw a group of horses. He pulled to the shoulder of the highway and got out of the car. There were five of them, four clustered together, heads down, grazing—and a large black horse that he assumed was a stallion, standing apart, like a watchful sentry.

He wondered how Shannon would have described the scene. All he knew was that the wild horses on that hill somehow captured the spirit of the people who lived here and for the first time, he could see the beauty of this part of Wyoming and could understand why Shannon had chosen to set her novel here. But he'd never know, nor would anyone else, how she would have woven the setting into the story she'd planned to tell.

He missed Shannon, but more than anything else he was saddened that the world had been deprived of someone with her talent and that her life had been cut short before she'd been allowed to experience all that she might have. He remembered when he'd taken her to a celebration dinner in Boston when she got her first publishing deal, not just how lovely she'd looked that night, but the way she'd spoken about her good fortune. She'd said, "Joe, I'm the luckiest woman on this earth, getting the opportunity to do what I've always wanted. I'm truly blessed."

He supposed she had been blessed, but it had been a short-lived blessing.

He decided that he didn't feel at all bad about what he'd done. Morse had said that he'd come into Waverly like a wrecking ball and destroyed people's lives—but that hadn't been his intention. He'd just wanted to make sure the cops were doing their job, and when he could see they weren't, he gave them a gentle shove. And he suspected, even if he couldn't prove it, that if he hadn't stirred the pot that the FBI might never have connected the I-80 killings. Certainly, Sonny Bunt wouldn't have been arrested for killing Jeff Hunter. As for Lisa Bunt, he hadn't forced the woman to try to kill him. That had been her desperate choice and hers alone.

The only one he had any sympathy for was Carly Turner.

When he got back to D.C., he'd go see Congressman Burns and ask him to use his influence to keep Jim Turner from being fired. Demoted maybe, but not fired. Turner hadn't investigated the people who might have killed Shannon because he'd been worried that his lover was one of those people. But in the end, Turner's failure to investigate Lisa Bunt, Lola Clarke, and his own wife hadn't really mattered. If Turner hadn't been married and a father, DeMarco wouldn't have done anything to keep Turner from losing his job, but he didn't want to see Carly Turner and her two boys suffer. And Jim Turner probably wasn't a bad cop when he wasn't screwing the people he was supposed to be investigating.

For some reason, at that moment, the stallion reared up on its hind legs and all the horses bolted and galloped over the low hill and disappeared from sight. DeMarco wondered what had spooked them. Some invisible predator? He wondered if wolf packs roamed this part of Wyoming.

Tomorrow he'd be back in D.C.—a place definitely inhabited by a variety of wolves.

He had no intention of investigating the freshman congresswoman from New York as Mahoney had directed. He'd spend a couple of days doing yard work that he'd been neglecting, and maybe reread *Lighthouse* to feel close to Shannon again. Eventually, he'd call Mahoney and tell him that the young congresswoman was as pure as the driven snow—although DeMarco knew she wouldn't remain that way. No one who worked in Washington remained pure.

He certainly hadn't.

# Author's Note

This book was based in part on events that actually happened. A rancher in a Western state refused—for about twenty years—to pay the fees for grazing his cattle on public land. When the amount he owed added up to over a million bucks, the Bureau of Land Management decided to round up some of his cows and an armed standoff occurred. I also learned that there are ongoing problems in Wyoming and other Western states when it comes to wild horses. It appears as if there are too many wild horses competing for rangeland needed for grazing livestock and there have been few instances where the horses have been illegally killed. It's a complicated situation when it comes to the wild horses.

In case you haven't figured it out, there is no town in Wyoming named Waverly. Waverly is roughly based on the town of Wamsutter, Wyoming, which is located on I-80 where I placed Waverly. I decided not to use the name of the actual town because some of my descriptions of it and its inhabitants—descriptions I sometimes invented for the sake of the story—are less than flattering and I didn't want to offend those who live in Wamsutter or cast aspersions on the town in any way.

In the book I talk about Shannon spilling a can of Coke onto her laptop. This actually happened to me, although it was an eight-ounce glass of water that I tipped into my laptop. At the time, like Shannon,

I hadn't backed up a book I was working on and had to rewrite a good chunk of it when I couldn't recover the file. Since then I've gotten religious when it comes to backing up my work.

Also in the book, I describe the town barber's experience with *Vanity Fair*, which also happened to me. My senior year in high school, an English teacher—one of the good nuns of the Sisters of Charity—required the class to read Thackeray's book, which, as I said, is about seven or eight hundred pages long. This was when I, too, discovered CliffsNotes. I learned in the course of writing this book that CliffsNotes were invented by a man named Clifton Keith Hillegass, to whom I shall be forever grateful and may he rest in peace.